The Last Villains of Molo

Kinyanjui Kombani

PUBLISHERS
expanding minds

Published by

Longhorn Publishers (Kenya) Ltd.,
Funzi Road, Industrial Area,
P.O.Box 18033 - 00500,
Nairobi, Kenya.

Longhorn Publishers (Uganda) Ltd.,
Plot 731, Kamwokya Area,
Mawanda Road,
P. O. Box 24745,
Kampala, Uganda.

Longhorn Publishers (Tanzania) Ltd.,
Plot No 4. Block 37B Kinondoni,
Kawawa Road
P. O. Box 1237,
Dar es Salaam, Tanzania.

First edition published by Acacia Publishers.

Cover design by Tuf Mulokwa.

978-9966-36-228-5

Dedication

Over 2000 people were killed and over 500,000 displaced in tribal clashes in Molo, Olenguruone, Burnt Forest, Njoro, Narok and other parts of Kenya in 1991. Some of these people, who were then only children, are now adults and assailed with the question: Why did it happen?

My friend and roommate at Kenyatta University was a victim of the ethnic clashes in the Rift Valley. The incidents of his childhood have affected him so much he cannot sleep with the light in the room turned off.

This story is dedicated to the innocent victims of the tribal clashes. Dedications also go out to God – for giving me the talent; to Mr. & Mrs. S.F.G. Mbugua of Eldoret – for giving me the power to read and write; and to Alice – perhaps my biggest source of inspiration, for being by me.

"The young refuse the bonds of the past, the bonds of hate…"
David Mulwa in *Redemption.*

Acknowledgements

This story would not have come to fruition were it not for the encouragement of Mr. David 'Keep-writing' Mulwa and Mr. Gachanja Kiai of Kenyatta University Literature Department. My thanks also go out to Prof. George Eshiwani, Prof. Everett Standa, Prof Oluoch Obura and Prof. Emmanuel Mbogo for their support.

And this story would have been grossly inaccurate were it not for the valuable statistics provided by the Kenya Human Rights Commission. I would also like to note the worthy contribution of Mzee Joseph Mbure (Kamwaura), Peter Muia (Kamwaura), and a man only known to me as Kip (Molo) who gave their account of what really happened.

This book contains quotes from local musicians (K-South - page 50, Kalamashaka - page 120, and Mashifta - page 27) which I thought best illustrated some events in the story. To these musicians I say, keep on singing.

I would also like to acknowledge the support of my friends Michael Owino, Nyambura Burugu, Tony Gichuki, Shibira Collins, Jennie Marima and Wangui Chege.

It would be unfair not to acknowledge the worthy contribution of Jimmi Makotsi.

Prologue

Ndoinet forest, Molo, 1992

From her hiding place under the bed, the young girl listened to the increasing noises as they came nearer their house. Her heart thundered in her chest as she heard the screams of her neighbours, and the crackling sounds of raging fires. Slowly, she peered upwards.

Her father stood in the doorway leading to the sitting room of their three-roomed house. Tapping his lips with a finger, he motioned to her to be silent and clutched the spear with renewed energy.

She tightly closed her eyes and sobbed. She had never witnessed such a traumatising experience - the slashing and burning was too much for her tender years. For the umpteenth time, she wished she had left with her mother and siblings when the call to evacuate the village had come hours earlier. But by the time she had been released by the Catholic nun at school, her mother and the others had already left, expecting their father to follow suit as soon as the little girl got home. But then, he had adamantly refused to leave and she couldn't force him.

The sound of footsteps came nearer and nearer, and she slid deeper under the bed in fear. Now she could only see her father's legs, but she could tell from the way they shook that he was as terrified as she was. Her heart beat faster with this realization.

She heard the attackers burst into the sitting room. The house shook with their entry. There was a long silence as they realized there was no one in that room. She could hear their sigh of relief at not having to face any adversary. An awful silence ensued before some footsteps indicated they were leaving. She gave a silent prayer of thanks.

Then she suddenly saw her father's legs move and she froze in horror. Almost instantly, she heard a loud, rough voice from the sitting room call out:

"Watch out!"

An instant later, she heard a violent thud as her father's spear plunged into the sitting room wall, bringing down half of the mud plastered on it. There was hurried movement, then she heard the clang of metal against bone. Something fell to the ground with a thud.

Her fear was replaced by apprehension. She crawled out of her hiding place and walked to the door.

There were two young men in the sitting room. One stood with a poised machete and the other was collecting himself. She gasped when she saw her father convulsing on the floor. Blood was gushing out of a deep cut in his neck, and he was shaking violently. An incoherent flow of guttural sounds escaped from his frothing mouth. Her whole body still in shock, she bent down.

One of the two attackers wiped sweat off his brow with the back of his hand as he surveyed his work. The other one touched him on the shoulder and said in a subdued voice, "Thank you for saving my life."

She looked from her fallen father to the intruders, her heart quickly filling with hatred. These were the two attackers who had done this to her father, her protector.

Suddenly, they saw her and started as if they had seen an apparition. One of them swung his axe to hit her and to her amazement, she did not move an inch.

The axe was stopped in mid-air by the other attacker.

"What are you doing?" her rescuer asked, still holding the axe.

"We are not to leave anybody alive, remember?" the other replied.

"Ah! Hell! Are we to kill a little girl for a crime she doesn't know, and in which she has not even participated?"

The axe-wielder looked at both of them with momentary hesitation. The room was silent again for some time, and all they could hear was the sound of the raging war outside.

She continued to stare at her father's killers without flinching. "Let's go," the one who had stopped her attacker said. The axe-man dropped his hand and walked out. At the door, they looked behind to see the cold form of the young girl. She was bent on her knees, one hand trying to stem the flow of blood from her father's body. As their eyes met, the hatred in hers hit the two attackers like a cold blade of steel.

"Let's get away from here!" One said to the other, and ran out. A second later, she heard an unfamiliar voice ask, "Is there somebody in?"

"Yes. We have killed him," came the reply.

"Right! Now, burn down the house."

one

Nairobi, 2001

". . . there are no villains or heroes here, just victims."

–Gerry Loughran, Sunday Nation

With a wide grin on his face, one of the five men — the one with the fake Adidas T-shirt — pocketed the 8-ball on the pool table. Instantly, a long argument followed. It seemed there were two rival teams playing the game. "What are you arguing about?" the shortest of the lot asked the opposing group. "The fact remains, we have won! Now where is the money?"

"*Usiwe hivyo!*" Don't be that way, the darkest of them, who was so dark that you'd think he was a chimney sweep, challenged. "We all know that this is not fair. I say we play another game!"

After much argument, the group came to a consensus. Looking carefully to see whether any of the pool attendants was watching, two of them suddenly flipped the pool table on its side. There was a clang that was muffled by the loud music in the club. That explained why they had been playing pool all night without worrying over the high cost of a pool game. They hadn't paid a cent!

The man in the Adidas T-shirt took one shot at the white ball then whispered something in the other's ear, pointing at the full dance floor. They could see Stella, the girl they had come to the club with, expertly dancing with some obese man. The Adidas man motioned his comrade and they followed the throng of people to the dance floor, dodging the drunks on the way.

Stella stopped dancing suddenly and the obese man bent over to ask her something. She motioned to her throat and the man dutifully led her to the bar. The man in the Adidas T-shirt smiled — there was the unspoken rule that in clubs, it was Stella who provided drinks; what with the high number of willing men! All that one had to contend with were the irate ones who demanded a refund of their beer when they discovered they were not going to get their beer's worth at the end of the night. Sometimes it turned into a fight. But then, none of the men now playing pool looked like a stranger to fights.

The obese man ordered four beers for himself and two for Stella. He was busy telling her something and was genuinely irritated when the Adidas man tapped his shoulder and enquired where the 'Gents' were.

"Get lost!" he hissed. He turned back towards Stella, but she was nowhere to be seen. Neither were the six beers. He cursed and swept his drunken eyes all over the club.

The Los Angeles Club was full to the brim tonight. The dance-floor was full of young school children, some hardly fourteen. How they gained entry into the club despite the age restrictions in the club was a mystery. The smell of cigarette smoke hung in the air. The booming hip-hop music reverberated everywhere.

The obese man looked all over the place, fuming in rage. He was half drunk, but his hazy mind picked Stella out of a group playing at one of the six pool tables. He stormed over like a wounded rhino. "Hey!" he turned her around and said drunkenly, "Where is my beer?"

The girl looked at him with absolutely no trace of emotion. "Which beer?"

"You slut!" he began, but then the five-man gang put down the cue sticks and closed in. He saw their bulging chests and hesitated. "*Iko nini?*" What is it? asked the shortest. He was well built, the very tight T-shirt he wore accentuating his large chest.

Outnumbered and intimidated, the obese man swore into the air and staggered away, mumbling something about bullies. The Adidas man smiled at the girl and gave her a pat on her behind.

"Thanks, Stella. That's why you are my number one!"

"*Kwani*, how many of us are there?" she asked in a slightly reprimanding tone.

The game resumed. This time the Adidas man was pitted against the short one. In a well-orchestrated manner, the girl moved away followed almost immediately by three of the men. The two players continued with their game. They sipped from the beer bottles sparingly.

The Adidas man opened one of the beer bottles by prising the top off at the corner of the pool table. Just as he lifted it towards his mouth for a sip, someone pushed him roughly from behind.

"Here they are!" he heard. He turned around to see five of the biggest musclemen in the club. They wore badges labelled 'SECURITY'. Leading them was the obese man whose beer he was drinking.

"Huh?" he lifted his eyebrows as if he had never seen the obese man anywhere on earth.

"Where is my beer?" the obese man asked roughly. "You thought I would let you get away with my beer?"

"Which beer?" the Adidas man asked. His colleagues, even the ones on the dance floor, now stood a round the table in readiness for a fight. Stella stepped behind her man. It was obvious they were used to such confrontations.

"I mean the beer that your slut stole from me. You can't get away with it just like that."

"Oh, so that's why you have brought all these bouncers?" The short one with bulging muscles asked arrogantly as he fingered the beer bottle in his hands as if ready to use it to crash it on somebody's skull. Already their stand-off had attracted the attention of other revellers.

"I just want my beer, that's all," the obese man said defiantly. "You people have become notorious. Can't you buy your own beer?"

"Okay," the Adidas man placed his cue stick on the table and faced them with his arms akimbo. "*Uta do?*" What are you going to do about it now?

The five bouncers moved forward menacingly.

"Mr. Odhiambo, what's wrong?" a lady's voice rose above the din. The warring sides hesitated. The obese man turned towards the voice.

The lady was stunning. The disco lights flashing on her face revealed beauty that no words could describe appropriately. She had lovely eyes, a well shaped nose and thick sensuous lips delicately laced with a trace of lipstick. Her long hair was neatly clipped at the back. She had a body any model would envy. The would-be fighters could not help staring at her as she stood leaning on the pool table while holding a can of REDDS.

"Hi my dear. What are you doing in this joint?" the obese man murmured lamely.

"I thought I could pop in here and have some fun," she replied. "Is something the matter? It looks like I have stepped into a confrontation."

"These hooligans here have stolen my six beers. I was going to teach them a lesson when you came." Mr. Odhiambo gestured towards the five men in anger.

"Just six beers?" the lady wondered, "That's only six hundred shillings!"

"It's not about the money," he replied. "If we let these hooligans get away with this, clubs will become ungovernable. Someone has to put a stop to it now."

The Adidas man and his cronies stepped forward. "Hooligans?"

"Yes! Hooligans, that's what you are!" Mr. Odhiambo countered as his bouncers also moved forward.

"Hey! Stop it!" the lady shouted. They all froze and turned towards her.

"Let's settle this amicably. Mr. Odhiambo, I am going to pay you for the six beers in contention."

From somewhere in her light green Dolce & Gabbana dress she fished out a purse. From inside, she extracted a brand new five hundred shilling note and handed it to the man.

Mr. Odhiambo declined the offer.

"I told you, it's not about money . . ."

"Sh!" she silenced him. "Take the money and leave these people alone."

He looked at her serious eyes and his obstinacy dissolved. "Alright," he said as he led the bouncers away. A few paces away, he wagged a finger at his five opponents, "But make sure not to cross my path again."

The Adidas man smiled and then turned to the retreating lady. "Thank you, whoever you are. You have saved your friend a thorough beating." His colleagues laughed loudly.

"Isn't that girl something?" one of them whispered when Stella was out of earshot. The Adidas man smiled in agreement and secretly made a thumbs-up signal.

*   *   *

It was already past midnight. The Los Angeles Club was now filled to capacity. Most people were on the dance floor gyrating to the loud music booming out of the large speakers. Around the bar, a few people sat on the stools with their beer. Some of them were fast asleep on the counter.

"Get off me!" a female voice rang out.

A youth, hardly seventeen years, with a shaggy mess of hair was trying to pull a girl off a stool. She was protesting vigorously.

The drunken teenager was all over her, mumbling incoherently and spitting saliva into her face. He was suffering from a bad dose of halitosis, the breath he emitted betraying a combination of the cheap spirits he had taken and complicating things further.

"Hey, beautiful! Why don't you join me for a dance?" the boy asked sheepishly.

"No, thanks. I don't feel like dancing."

"I know you want to!" the boy insisted, bringing his half-open eyes and his sagging mouth closer. "That's my best song. Come!" He got off the stool and tugged at her arm.

"No! I don't want to dance," the girl said with finality.

"I know you women are like that," the boy insisted. "You always, say 'no' when you mean 'yes'."

A slap rang out, followed by an 'ouch!' of pain. Some people turned to look. The girl was holding her face while the boy was jerking her other hand.

"Bloody...!" the boy swore.

The man in the Adidas T-shirt came out of the gents, still buttoning up his trousers. He recognized the girl as the one who had hours earlier stopped him from beating up that Odhiambo man. He came closer and held the teenager's hand tightly. The girl looked up at him, her eyes asking for help.

"Hey, *kijana* – the lady does not want to dance. Leave her alone," the Adidas man said calmly. "There are many other girls on the dance floor. Go get your choice."

"Bastard!" the boy drawled drunkenly. "Mind you own business."

"Okay, okay. I'm leaving." The Adidas man turned away. He could almost hear the sigh from the girl who had thought she had found a saviour in him.

Then he pivoted suddenly, at the same time kicking out. His low kick got the teenager right in the groin. The boy doubled up in pain. The Adidas man hit him hard on the back of the head and he fell on the ground, writhing in pain. Then he kicked him thrice in the ribs.

"I think you should let him rest," he told the bewildered girl, pulling on such a gentle face you would think he had done something most commendable.

"Thank you," she whispered. She was still amazed at the brutal way in which he had handled the matter.

Suddenly, two security men burst onto the scene, attracted by the commotion. One of them recognised the Adidas man.

"What is it this time?" he growled. He was one of the five bouncers who had accosted him a while earlier during his altercation with Odhiambo.

"There is nothing wrong," the girl said calmly. She took the Adidas man's hand. "Come on, let's go."

The Adidas man's colleagues rushed over to rescue him.

"Everything's okay," he assured them.

"We don't want more trouble from you," the bouncer warned them, eyeing each of them sternly.

The girl led the Adidas man back to the pool table.

"Better be careful with those bouncers," she warned him. "Next time they are going to throw you out."

"I don't care," he answered. "Do you play pool?" he asked as an afterthought.

"A little."

"Then let me challenge you to a game."

She smiled, revealing a set of the most dazzling teeth he had seen. He raised his eyebrows slightly in awe.

"Challenge accepted," she replied in a husky voice full of confidence. She had an accent and spoke like a radio presenter. There was no telling whether it was real or faked though, he thought. These days, almost all girls tend to talk with a nasal twang in imitation of foreign role models.   She calmly sipped from the can of REDDS.

"How do you want to play?" he asked. There were two options: Loser Pays or Bet Game. The former meant that the loser would pay the cost of the game while in the latter option both players paid for the game, and then the winner collected a prize.

"I have seen how you open the game," she told him matter-of -factly. "Why don't we pay for this particular one and see whether all those free games have sharpened your expertise?"

The man winced, then smiled. She knew he was surprised by how much she knew about them.

"What is the bet?" he asked. He didn't want to bet any money. In pool, only a fool risked his money playing against someone whose expertise he didn't know. He opted for another choice where he would have nothing to lose.

"If I win," he grinned, "you dance with me the rest of the night." The remark elicited another smile. Her teeth sparkled under the white fluorescent tube hanging over the table. Her dress reflected the disco lighting beautifully.

"*Ni sawa.*" Okay with me. She switched to Kiswahili, though the accent was still there.

"You break," he told her.

"She bent down and with a surprisingly powerful shot, broke the triangle of arranged balls on the table. He stared at her firm behind, made even finer by the woollen dress. It took him quite some time to realize that some balls had dropped into the holes. With a slight 'Oh!' he bent down to see what type of balls she had pocketed. Stripes.

"You play 'stripes'," he informed her, and she nodded in agreement.

He moved back to let her access the best angle for her next shot. Another clean shot. He thought he heard a gasp from his colleagues. He pulled his eyes from behind her to the game.

Damn! he thought. He had underestimated her skills. She arched her hand expertly and hit the white ball with enough force to get two of her balls sliding slowly into the hole – double shot. "This lady is a professional!" he said.

Suddenly, he realized he had not pocketed any of his balls. A wary smile crept up his face when he saw his own seven balls in very unfavourable positions. If she finished all her balls before he'd put in any of his, the game would be over. That would be a disgrace! In pool, that was the most shameful defeat!

Luckily, she hit her next ball a bit too softly and it stopped a centimetre away from the hole. He smiled triumphantly.

"Your turn," she said as she slid back. Damn! he cursed inwardly as he studied his balls to see which among them was best placed. He could not lose the credibility he enjoyed as the local pool champion. A glance at one of his colleagues across the table showed him he was fast losing it. He ignored him and concentrated on the game.

Ball number six was nearer the hole. If he got it, it would be easier to pocket ball number seven, then number one. If it failed, the white ball would fall behind his other balls, making it harder for her to hit her remaining ones. He aimed. From the corner of his eye he saw her move opposite him. She smiled again. He missed the ball by a whole inch. Hell!

"I get two shots?" she asked irritatingly.

"Sure," he answered with clenched teeth.

There was no way she could get at her ball – she was completely snookered by his ball number four. He smiled. She frowned in concentration, then walked over to the other side of the table and hit the ball off the side of the cushion. He tensed as the ball slowly passed his balls and hit one of hers, edging it close to the hole.

"Good!" she whispered as she took her next shot. She remained with only one ball.

He took a wild aim and hit the cue ball with all his strength, something he had not done for ages. His balls flew all over the table. Mercifully, one of them slid into the pocket. He breathed a big sigh of relief.

His next shot was disastrous. Not only did he fail to pocket any of his balls, but he also let the white ball stay right in front of her remaining one. He cursed yet again – this kind of play was very unlike him. His colleagues gave him a look of disapproval from across the table.

One shot was enough for her to pocket her two balls. She looked at him, smiled and pointed at the most obvious destination hole for the black ball. He nodded, all signs of defeat on his face. She aimed at the hole for a whole minute.

Damn! he thought angrily. She was taking ages to make the decisive shot, as if she was teasing him! It was more humiliating to watch her doing this when he knew the game was over, and he was about to shout, "Go ahead! Finish the game, godammit!" when he suddenly noticed that she had the cue stick tilted in her hand. He paused. This kind of shot would make the white ball follow the black ball into the designated hole. He was puzzled that she did not see that, experienced as she was.

She took the shot and true to his word, the black ball dropped into the hole and the white ball followed along.

"A *follow-me!*" he almost shouted. She had lost! He sipped his beer and smiled at her.

"I've made a fatal mistake," she complained with no hint of regret in her voice as she stretched out her hand to congratulate him. She had the softest of hands.

"Hi. It's nice to meet you all. I am Nancy," she smiled at them. The looks on their faces told her she had somehow impressed them. The dark one threw the cigarette butt on the ground and placed his drink on the table.

"My name is Bone," the one in the fake Adidas T-shirt said. "Bone, *mfupa*."

He set about introducing his crew. The dark one – the epitome of blackness – was called Ngeta. She loudly wondered what the name meant, but nobody answered her query. He too was dressed in imitation clothes, just like Bone – a fake Nike top over brown corduroy trousers. He wore a permanent scowl on his face. Not the kind of a guy you'd want to meet at a dark street corner, she concluded.

The short, heavily set one was Bafu. He looked less menacing, but there was an unearthing glint in his eye. The small eyes darted in all directions like those of a pickpocket. His face expressionless, he squeezed her outstretched hand and fondled the big chain round his neck with the free one.

The one with the stylish hairstyle was Bomu. He had frighteningly bloodshot eyes that bored into you unseeingly. Bomu wore a bright yellow vest and stared shamelessly at her chest when she stretched out her hand to greet him.

Rock looked more presentable than the rest. He wore a beach shirt under a black coat, and on his left ear was a copper ring. Just like Bone, he had ruggedly handsome features. With the right grooming, he could pass off as an attractive man.

"Hey," Bone said, "you owe me a dance!" He winked at the rest of the crew as he grabbed her by the waist and led her to the dance floor. He placed his hand on her behind feelingly. Her woollen dress looked and smelled new. He was almost ashamed of his second-hand clothes. He slid his hand down her waist and as she placed her own delicate ones round his shoulder, he almost whispered, 'Whoa!'

The night wore on. She was a pretty good dancer. Had he not been frequenting dance halls, he could have been totally lost. The girl employed many styles he had not seen before. The DJ on the turntables switched onto Lingala and they stopped dancing. As if by some telepathetic connection, none of them was interested in dancing to Lingala.

"Care for a drink?" she asked.

"No, no. I'm fine!" he hastily replied. Another rule of thumb for the crew was that you didn't buy girls drinks before four in the morning. You got broke, and they would leave you for greener pastures. If you wanted to take a girl home, you started buying her drinks in the wee hours of the morning.

As if reading his thoughts, she added, ". . . It's okay, I'll buy."

"Well, in that case . . ." he shrugged. This must be the most inexperienced girl he had ever seen. Why in God's name buy a man a drink while hordes of men would fight to buy you until you collapsed?

A girl as exquisite as she was needed not to look far before a stupid man came with offers. Bone could see the looks of envy as they walked towards the bar. He thought he heard surprised guffaws from his group – they imagined he was the one doing the buying.

She ordered REDDS and he a Tusker. There was an ongoing competition, *Mavuno Kenya Nzima!* and he secretly thought he would strike it rich.

The DJ played the hit song, *Ni Wakati,* and the crowd went into a frenzy. Nancy was puzzled by the excitement.

"It's been a while since the DJ played such music," Bone explained, sipping his beer. "He has only been playing American tunes. You know that group – *Kalamashaka?* It's the equivalent of America's Lost Boyz. We have enough talent here."

"Well, it's all about taste," she said, not quite interested in Kalamashaka.

To change the subject, Bone asked, "Excuse me, but who was that Odhiambo man?"

"Just an acquaintance," she replied, not divulging much. He did not pursue the matter further. Some of the ladies he knew had sugar daddies who looked worse than Odhiambo.

He smiled tolerantly then said, "If you don't mind, let us speak in Kiswahili. Where I come from, you'd get mugged for speaking English."

There was a slight frown on her face. She had a pair of the most startling eyes he had not seen in a long time. Even her frown was beautiful. She was breathtaking, he concluded. The reigning Miss Kenya would certainly pause on seeing her. He was already plotting how he would get to enjoy her company without the knowledge of Stella.

"*Kwani,* where do you come from?" she asked.

"I'm sure you wouldn't like to know that," he smiled.

"I would like to. That's why I asked."

"There is a song by some guy called Ndarlin' P," he explained as he fingered the bottle top, looking under the liner to see what he'd won. She knew he had not won anything when he flung it onto the crowded dance hall. "He talks of chips and *mandazi* worth five bob. I come from one of those places."

She looked at him innocently, as if she was picturing the locality in her mind.

"Do you mean to say that all that stuff in the song is true? That there are places where chips are sold at five shillings?"

"Sure. My immediate neighbour sells them at that price."

" Do you come from a slum?"

"We call it a ghetto. It's less demeaning."

"A real slum, like Kibera?"

"Kibera is a different case altogether," he informed her as he bent forward. It was time to deliver the winning line. "If you wish, I could take you there free of charge. Then you will see all these things for yourself."

She hesitated. "I'll think about it. Give me until morning to decide."

He smiled. Now, all he had to do was keep Stella out of the way. "Let's go dance," he said.

*   *   *

They occupied the back seat of an old Kenya Bus. All of them were haggard and tired, a far cry from the vibrancy that they had exhibited on entering the club the previous night. Bafu had his head in his hands, while Bomu was struggling to keep his eyes open. Ngeta had given up and now slept, his head thrown back and his mouth wide open. At the far end of the bus, just after Rock, a man they had seen at the Los Angeles the previous night was fondling a small drunken girl. Man, Bone thought, she is barely fourteen!

Bone was still tipsy. The girl – what was her name, Nancy? – had spent over three thousand shillings on him and his friends, which explained why they looked that 'stoned'. He glanced outside at the Sunday morning scene as the bus sped out of the station. Evidence of the previous night's escapades was strewn all over the streets in the form of broken bottles and crushed cans.

He glanced at Nancy who looked petrified as she clutched the seat in front with her well manicured hands. It was as if she had never experienced anything like this ride before. The bus hit a pothole at top speed and she lurched forward. Bone took the opportunity to slip his hands round her waist, for the hundredth time thanking his lucky stars that his girl, Stella, had gotten bored with Los Angeles and decided to move to Hollywood Club where they played pure reggae. The slum girl would have torn Nancy to shreds.

The bus stopped to pick more early morning passengers. Most were vegetable vendors coming from Wakulima Market, commonly known as Marigiti. By the time it reached Kenyatta Avenue, joined

Ngong Road, briefly left it at the library and rejoined it near Kenyatta National Hospital, it was already full. There were more people standing than seated. Bone watched the small overworked conductor coming towards them, weighed down by the heaviness of the ticket machine. He saw Bafu throw quick glances at him and instantly understood his friend's consternation.

You see, this group never paid bus fare. There were scores of ways of avoiding paying. Sometimes one would alight just when spotted by the conductor and waited for the next bus and repeated the same until one reached the stop. Or the colleague in front paid, then passed the ticket to the one behind who displayed it to the conductor before passing it to the other behind. Sometimes the conductor caught you, and you had to pay. You could cheat on where you were alighting and pay half the fare. In most cases, however, it was better to wink at the conductor then give him half the fare. You wouldn't have the ticket, and he'd keep the half fare to himself, unreceipted – a benefit to both parties.

Bafu's worry today was that they could not pull any tricks with such a lady in their company.

Smiling, Bone sought to allay his fears.

"Don't worry about the bus fare," he said as he squeezed Nancy tighter. "The lady will pay!"

Nancy looked surprised even as she removed a crisp two hundred shillings note to pay. She was amazed because Bone had not consulted her about it.

"Kenol!" He told the conductor. "We are alighting at Kenol." The heavy roar of the engine dampened any efforts of him conversing with Nancy as the old bus ambled on past Dagoretti Corner. Bomu and Ngeta snored loudly. Occasionally, Ngeta would stir awake, look around him and bless anyone looking at him with a scowl that intimidated them and made them hastily look away .

As they alighted at Kenol near the Commonwealth War Cemetery, Nancy looked at the serene and subdued atmosphere. It hardly fitted what Bone had described the previous night. The Kenol Petrol Station from which the stage acquired its name stood beside the huge Kazi Plaza and the equally imposing Sterling Crafts. They crossed Ngong Road which was now deserted because it was on a Sunday, at seven o'clock in the morning.

A mound of debris blocked the narrow, one lane dirty road that passed between Sterling Craft and another compound with a well-decorated fence, evidently from the construction of the wall beside it. The six of them had to walk in a single file.

"Ah!" Ngeta grumbled as he slid near the place carved out of the fence where water was sold at five shillings per jerrycan according to a handwritten sign on the wall. "*Kwani,* When is this man going to finish this construction work?"

"He is inconveniencing hundreds of people!" Bomu added as he lit a cigarette,

Nancy looked at Bone and asked, "You mean, it's one man who has done this?"

"He happens to be a big man in our society. There is nothing we can do about him," Bone explained.

"The whole neighbourhood can sue him!"

Rock laughed. He hit a piece of broken pottery with his shoe. "I don't know where you lived before you fell onto this earth," he said, smiling to show he meant no insult. "This is Kenya. This guy is a lawyer and a politician. He is untouchable. So, if he decides to build his wall and block off the road, he need not apologise to anybody."

"Besides," Bafu said, "Rumour has it that a group of shop owners went to see him about this. He threatened to close the whole road. I think it falls on his land."

"You can go to the local MP!" insisted Nancy. All the five men laughed at her naivety.

"The local MP indeed!" scoffed Rock, then he went on: "We are lucky to have him as one of the most active members in Parliament. He is great in the House, contributing in to all the debates, tabling controversial motions and so on. Unfortunately, I've only seen him once when he came in a convoy to thank us for voting him in."

Bone stretched out his hand for a share of the cigarette now reduced to a stub. "I heard they are in the same political party, the lawyer and the MP," he explained. "You don't expect them to disagree, do you?"

They were now approaching Ngando. The slum lay wedged in between Santack Estate, Key-West and Ghettos – the latter two being shanty dwellings as well. It was divided into two by one major road with many smaller outlets that led deeper into the rusty *mabati* and mud houses. You could smell the decay in the air – the whole place smelled like a pigsty. A sewer had evidently burst ahead and a thick greenish viscosity flowed along the road, weaving in some places.

A heavily pregnant goat was nibbling at rubbish from a foul-smelling dump beside the road. Across its protuberant belly, someone had scrawled, 'ASK FOR TRANSPORT' in charcoal. Nancy laughed loudly, though the others did not seem to find anything amusing.

The group filed out into one of the narrower lanes. The lane filtered into another still narrower one. Nancy was perplexed by the situation. She had never known this place even after a hundred visits. The small, derelict houses leaned dangerously on their sides. A man lay sprawled out in the mud, and the five men laughed at his familiar face.

"That's the effect of *mugacha*," Bone explained without feeling as he kicked a pebble at the man in the puddle. "Most likely he spent the night drinking the illicit brew."

They walked between two rows of *mabati* houses whose doors faced each other. Nancy gasped. The space between the rows was less than a metre. A small ditch meandered the whole length of the narrow space. Above them, on the two lengths of hanging wire, were wet bedding and not so clean clothes still dripping. At a door at the end of that row of houses, Bone unceremoniously stopped, produced a rusty key from somewhere at the rafters and opened the corroded padlock. Nancy looked up at the rickety door. In a small untidy scrawl, written in chalk were the words: *The Slaughterhouse*. Under it was scrawled in capital letters:

THIS IS THE ROOM YOUR MOTHER
WARNED YOU ABOUT

They entered like a flock of tired sheep.

Nancy sat on the only bed in the room and surveyed it curiously. Apart from the bed, the only other furniture were three stools and a small table on which a draughts board was roughly drawn. On the checked design were burnt-out cigarette ends strewn amongst many bottle tops. At the far corner of the room stood a sooty stove amid a pile of dirty dishes.

Nancy looked at the darkened side of the wall above the stove, then turned her face to the adjacent wall where, also in chalk, was laconically inscribed:

'Ladies please don't fight,
Bone is here all night!'

She chuckled at the author's attempt at rhythmic arrangement, and then yawned. As if on cue, the four other men stood up and prepared to leave.

"See you later at Thiong'o's," Bafu said to Bone as he and Nancy were left to themselves.

Shortly, they heard a giggle from outside and suddenly, a little girl skipped playfully into the room.

"*Sasa* Bone?" she jumped at him.

"Cecily! Isn't it too early to visit?" he whipped her in his arms and swirled her in the air. She screamed in delight.

"Come, Ngeta will go buy you something," he told her. Instantly, she jumped from Bone's hands and ran out after Ngeta.

Bone stood at the centre of the room, his hands akimbo as he faced Nancy's inquiring expression.

"Cecily is our friend. Her mother's always beating her whenever she comes to visit us, but she never stops coming. She is the only neighbour, I guess, who likes us." He caught Nancy's eyes as relief flooded into them.

"Well, this is the home you so much wanted to see," he announced. "You'll get a chance to see around the place, but first, we need to rest." He removed the T-shirt to expose a well-muscled body.

*   *   *

It was the sweltering heat that woke her up at noon. She was startled at first, not knowing where she was, but then she relaxed after seeing Bone at the corner, cooking something over the stove. "God!" she exclaimed. "It's really hot in here." "Yes. In these *mabati* rooms, it gets quite hot in the afternoon." She saw a large mosquito slowly float in the air, then settle on the table before lifting away again. She stared in amazement at its sheer size.

"I thought mosquitoes only came out at night," she ventured.

"Not here in Ngando," he laughed. "Here they work twenty-four hours. . . like petrol stations!" he said mirthfully. "They breed in the filth out there, and then come to suck our blood. We've tried everything – once we bought a mosquito coil, but we stopped using it when we woke up at night to find them warming themselves by it."

She laughed loudly. Then she froze as the insect purposefully buzzed towards her.

"No! It is going to bite me!" she cried out.
Bone slammed his palm onto the wall, and removed it to expose blood smeared over the *mabati*. As if he had done nothing, he walked back to the stove, wiping his hands against his trousers, and continued with his culinary preparations.

He placed the sufuria down and, using two torn pieces of paper, took the stove outside. She heard the hissing sound of water upon fire. Suddenly, he came in running and slammed the door shut behind him. Her heart skipped a beat.

"Sorry," he told her when he saw her petrified look, "I'm shutting out the smoke. Some *fundi* messed with the stove, so it cannot be turned off. We have to use water."

Nancy rose off the bed just as he sieved the tea he had prepared into two battered cups. Then he passed one cup to her and handed over a large steaming *ndazi* as well.
And so Nancy, for the first time, tasted the famous *mandazi ya kobole*.

two

Nairobi, 2001

Ngando's population was made up of drunks, the unemployed and idlers. Well, not exactly idlers but people who you thought were idlers until you found yourself upside down with your pockets frisked and wallet gone. *Sheng* was the locals' official language and *chang'aa* the official brew.

The hub of activity was the collection of shops along the one main road. There was Nyang'anya's shop, Gitau's butchery and Njogu's 'Dot-com' Kerosene depot. The other side was more lively, housing Thiong'o's Pool Bar where all the idlers met, and Mama Pima's Parlour – the *miti-ni-dawa* place. Standing curiously among these was the East African Church of the Holy Spirit, Kenya Chapter. When each of the businesses was in session, the area was rowdier than a Gor Mahia versus AFC Leopards football match.

Nyang'anya operated a general shop. He was aptly named so because of his well-honed, uncanny ability to short-change his customers. He was one of the most arrogant and spiteful shopkeepers in Ngando. It was surprising how he managed to maintain a steady flow of customers. Perhaps, It was because his was the only shop that sold goods in the smallest affordable quantities. If you wanted sugar worth only five shillings, you'd get it from him.

Njogu, the kerosene dealer, had the shop next to Nyang'anya. He was more popular than his next door neighbour. His only letdown was that he drank heavily. Njogu was otherwise a very humble and pleasant man until he got drunk. Funnily, only then did he discover that chips were, after all, potatoes, and he asked his customers, "*Kumbe chivus ni viazi?*" He could be quite stupid when drunk.

Ngando was the home of some of the weirdest human beings. It was the home of comedians like Charlie, the short young man who looked ten years younger than he really was and who took advantage of this fact fully. He would purposely irritate you, and if you grabbed him in a fit of anger he would shout, "*Wachana na pesa za mamangu, nimetumwa!*" You would, of course, be embarrassed when everyone around looked at you accusingly as if you were indeed robbing a minor.

Nevertheless, there were several well-meaning traders, like Mali. Same as hundreds of others, nobody knew Mali's real name. He was the '*mali kwa mali*' man who exchanged plastic containers for anything from your house: bottles, old shoes, clothes, and even old newspapers.

*   *   *

Word that Bone had brought home an extraordinary girl reached Thiong'o's even before Nancy was out of The Slaughterhouse. When Bone went to Thiong'os, everyone milled around him, trying to find out how she was. Charlie, touted as one of the meanest men Ngando had ever produced, bought him a sachet of Cane liquor in congratulation. Even Thiong'o allowed Bone and the others to play three free games.

Bone tried to be modest. "Oh! She is just like any other common floozy you meet at the Los Angeles. In fact, there is nothing she has that your Waithera doesn't have!"

Charlie surveyed the room for a moment, then shot back. "Nonsense! Waithera cannot buy me beer! If she bought me a drink, I would get saved." When the laughter died down, Bone cautioned them about spreading word of it around. If Stella got to hear about it, he said, she would kill both of them. One never underestimated the temperament of a ghetto girl.

"Anyway, I don't even think she'll come back here again," he finally said. "She is not used to stepping on mud. So it was a one-night stand."

"Yeah," piped Rock. "She's now probably in Lavington or Runda, watching *No One but You* on television!" Neither Bone nor the others said anything more about Nancy for that day.

*   *   *

The residents knew nothing about the five-man group that stuck together like Super Glue and rubber. They didn't even know where they had come from. They had never told anyone the meaning of their strange nicknames or revealed their real names. It was really strange. But then, that was the changing Nairobi or may be Kenya. Strange names, strange music, a very new and strange world.

Most of the now famous musicians in Kenya today owe their success to the 'Showtime' sessions at Florida 2000 and New York discotheques. Successful groups like Kalamashaka, Zulukru and K-South first started out from these clubs where their talents were noticed by the producers of the time.

Bone was a product of 'Showtime'. However, despite the immense popularity he enjoyed with his friends from the ghetto, the situation outside was different. The world outside was not ready for the kind of lyrics he sang. He had had numerous arguments over this with a top producer.

"Come on, Bone," the producer would say. "You've got to sing something that's going to please the masses. We want songs people will dance to, not dirges!"

Bone did not like the idea of toning down his language. He scoffed at the young rappers emerging from obscurity, trying hard to ape Western musicians with meaningless rhymes.

"I can't waste my time rapping about my lyrical supremacy and my wealth while there are millions of Kenyans living below the poverty line!"

Puffed with this determination, he looked for some money and produced his own music. But then, the radio stations refused to play his music, citing inherent incendiary phrases!

"Damn!" he swore at one radio producer. "Those foreign musicians are taking up all our airwaves! Just think, this American rapper shouts about raping his own mother and killing his wife and you play his music five times a day, yet you can't play my music because I speak about corruption!"

"It's not only about the message," explained the producer, "it's about popularity and demand. We play what our audience requests. They request those songs, so we play them!"

"Nonsense! You have made sure that the audience doesn't know about local musicians. How can they request for my music if they don't hear it and get to know me?"

"But we feature local music as well," the producer was adamant.

"Local music "indeed!" Bone retorted, and then added reflectively,

"When I switch on my radio each morning, the presenter tells me which American personality is celebrating a birthday. They go to the extent of telling me every detail about American musicians – from who is dating who to what size of shoes the rappers wear, or the size of a diva's rear. We don't get to hear anything about local musicians. Really infuriating!"

Slowly, he lost interest in music and could only be found writing rhymes occasionally. Even with the sudden promotion of local talent by music houses and radio stations, he refused to record any more music. When the producer had come back to him asking to promote him, Bone had told the guy off.

Some residents of Ngando remember that when the five young men arrived there many years ago, Bone was known as *Mfupa*. All of a sudden, his friend Rock started calling him the English equivalent and the whole slum followed suit.

Most of the time, Bone was seen working out at the local 'gym', where the work-out machines were a collection of stones ingeniously joined together with metal bars, or at Thiong'o's, or with his girl, Stella. Many thought he had wasted his twenty-something years, but to him nothing really mattered.

Bafu was Bone's favourite within the group. They stuck together, and many times got involved in brawls. He was short but sturdy. He was also known to instil fear into notable weightlifters including Gosti, the local body builder. He wore a small, almost unnoticeable moustache and spotted a permanent 'Jordan' hairstyle.

The significance of his name was lost on people. It could have meant the Kiswahili term for bathroom, or a phrase coined from the sheng *kupiga bafu*, roughly meaning to outwit. Bafu was known more for the latter than the former. He was always looking for ways to make money. He could, as Bone rhymed, 'sell water to a well and fire in hell'. Any time his lips parted, his audience braced itself for a tall tale. His ridiculous talent earned him quite a number of female friends, most of whom were gullible schoolgirls.

Initially, Bafu's main interest was in football. When he was not playing a card game called *kameda* or conning someone, he was to be found training at Kaharo, a small field just near the Ngong Racecourse. He had once harboured dreams of making it to the national team and later graduating to professional football.

His dreams were, however, unceremoniously shattered when it was discovered that the money he and his teammates had collected had disappeared mysteriously. So had the coach who handled the team's finances. Then, a few months later, a stone fence was hurriedly constructed around the training field. After numerous complains, the residents were informed that the land had been allocated to the area councillor.

Some of the team members had continued playing on a small strip of land left on the side by the developers, but had soon given up, unable to train on the bumpy ground. There was the option of playing at the Telkom field just a kilometre away, but Bafu had lost interest in the game altogether.

Bomu was a tout on the busy route 111. He plied that route on the attractive and popular Nissan *matatu* named 'Snoop' after some American rapper.

Years earlier, touts had been considered the scum of society. It was abominable to be a tout. It was a career chosen by school dropouts and illiterates, and parents had no need to keep their daughters away from touts because they were not appealing to anybody. They were shaggy and dirty, and abused people flagrantly while at the same time shoving them into their vehicles.

Lately, however, society had apparently changed its opinion of them. Suddenly, touts wore the flashiest and most appealing clothes. They sported nice, clean and stylish hairstyles, and became trendsetters. Teenagers flocked into *matatus* manned by flamboyant touts. Suddenly, young girls started playing truant to be with touts, and even some, eloped with them. It had reached a point where being a tout was the in thing. Many a time, Bomu had stopped fights between girls in his matatu over him.

Despite all the hype and almost celebrity status they enjoyed, life was not easy for both the touts and the *matatu* drivers. They had to contend with a 5 a.m.-10 p.m. work schedule. They left home with orders from the matatu owners to bring an astronomical amount of money at the end of the day. During the day, they had to deal with arrogant customers as well as corrupt traffic police officers who demanded unreasonable bribes. Besides, there were those opportunists who thought that simply being a neighbour to a tout or driver was enough to earn them a free ride.

"So you want to pay five shillings to town?" Bomu would ask a passenger on one of his bad days. "Why don't you buy a piece of roast maize worth that money and go on foot?"

He was sick of passengers who boarded the *matatu* knowing very well what the fare was but still wanted to bargain. Come end-month, the same passengers would arrogantly pay their fare with large-denomination notes, knowing very well there was nowhere he could get change that early morning.

Maybe it was this hectic life that fuelled Bomu's phenomenal love affair with bhang, commonly known as *boza* or *bomu* among other synonyms in Ngando. His eyes were always dazed and bloodshot from smoking the drug as well as chewing miraa endlessly. It was rumoured that he grew some *bomu* at the small forest between the road to Lenana School and Ngong Road, but these rumours were never confirmed.

Rock was the other interesting member of the group. Unlike the rest of his friends, he was married – not in church, but in the common 'come-we-stay' fashion. He was loyal to Mary, his spouse, even though he spent most of his time in the company of his friends. Unlike what most girls would do, Mary never seemed to mind his liaison with the rest of the group. It was as if she had been let into the secret of their bond and promised to stick together.

Rock had like most greengrocers in Nairobi, graduated from the porter business in *Marigiti* market. He had learnt the secrets of the trade and, as soon as he had saved enough, he had left the market to set up his own business. Most of the days, it was Mary who manned the green grocery.

What nobody in Ngando ever knew was that it was one of Kenya's greatest calamities that helped Rock into this business. When, in August 1998, a bomb blast had rocked the city of Nairobi, he had been one of the first people to get to the scene. The bomb, targeting the U.S. Embassy, had extensively damaged Co-operative House. The smaller Ufundi Co-operative House which had borne the brunt of the explosion had collapsed, burying underneath many people. Over two hundred people had died and over five thousand injured.

Rock had rushed to help rescue the victims from the rubble. It was then that he stumbled upon a briefcase with a government logo on it. Instinct told him to tuck it in some corner. Unfortunately, some of his colleagues from *Marigiti* had seen him sneak it away. When the briefcase was forced open, they realized that it was stacked with money. In the ensuing fight for the cash, Rock had managed to grab a handful of the crisp, new notes. Later in the night, as he planned how to start some worthwhile business, he had heard it announced over the radio that a minister had lost his pocket money in the blast – Kenya shillings 300,000! He had used his portion of the money to open the grocery.

The astute manner in which his wife, Mary, handled the business earned her a steady string of clients. Rock saw the business as a great blessing. He praised the minister for giving him manna. He was, in fact, thinking of registering as a voter in the minister's constituency so as to vote for him.

If Ngando residents didn't know much about Bone and Rock, they pretty well knew something about Ngeta. The well-muscled black man was as abominable. Like Bomu, he too worshipped bhang and *miraa*. He had become frustrated with looking for jobs. He had always worked as a casual labourer and was quite an experienced construction worker. It was his wish that one day he would be made foreman, but then he realized that to be made a foreman one had to know how to grease and oil the right hands. To do this one had to have money. He didn't have the money, so his experience went to waste.

Ngeta was more famous for the nocturnal activities he engaged in, especially *kupiga ngeta*, meaning to mug. He 'owned' the territory behind Kenol Petrol Station where he hid in the dark corners and waylaid passersby. His armlock was reinforced with a piece of wood tied expertly on his arm in such a way that, if he got your neck in a strong hold, the single breath you exhaled was only to declare where your wallet was and how much was in it.

Ngeta's black cap was infamous. When he walked towards you with his head bent low, his cap covering half his face, you'd dismiss him as just another madman suffering from disillusionment. Suddenly, he would attack in a first and surprising move. Then, it would be too late to notice that the cap had two holes bored into it, and that he had been watching you all along. By that time, your wallet would be gone.

Fortunately, Ngeta never attacked people he knew. Actually, if you passed near his hideout and whispered into the darkness, "*Niaje Ngeta?*" nothing would happen to you. Sometimes, he returned useful things, like people's ID cards. That is probably why the residents had not lynched him as yet, even though most wished he contracted something bad like AIDS, or got shot by the police.

If there was anything Ngeta hated most was to be woken up early in the morning. You could get a fist in your face for that. Bafu had once tried to rouse him:

"Come on, wake up! The early bird catches the worm."

He had woken up just to retort, "Shut up! What about the early worm?"

Ngeta was in an on-off-and-on-again relationship with an equally weird girl from Kibera who frequented reggae clubs and competed with him in smoking bhang.

*　*　*

So, Bone, Bomu and Bafu were the bona fide owners of The Slaughterhouse. Ngeta and Rock were like extended family members. It was however, rare to find even two of the three in the house, because each was on his own money-making exploits. And life for the five men was like a verse from '*Pesa, Pombe, Siasa na Wanawake*' (*money, alcohol, politics and women*) – the popular song by Mashifta:

Naishi leo ni kaa hakuna kesho. . .	*I'm living today like there is no tomorrow. . .*
Siku za wiki kwetu ni wikendi,	*Weekdays are weekends to us,*
Kila ndururu tunaspendi,	*Every cent we spend,*
Kaa hunipendi,	*If you don't like me,*
Sikupendi!	*I don't like you either!*

The Slaughterhouse was the local den of iniquities. A lot of activities which would interest the police took place there. Kameda was played into the dead of the night, most of the times ending in fights. Sometimes, the room was rented out to one-night stand couples. Such lodging services were offered at fifty shillings per night.

Not that the neighbours did not mind or did not try to stop the heinous activities. The one who came nearest angrily knocked on the door during a scuffle when a woman had refused to participate in a sexual orgy known as a *kombi*. The neighbour had been met by Ngeta at the door, with a scowl that made him forget what had brought him there. He had hastily left. The only neighbour the gang was in good terms with was Chomelea, the man who made a living repairing other peoples' plastic objects at a fee.

Exasperated tenants had complained to the landlord once, but he had simply mumbled something about the spoilt young generation, then he had abruptly left. It was rumoured that he feared the five young men much more than he feared being broke. It was said that he had once removed the door to The Slaughterhouse when the occupants had failed to pay rent. He had allegedly returned the door the same day, having mysteriously suffered a broken nose. It was also whispered that since then, The Slaughterhouse's rent was paid when and if the occupants wished.

Nobody really knows who exactly floated the idea of bringing a peer counsellor to talk to 'The Slaughterhouse Five'. It had been mooted by the neighbours during one of the days none of the gang members was around. There had been a hurried meeting and it was decided that if the infamous neighbours could not be evicted, then something should be done to redeem their behaviour.

The day the peer counsellor showed up is always talked of during one of their more nostalgic times, when they feel the need to laugh. The girl was probably twenty. She was pretty and fresh from college. Having attended training on peer issues at a local youth institution and also earned accolades from a non-governmental organization specializing in counselling young adults, she believed she was well equipped to get into the men's hearts and change their ways. She was quite unprepared for what she received.

To start with, she had chosen a very wrong day. For one, everybody in the house was broke and irritable. Bafu had been injured the previous day during a football match. Ngeta had been involved in a brawl a few hours earlier and was in a foul mood. Rock and Bone were nursing dreadful hangovers. Bomu had just broken up with one of his many girls. She had used a series of expletives. He was incensed by the words and kept on swearing as he chewed furiously on his miraa.

The previous night, they had gone to the aid of one of the women in the plot whose husband had come home late, dead drunk and started pummelling her. Her heart-wrenching screams had raised much debate. Could they intervene? It was a domestic issue and they had no right to poke in their noses. But when the man had started beating up the children as well, they had all trooped out.

"*Wacha ujinga ama tuingie na huu mlango !*" Stop this stupidity or we break open the door! Ngeta had warned him.

Sure enough, they had smashed the door and proceeded to give the man a few slaps in front of his relieved family, and left him with the warning that if they heard as much as a whimper from the house, the man would pay for it in kind.

"I love fights, but not when the weak are on the receiving end!" Bafu had said as he limped back to The Slaughterhouse.

And now the peer counsellor knocked, said a casual 'hi' and stood at the door waiting to be welcomed in. Bone lifted his head, tried to see through the maze, failed and fell back. Bomu chewed on the miraa as if he was on another planet altogether.

"Hallo everyone," she now started confidently. "My name is Florence and I've been sent to talk to you about. . ."

"*Hatukuelewi!*" We cannot understand you, Ngeta said. "Talk a language we can understand. We don't speak German."

She was taken aback, but she took it in her stride and smiled, then switched from English to Kiswahili.

"I was wondering . . . er, do you know about AIDS, and . . ."

"Yes," Bafu said as he shifted his injured leg and placed it on the only stool. "It is spread by having unprotected sex with an infected woman, through blood transfusion, bla, bla,. .. It's not spread through shaking hands, playing together, etc. . ."

It was evident nobody was interested in what she was saying. That line of approach discouraged, she chose another path. "I'm wondering if you'd mind to use protection," she fumbled for something in her bag. "I have in my possession. . ."

"Don't bother," Bone said, his eyes closed. "There are hundreds of condoms in a box just outside Kax Kinyozi. We'll go there when we need some!"

"Well, I really think you should think about the 'True Love Waits' approach." She fumbled for another pamphlet.

"Ati, true love waits?" Bafu chuckled. "True love waits for what?"

"Listen, Siz," said Bone. "I've not met the girl I'll marry. When I meet her, maybe we will wait. But now. . ."

"You see," the girl countered, "it's just that attitude which makes AIDS take such a heavy toll on us. At the moment, 700 people are dying everyday, and 23 are being infected each hour, and the figure is rising. . ."

"That's the problem with you people," Rock spoke up now. "You bombard the youth with strange facts and frightening statistics. You make us see the scourge as an abnormal thing that cannot happen to them. Why don't you people address the real issues, like the poverty that makes the infected people die, or the unavailability of drugs for the sick?"

"The government is importing drugs worth millions of shillings and they will soon be available."

"And is the government also importing food for all those dying because their bodies do not receive enough nutrients to fight AIDS related diseases?" Bone asked.

"The government cannot do everything," she continued. "We, must also do our bit."

"Like wearing condoms?" Rock asked sarcastically.

"Yes," she answered. "That's just but one of them."

"I have a slight problem, young lady," Bafu chipped in. "It's about the size and strength of the condoms you people distribute. Have you looked at the ones available in these tiny satchets your organisation offers? I bet you would not use them yourself – they are so weak that you have to use at least four so as to think of protection, and then it feels like you've covered yourself with a Mumias Sugar wrapper!"

Florence was visibly embarrassed. She had never encountered this before. The conversation had become so grossly graphic.

"Still," she was not about to give up that easily, "you don't have to use those free ones. The price of condoms is relatively low. You don't have an excuse for not using protection . . ."

"Maybe it is to you, but not to the thousands wallowing in poverty," Bone said. "The cheapest one and the poorest in quality is ten shillings. To you, that is not much because your boyfriend buys them. But to me, that is equal to three cigarettes. To a family here, that is two bundles of *sukuma wiki*."

"And really," Rock added, "don't you think that poverty is the real cause of AIDS?"

She was now speechless. "Why? How?"

"A prostitute was being interviewed the other day on why she continued practising her trade even with knowledge of the risks involved. She said, 'I'd rather die in ten years with AIDS than in ten days due to starvation.' Huh? Go and tell your instructors that."

She was going to add something, but then she saw the sudden interest the men were developing in her. Bomu was nibbling at the miraa twigs while thoughtfully looking at her legs. "You know," he said "If I were you, I wouldn't waste my youth telling people to beware. . . You have such nice legs." She gave him a horrified look.

"Yeah," Bafu concurred. "If I had such legs . . ."

She flew out, livid with anger, trying to shut out the hearty laughter of the men in The Slaughterhouse. Bomu, Ngeta and Bafu later lent out a tirade of abuses at the neighbours, warning them to mind their own businesses.

"Why is our room bothering you so much?" shouted Ngeta at the closed doors.

"Just don't let us collide with one another," Bomu added. "What we eat won't make you constipated!" He warned them not to send any more peer counsellors to them.

"The fools! They cannot even come out to face us!" Ngeta said, as always spoiling for a fight.

It is said that the neighbours stayed indoors the whole of the following day, except Chomelea who came in to have a good laugh with them about the crazy, nosy people of Ngando.

That had come to pass, but still it puzzled the neighbours how anybody would lead such a reckless life in this era. Psychologists say all behaviour is caused by something. So, what could it be that was causing this behaviour of The Slaughterhouse Five?

three

Molo, January 1992

M olo is a fast growing town fifty kilometres after Nakuru on the way to western Kenya. In 1992, there were several major routes through which you could reach the town. First, there was the route off the Nakuru-Eldoret highway, branching off at Kibunja and which was four kilometres in length. It passed through the now cleared forest and by the Kenya Co-operative Creameries factory near the post office. Another route was the one through Njoro, Elburgon and Turi which entered Molo through Munju. If you came from Keringet and Olenguruone in Molo South, you would stop at Keep Left and go either left towards the post office or right towards the *matatu* terminus. The other route was the Tayari one. Vehicles travelling to Kisumu and Kericho left the highway at the Total Petrol Station junction at Mau Summit, branching left into a not-so-good road that led to Molo.

Through this route, interestingly, one was able to enjoy the beautiful Molo scenery. Set in the undulating forest hills, the elegance of The Highlands Hotel where healthy, handsome horses grazed on the green grass would enthral you. After leaving behind the serenely attractive St. Josephs' Seminary, the sight of the expansive town would hit you as you rounded the bend at Tayari Farm. The first of the most notable buildings on that side of town would be the Green Garden Lodge where most children peeped in through the white fence, trying to get a glimpse of the lovely swimming pool.

The town was divided into two by a small river near the police station. One side of the town consisted of the District Hospital, the DO's office and the *matatu* terminus, while the other side held most of the banks and petrol stations, as well as hundreds of other businesses.

Molo, like many upcoming towns in Kenya, was a commingle of many tribes, though the most predominant was the Kikuyu. There were Kalenjins, Luo, Luhya and even a few Maasai. There were also, several Nubians who lived near Kimotho Mbembe Hotel, as well as a few Turkana – including Mutani, the shepherd – who lived near Mugumo Secondary School. Until the unfortunate twist of events disturbed the relative peace in the area, tribal affiliations did not matter.

Mutai owned a butchery in the heart of Molo township. His business was situated in a strategic position overlooking the bank on one side and the big bookshop on the other. His was the only butchery in the area owned by a Kalenjin. Kikuyus, it is true, owned most of the businesses. Mutai had carved a niche for himself in the area as a most astute and honest businessman who sold the freshest meat. In fact, he had a big clientele and his butchery was always full. He was considering employing another hand to help Karuri, his only employee. But then, another butchery had been opened adjacent to his by a notable personality and Mutai hesitated, waiting to see if it would have an effect on his business.

One Monday morning in 1991, he entered his butchery whistling softly to a Kalenjin tune. He had not been in for most of the previous week and was anxious to know how Karuri had fared on. As he slipped under the counter and emerged behind it to reach for the white coat hanging on the wall, a fetid stench assaulted his nostrils. Puzzled, he turned round.

"What is that smell?" he asked. The assistant looked up from the weighing machine.

"*Mzee, hiyo ni nyama.*" That is meat.

Mutai opened the framed glass compartment in which meat was usually hung. The smell now hit him full in the face. He stared at the flies around the meat in amazement.

"Kwani hii nyama ni ya lini?" he asked. How long has this meat been here?

It was then that he noticed that the meat was a lot more than what he normally would have expected on a Monday. On regular Mondays, it would be quarter this size. They must have had bad sales that weekend, or had Karuri not opened the butchery the previous day? But no, if that had been the case, he would have been stopped by his many customers in the street and asked why the butchery had been closed. Mutai wiped his wet brow with a handkerchief and looked round the meat shop. The last time he had such dismal sales was when he was trying to gain a foothold in the business, six years ago.

"You mean the opening of the new butchery has affected our sales this much?"

"Not really," explained Karuri as he counted the few coins in the cash box. "Kamau, the politician, has opened another butchery just across the road. That is the problem."

Mutai leaned over to catch a glimpse of the new establishment. It was directly opposite his and had a large 'Special Offer' sign over the door. As he gazed at his competition, his heart sank.

History has an irritating way of repeating itself! Mutai thought.

*   *   *

For Mutai, growing up had been an uphill task. He was the sixth in a family of tea farmers in Kericho, his goal in life was to get out of the impoverished life and settle in a town somewhere. His father owned a piece of land near Brooke Bond that never seemed enough for the polygamous family with a horde of children. Life was a monotony that started and ended on the tea farm. His older sisters were married off by the age of fourteen, All the children never went past standard three. Sitting in the small smoky kitchen next to the dung-filled cowpen that housed their only cow – a bony creature from which not even a cup of milk could be squeezed – Mutai decided he was fed up.

"I'm going to town to start my own business," he declared.

Instantly, the kitchen thundered with laughter. "Tell us how you'll do that, Mr. Clever," his eldest brother challenged him.

Mutai bore his family's derision with gritted teeth. They did not take any initiative to improve their position, he thought. It seemed that he too would go the way of his elder brothers – with nothing better to do they got married as soon as they were initiated. One day, he would show them, he promised himself grimly.

"Mutai, my son," said his mother softly, "don't think that out there life is fun. The world is a jungle; many have gone away and got lost."

Nonsense! The small boy thought bitterly. None of you has tried it out! I'll try one day! This family did not feel any shame, being laughed at by everyone about their torn pants. They didn't! They just accepted their fate, the losers! His mother looked at him sadly, remembering with pain the days when her husband was a real man. The days when getting food on the table was not a task to contend with. He had then been a successful farmer who was beginning to put together some little wealth from the sale of tea. He was also employed in the tea factory as an assistant manager.

Things had started going wrong when Bwana Rono was suddenly sacked from his job. Grapevine had it that he had differed with his boss, a new man called Mwangi. Suddenly, it became impossible for him to sell any tea to the factory. Tea leaves got spoiled on the farm and the family found itself without any source of income.

Then one day, Mwangi had come with an interesting offer. Mzee Rono had agreed to sell off a huge chunk of his land – after all, why own land whose produce you could not sell? One thing he did not think about was where he would graze his large herd of cattle. The small piece of land left was not enough for the family and the cattle together. It was evident one had to go. Mzee Rono had approached the rich entrepreneur once again.

Mutai finally escaped one cold morning after a bitter row between his father and Mwangi, when the poor man's cow had eaten into the latter's farm. Mutai had been charged with caring for the animal and knew that his father would come for him as soon as he had finished with the rich man. He had hidden in one of Mwangi's lorries and got a ten-kilometre ride to Kericho town. His first night was spent in the cold.

It was the ambition, to make something of his life, that kept him alive, braving the hunger and the cold. One day, he dreamed, people would stop him in the streets to greet him.

His lucky day came when Rotich, a butchery owner, found him sifting through garbage at the back of his shop. The businessman was looking for an assistant in his butchery. Rather than rebuke the teenager, he found himself making a business proposal.

The rest was history. The two became great partners in business, with Mutai ardently working for Rotich and the latter paying handsome dues. Half-fuelled by the desire to make his name great and gratitude for being rescued from the streets, Mutai furiously worked sixteen-hours a day without complaining. The business flourished.

It was five years, though, before he was able to stand on his own feet. Rotich's fortunes began to change dramatically. The first blow to his source of income was the opening of the three new butcheries, two of them right across his own, by a newcomer. The business pulled away customers from Rotich like a magnet. Then, one of Rotich's butcheries, the best performing one, was closed down by health officials led by the Municipal Health Officer who happened to be Mwangi's friend. Rotich made the painful decision to sell the businesses.

Mutai paid off his employer in easy instalments, moved into the business and struggled on on his own. Unfortunately for him, competition was coming from all sides. He now felt it was necessary to leave Kericho town completely for greener, pastures.

Molo was a fast growing town that had enormous potential for meat business. The street boy-turned-businessman had settled there and climbed his way up the ladder.

Now, as he saw the short, bald, potbellied Kamau emerge from his premises across the road, Mutai wondered why history always repeated itself. What had happened to his father and to Rotich was happening to him too.

Subconsciously, Mutai verbalized the thought that had been forming in his mind: "I hate Kikuyus!"

He was perplexed when his assistant, Karuri, looked at him with petrified eyes. He had spoken aloud.

*   *   *

Friday night. The Highway Bar was crowded with noisy revellers. Angelina Chebet took another long swig at her beer, straight from the bottle, and brought it crashing down on the new counter. The frothy drink had an acid taste. Does barley taste this bad? she asked herself as she gulped it down.

She chuckled softly and ordered for another drink. It was funny that after more than ten years, she should be drinking like a veteran again. Many of the patrons at the bar who recognised her gave her surprised looks. Those who came to say *habari* looked at her strangely, as if she had just sprouted horns. She downed a Tusker in one long gulp.

She ordered another, this time a Pilsner. Tusker was not working for her. Her clouded eyes surveyed the large bar. She was disconcerted when every figure dancing on the floor to a popular Queen Jane's song took on the large form of Macharia, her new archenemy. One of the Macharias came closer, said 'hallo' and took the stool beside her.

She was going to throw a punch at him when the figure diminished in size and there sat Mutai, the famous butcher.

"So it's you!" she said drunkenly.

"I didn't know you drank. I thought you were a teetotaller."

Angelina Chebet was a big woman. In fact, she generally instilled fear in most men who dared confront her. This was her biggest asset in this male-dominated world. A widow, she had never remarried. Men would of course be more likely drawn towards her purse than herself. She was a successful businesswoman with the sole tender to supply firewood and vegetables to Molo District Hospital. Her name featured prominently in the *Who's Who* of Molo. She was said to have a firm grip on the tender business. It had, therefore, been a shock to her when she went to Nakuru earlier that day to follow up on the renewal of the tender and was told she had lost her bid. She was even more surprised to learn to whom it had been awarded.

"That fool, Macharia, grabbed my tender," she told Mutai as she drained her sixth beer.

"But Macharia is your most trusted assistant!" exclaimed the butcher. It was a known fact that the two associates were inseparable.

"The most trusted assistant?" she scoffed. "All these years I have employed him, he was planning how to steal from me. And to think I have entrusted him with all the secrets of my business! Trust a Kikuyu to smell out rich feeding!"

"You are not the only one who has suffered," Mutai consoled her. "I have sold less than a hundred kilograms of meat all week. Imagine! Two Kikuyu's have opened butcheries right across mine and stolen all my customers." Bitterly, he leaned on the counter and placed his head in his hands.

Angelina put out her hand to pat him sympathetically.

"Sorry about that," she drawled drunkenly. "The customers will come back eventually. This is just but a passing storm."

"No. It's more than that," Mutai told her. "They have stolen my employee from me. The young man, Karuri, tendered his resignation just before I came here. Kamau has given him a more attractive salary, telling him they are brothers. I'm ruined!"

"These Kikuyu's are like that," she replied. "Give them something small to eat and they take the whole lot. Like pigs!"

Suddenly, Mutai rose from the stool, raised his fist in the air and announced, "Well, I have news for you. That was the last meal. The last meal these robbers are going to eat off me!"

He looked round the bar as if in a trance. Everybody had stopped dancing and was looking at him with mouths agape.

*   *   *

Three years earlier, deep in Ndoinet Forest, Molo South, Mzee Kipyegon had watched as his young sons brought in the sickly herd of cattle. The cows' hooves stamped in the slosh as the animals sought a place to settle. The clang of the bells strung on the cows' necks made a racket that jolted the old man from his thoughts.

Dusk was approaching fast and the *boiyo* could see the children silhouetted against the last rays of the setting sun. Their tattered clothes fluttered in the evening wind. He watched them as they locked in the three cows and ran to the kitchen, undoubtedly eager for the evening meal of *mursik* and *ugali*. The old man was hungry, but the thoughts that whirled in his mind had blunted his appetite. He walked out of the gate and headed downhill towards the shopping centre.

It was shortly after the harvesting season time and the neighbourhood smelt of the cooking of the staple food of the season – *ugali*. The usual atmosphere of toil and hard work pervaded the air. These people were crazy, he thought. Always planting, weeding, harvesting and starting all over again with the same zest. They really had a calling for farming.

Cultivating the land was not meant for his ethnic communty, and those who tried failed. Even Chebongolo knew this – wasn't that why the creator sent the first man on earth on a cowhide? But his tribesmen were busy trying to imitate the Kikuyu – despite his warnings. On numerous occasions, Mzee Kipyegon had argued with his people on why they let their land go away with these newcomers.

"Be wary of the Kikuyu," he repeatedly told his family as they gathered for the evening meal. "The Kikuyu and the Kalenjin can never mix. Look, the Kikuyu are very well-known thieves. Us? The only time we stole was to raid iron from the white men who came to plunder our land and destroy our ways. Our fathers uprooted the plates they laid down on the railway and used them to make spears.

We did it because we wanted to stop them from interfering with our way of life! Now, the Kikuyus have invaded our land and changed that way of life as well, only this time we have let them!"

Another time he would argue: "The Kikuyu are cultivators of land, we are pastoralists. How can we mix? They will want more land to farm, and we will want more land to graze our animals. The only solution is for them to go back to where they came from."

To his chagrin, none of the members of his family agreed with his sentiments. His son Kipruto, who was now a teacher in Molo town, disagreed with him vehemently.

"*Mzee*, I beg to differ," the foolish boy would say. "We are not living in the past. Pastoralism is not practised now, and we are embracing modern agricultural methods. If all of us were to think like you, there would be a civil war!"

Mzee Kipyegon would have thrown his walking staff at him were it not for the fact that he was too far away. And his rheumatic bones would not allow him to run after him and give him a nice whack on his shoulder to wake his brain. It is this education of these days. Education that makes our sons and daughters blind! *Takataka!* Rubbish! He only hoped his younger sons, especially the bright Kiprop, would see the light.

The Kikuyu were the proverbial camel that was allowed only one foot inside its master's tent during a storm. They had begged to be allowed the head, then after some time, the legs. Suddenly their whole body was in the tent, which was now ripping apart, leaving the Kalenjin drenching in the rain!

They had encroached the whole country. Go to the Coast, to North Eastern, Nyanza and you will find that Kikuyus owned three quarters of the businesses there. You'd think they alone had fought the British. The fruits of independence should be eaten by all, thought Kipyegon, not a single community!

What bothered him most was that his people's ancestral land was being bought by Kikuyus. The government had allowed Kikuyus to settle in the Rift Valley in the 1970s. The unsuspecting locals readily accepted the newcomers, and sold them land. It was now too late – now his people had no more land to graze their animals the way they had been taught to do, the way their forefathers had done.

Now, seated in the chilly evening of the darkening period, Mzee Kipyegon sighed heavily. At least, something was going to be done. It was about time.

four
Nairobi, 2001

A typical Ngando day. It was almost noon. Bone, Bafu and Rock were playing pool as usual at Thiong'o's. Bafu was pitted against a visitor who had chanced along and wanted to bet on pool. Knowing that they would need money for the jam session at New York Club the following day, Bafu was playing a bit more cautiously. He was now on his fourth consecutive win and the crowd that milled round the pool table was ecstatic. Bone, the undisputed pool coach, pulled him aside and whispered into his ear.

"You fool! You don't win all the games. You'll discourage him. Let him win a game once in a while."

"*Tuliza boli,*" keep cool, came the brusque answer. "I know what I'm doing. The guy will win this game."

And sure enough, Bafu made a 'fatal mistake' and the man won. The elated fellow agreed to another game with the 'distraught' Bafu. He even increased the stake. The onlookers smiled knowingly. It was exactly one week after Bone had come with that girl, Nancy, from the Los Angeles Club. The entire furore about her had gradually died down. In a week, a lot of things had happened in Ngando and Nancy was stale news.

The most notable was Ngeta's arrest for assault the day before.

It was not really assault, though the victim's nose had bled. It had happened during a name-calling session called *kutoana rangi*, where the local youth met to chew *miraa* as they contested to see who could ridicule the other the most.

"You are so tall that where you come from aeroplanes have blaring horns!" someone told another. One of the younger chaps had then derided Ngeta with: "*Manze!* You are so black that a mosquito would have to light a torch to see you and suck your blood." Incensed more by the laughter elicited from the jibe than the jibe itself, Ngeta had charged at the insolent fellow. It was unfortunate that at that very time, two police officers on patrol were passing by. They refused any offers of *kitu kidogo* and handcuffed him. Most probably, they had collected enough and were looking for a genuine law-breaker to show for their day's work.

Anyway, everybody knew Ngeta could be booked in on a lesser charge; probably being drunk and disorderly!

Then City Council *askaris* had come in full war regalia and demolished all the kiosks along the main road. There had been a near riot, especially when the leader of the demolition squad had tried to explain that the kiosks were blocking the road. How? The irate crowd had shouted, yet the kiosks were along the road, not on the road? When the man had started to explain that the kiosks posed a security and health risk, he was pelted with stones. The squad had to call in anti-riot police who battled the residents while the City Council continued with the demolition.

Another pool game was opened. The man had obviously lost. He still had hope of beating Bafu though, and agreed to another bet. Bone smiled as he took the rack and prepared to arrange the balls for a new game.

Suddenly, the room went totally quiet. Somebody gasped, "Wa!" and Bone instinctively looked up. Everybody was looking outside, their mouths agape. Puzzled, he turned round to see what was happening. He knew it was not the police because then the crowd would have scrambled out instantly through the secret back door. True, there was no police Mahindra out there. Instead, there was a gleaming white Toyota Corolla saloon. Nancy, her face masked in dark sunglasses, was walking from the car towards Thiong'o's. She walked with the confidence of a model who knew that all eyes were on her. Then she calmly paused outside Thiong'o's as if she was a queen on the catwalk.

Her hair, held together at the top by a metal clasp, was let down at the back of her head. She wore a white T-shirt over a pair of white jeans shorts. On her feet were white sneakers worn over brief white socks.

"Oh, my!" someone whispered in admiration. She walked over to Bone, who was still holding the pool balls in both hands.

"Hi. I've been looking for you all over. They told me I would find you here," she announced, her smooth voice filling the entire room. She leaned over him and gave him a light peck on his cheek. Then noticing his astonished colleagues, she turned to them and shook each by the hand. One of the chaps quickly stamped out his cigarette before shaking her hand – something that he later on vehemently denied having done. Charlie, the last of the lot, was so confused he offered both his hands in reverence and accompanied them with a curtsey.

As she turned back to him, Bone could only manage, "Niaje?"
"*Poa*," she replied, removing her designer shades and polishing them with a white handkerchief.

He realized that all the eyes in the hall were trained on them. All business at Thiong'o's had been brought to a standstill. Nothing would go on unless something was quickly done. He got hold of her and gently eased her out of the door. Inside the pool hall, nobody spoke for a whole three minutes.

The gleaming car stood out against the Ngando backdrop like a white man in a Mungiki ritual. Nyang'anya, the shopkeeper, unknowingly dropped the newspaper he was holding when he saw Bone step into the car. He watched it keenly as the couple tried to manoeuvre round and look for a suitable parking place to avoid blocking the road.

As they headed to The Slaughterhouse, Bone remembered how untidy the place had been when they left. When they got there, Nancy offered to clean the dirty dishes but he brushed her off. What? With those manicured hands? You could see very clearly that she had never touched a scouring pad.

"If you are hungry, there is a place down there where we eat," he said with finality.

Kazee's place was twenty metres from The Slaughterhouse. It was really a small *mabati* structure scrawled in an untidy style on the wall were the words: *Karibu Supu, Mutura na Chemsha*. It stood opposite Gitau's butchery. In fact an extention of the butchery since the surplus meat was taken there and made into all types of delicacies. A thick cloud of smoke came from the kitchen area at the corner.

The establishment boasted of two large tables, both sides of which stood benches. Kazee peeped from the kitchen, saw the strange visitor with Bone and rushed to the eating area. Bone was impressed at the small man's sudden display of customer service.

"What I can do for you, Madam?" he asked in broken English, wiping his dirty hands on the equally dirty apron. He ignored Bone and did not even spare him a glance. Bone was surprised that Kazee actually spoke English.

"What do you have?" she asked in a perfect drawl.

Kazee was taken aback. He had hardly grasped the question. He therefore looked at Bone for help, but Bone too ignored him in a tit for tat gesture.

Er, we are have *sembe, surwa, mutush. . ."*

Nancy looked at Bone, confusion written on her face. He explained that surwa was the slum equivalent of soup, *sembe* meant *ugali,* and *mutush* was . . . well, *mutura.* He could not find the English equivalent for that delicacy. Turning to Kazee, he ordered two plates of ugali and ox-tongue.

As they sat down, Nancy looked up at him and said, "I really missed you, Bone. That's why I came."

"I thought you had forgotten me," he said after a short pause.

"If it were so, I would not have come, would I?"

He shook his head.

Two thick slices of ugali and some unclassifiable bits of meat were brought in a large tray. Nancy remarked about the enormousness of the ugali.

"Here in the ghetto, things are relatively cheap," Bone explained as Kazee poured cold water over their hands. "The *mandazi* you get here at five bob is twice the size that you get in town for ten. It's just that even then, people are still too poor to afford such food."

She waited for the cutlery to arrive but when she saw Bone dive into his piece of ugali, she realized that no fork or knife would be forthcoming.

"*Haiya! Kwani wewe haudemi?*" Aren't you eating? he asked.

"I'm not really hungry," she declared as the table began to attract flies. Then just to please him, she took a large piece of ugali and washed it down with a mouthful of soup. A large green fly sailed over the tray, then rested smugly on the lump of ugali. Bone brushed it away with a sweep of his hand and continued to eat. Nancy looked at him incredulously, caught between genuine disbelief and disgust.

"One day, you'll be eating this food like a malnourished child," Bone predicted good-naturedly when he saw the amazed look on her face. She laughed softly, unable to imagine what catastrophy would occur to dawn into such a day.

"Me pay for lady," Kazee announced when they were through with the food. Bone was genuinely astonished. It was totally inconceivable that Kazee could be that philanthropic to buy anybody a meal. But then, strange things cause strange reactions. They walked back to The Slaughterhouse.

"Have you ever met someone for the first time, then decided he is the person you would like to be friends with for life?" Nancy surprised Bone with her question.

"Yes, sometimes," he replied after some reflection. At the many clubs he frequented, he met many girls who all turned out to be opportunists eager for a beer. To him, love at first sight was something that only happened in movies.

Almost at the door, she looked around the derelict houses. "I wonder how the toilets are like," she said.

Bone pointed at the small structure which leaned precariously on one side. As she approached it, an acrid smell hit her nostrils. She took only one look inside and the expression on her face told everything.

"My God! The place is dirty," she said as she quickly retraced her steps.

"It caters for fifty or so houses over here, that's why," Bone explained. "The neighbours have been trying to draw up a duty roster for cleaning the place, but it fails whenever it is our turn," he laughed. He chuckled even more as he told her about the time when the neighbours had locked up the toilets in protest. Bomu and Ngeta had broken the new padlock. Nancy shook her head in disbelief.

"By the way, this is one of the cleanest around here," he added as an afterthought. The expression on her face changed. "And there are places where there are no latrines, like the worst parts of Ngando where people use *Choo* FM."

"*Choo* FM?"

"Yes, that is, Choo Flying Method. You just do your thing into a polythene bag then let fly in the air!"

She grimaced. Well, she concluded, she had a lot to learn about the ghetto. They were about to reach The Slaughterhouse when Nancy suddenly stopped, her gaze fixed onto the car they had parked by the road.

"Oh my God!" she gasped. Bone followed her eyes to the car. One of the side-mirrors was gone.

"How did it disappear?" she wondered. "I mean, it was there only ten minutes ago!" They walked to the car and shortly, Rock and Bafu joined them. The four examined the gaping hole where the mirror had been fixed.

"Now I will have to pay for it," Nancy said, explaining that the car was rented. Bone then saw the 'CAR RENT LTD' sticker on the side window.

"Stay with her," he told Rock and Bafu. "I am going to make a few enquiries."

He walked quickly to Nyang'anya's shop where he stayed for a few minutes, then left and went down the road. Rock and Bafu took Nancy back to The Slaughterhouse.

When Bone came back an hour later, he was clutching the side mirror in his hand. He was not talking and ignored Rock's query regarding where he had retrieved it from. It was much later that details emerged that Bone had been declared 'wanted' in Keywest after beating up one of the rival shantytown's residents.

"*Wewe tothi sana!*" You are a big fool, Bafu told Bone when he heard of it. "You dare go to Keywest to beat up people over a woman's side-mirror. Now you are a marked man!"

Keywest and Ngando were two rival slums. No one knew where the conflict stemmed from. Attacks and counterattacks were prevalent, especially between the youth gangs. If one was dating somebody from the opposing side, it would be very unwise to show it openly. Gosti, the weightlifter, had almost been lynched when he had tried to flirt with a Keywest girl. That incident alone had led to a whole week of fighting.

During such wars, both Ngando and Keywest became places where even the anti-riot police hesitated to enter and quell confrontations. By morning, they were just a heap of iron sheets. And now Bone had aggravated the already volatile situation. The expected backlash would not be pleasant at all.

"Why didn't you take us with you?" Ngeta asked.

"I didn't want you to get involved in a matter that had nothing to do with you. It was I who advised her to park there," Bone explained.

Ngeta was unimpressed.

"You don't expect them to take it lying down, do you?"

"Ah!" Bone retorted angrily. "Then they shouldn't go stealing from my woman."

"Your woman my foot! What do you know about that woman?"

"I don't know much about her," admitted Bone, "but I know she has a soft spot for me. She has just invited me to her place."

"What?" they all exclaimed.

"Yes. She will be picking me up on Monday."

"You've got yourself a real one!" said Bomu as he puffed at the cigarette dangling from his lips, not sure at all that he was pleased with the latest development.

"*Uliona hizo mahaga?*" Did you see her behind? Rock asked mischievously. "Man, if she gave it to me, I would not bathe the whole week so the sweetness wouldn't fade away!" The room exploded into laughter.

"But beware of such girls," cautioned Bomu.

Bone understood why Bomu detested rich girls. He had struck a relationship with one such girl from South B. The rich girl fell for his flashy style and thought that he was heir to some big fortune. Bomu had made the mistake of bringing her to Ngando during the rains, a time when the dirt road was absolutely impassable. Her sandals had stuck in the slush and she had been forced to dip her hand inside to retrieve them. Needless to say, she never came back. When Bomu had called her to ask why she had suddenly gone quiet, she had candidly told him, "Darling, I'm sorry to have to say this, but it is plain obvious that we cannot go on. I mean, I am from the suburbs and you are from the ghetto. What will my friends say?" They had earned herself an unprintable list of insults for her question. So, Bomu had detested rich girls ever since. Actually, that story had formed the subject of one of Bone's songs, but just like the others, it was never played on radio.

"Are you serious about Nancy?" Bafu asked suddenly.

"I'm not sure really," Bone replied truthfully. "It's too early to know if what I feel for her is real love or just an infatuation. And there is still Stella, you know."

"If she is really into you, it can only mean that you will be out of the ghetto in a few days," Rock predicted.

"But one thing you should remember," cautioned Bafu, "don't

forget who you are or where you come from. Do not be like Jamaa."
At the mention of the name, the whole room went silent.

Everybody knew Jamaa. Years earlier, he had just been one of the Ngando idlers. Like the rest, he had been trying hard to eke out a living by doing anything that came his way, legal or illegal. He had even once been a houseboy.

Nobody knew how he had met a rich white woman. Some rumour-mongers said he went to look for work at her hotel and his well-toned muscles attracted her. Others said she had sent agents to help her get a young man with strong features and he had passed the interview. However, it happened the woman had taken him in regardless of the fact that he was way younger than her. Some people said that he was younger than the white woman's own daughter, but that claim was never substantiated because Jamaa never took anybody to her Runda Estate home to see.

He had disappeared for a whole year. When he came back, he had turned a new leaf. He now only wore designer suits and imported sports wear. He changed cars as often as one changed undergarments. The most remarkable change, however, was his attitude towards his former friends. He derided them for 'remaining stuck in poverty and doing nothing about it.

"You people are just too lazy!" he scolded them, waving his cellphone at the hungriest of them all. "You should know that in life, if you can't take the stairs, there is the lift!"

Many Ngando residents disliked him. Unfortunately, their pecuniary disposition forced them to come running each time his Mercedes was spotted. Everyone laughed at his jokes no matter how tasteless they were.

That is, everyone except Bone and his close friends. The Slaughterhouse Five would not bring themselves to worship him. There was no love lost between Jamaa and Bone. As Bone said one day, the group called K South must have had Jamaa in mind when they sang:

'Now, unajiskia mwenyewe,

na tenee ulikuwa umesota, huna any.
Sasa unaendea ma dame kama mende,
pia kilindi ya mtaa ume decide waende'.
'Now, you are feeling good,
while before you were broke.
Now you are going after girls like a roach,
and the local comrades you decided to do without'.

After a long silence, Bone finally spoke solemnly. "No. I would never forget you. We are a family, men."

five
Kamwaura, Molo South, March 14, 1992

Kamwaura is a small, dusty shopping centre situated 23 miles from Molo town in what is now called Nakuru County. The people there in 1992 were a mixture of many ethnic groups, the most common being Kisii, Kalenjin and Kikuyu.

Various personalities among Kenya's political elite owned large tracts of land in Molo South. Most of the locals, however, had small two and five-acre plots, and a few as many as ten.

It was on one of these smaller farms to the east of the centre that two boys worked, sweating in the afternoon sun.

"This is why I hate weekends!" grumbled Kimani as he sank his hoe into the soft earth.

"*Kiguta giki!*" You lazy one! his companion admonished. "You are lucky to be in school, otherwise this would be your daily chore."
Kimani hated *shamba* work, especially now that it was the season of preparing the land for planting. He paused and looked towards the extremes of the eight-acre farm. He despaired, wondering when the whole *shamba* would be done.

"Why doesn't your father hire a tractor to plough this land instead of relying on child labour?" asked Irungu. He had come from his home at the shopping centre to help his friend. During the days they were at school, the rest of Kimani's family tended the farm.

"He says he doesn't have the money," replied his friend, standing with one hand to his waist and the other balancing on the jembe.

"Then he should sell part of it!" Irungu said half-jokingly.

Kimani surveyed the shamba pensively.

"He wouldn't sell even a handful of the soil," he said. "It is said that my grandfather left a hanging curse on anybody who would dare sell this land."

This Saturday's sun was fiercer than ever. Irungu took off his shirt and continued working. The afternoon sun raged on. Kimani often wondered why his father, Waweru, did not employ modern agricultural practices. The old man always said he did not have money: what with the high cost of education and skyrocketing food prices to feed the family? Kimani, the elder of his two children, was now in Standard Eight at Banana Primary School. It was a lucky thing that the children in the family were well-spaced, and the *ikumbi*, granary, could sustain them for the better half of the year, until the beans were ready.

"Let us rest a little," Kimani implored, sitting down. Irungu followed suit, calling his friend a lazy wimp but also happy for the break.

A few minutes later, Wanjiku, Kimani's small sister, arrived to announce that lunch was ready. A look at the overhead sun informed them it was about three o'clock. The two teenagers rose up immediately and headed for the homestead from where a small cloud of smoke was billowing into the sky from the kitchen.

Their friendship had stood the test of time. They had struck a good and easy rapport since their first day at school. They had grown up together, graduating from stealing fruits from other people's farms to stealing sweets from Irungu's father's small shop at Kamwaura Centre. They enticed young girls to chat with them using the sweets and fruits. They helped in each other's farmwork alternately, although Irungu's family *shamba* was smaller than Kimani's father.

Now that they were going to finish school together and get initiated into the adulthood, the strength of their friendship was boosted. This was despite the ethnic tension that had struck the area in recent times.

The whole village was at the moment held in a serious wave of fear and anxiety. Ever since leaflets had been found thrown all over ordering all 'outsiders' to vacate the area immediately, Kamwaura had ceased to be a peaceful village anymore. The leaflets were read by everybody who could read until they became tattered from manhandling. The frightening messages announced that outsiders included anybody who was neither Kalenjin nor Maasai or any of their sub-tribes. The eviction threat gnawed at Kamwaura, heightened especially by an apprehensiveness for strangers.

The tension caused by the circulation of the leaflets had scarcely died down when other rumours came. It had been reported that if you listened keenly in the wee hours of the night, you could hear frenzied war songs and dances from deep in Ndoinet Forest. Now everybody kept a weapon within reach. Doors were closed tightly at sunset.

These happenings did not bother Kimani as much as the events of the previous day did. Even now, as he dug into the soil, he felt a tremor of trepidation in his heart. In class the previous day, the behaviour of Koech, one of his classmates, had been noticeably odd. The boy, unusually, could not concentrate in class and kept on looking outside the window as if he was expecting someone. He did not touch a book, though all the other pupils were busy studying.

"Now," he would ask every ten minutes or so, "why are you studying? If I were you, I would go back home immediately."

All the other classmates had been puzzled by this very strange behaviour. It had bothered Kimani all day. To add on to that, Kimani's father had received a rather unexpected visit from Mwalimu Kipruto, the son of Mzee Kipruto who lived in Ndoinet. Kimani had peeped to hear the two of them speaking in hushed tones. He could not help eavesdropping.

The youthful employee had been very agitated as he hastily whispered to Waweru that something bad was going to happen, and he should think of leaving Kamwaura for a while. Despite much coaxing, the teacher would not elaborate.

"Thank you very much, Mwalimu. You have proved to be a good friend and I am proud of you. Thanks," Mzee Waweru had said, patting the younger man on the back.

"So? Will you go away?" Kipruto had anxiously asked. From his hiding place, Kimani could see how troubled the teacher was. Kipruto had kept glancing behind him as if he was afraid he was being watched.

"I don't see why I should leave my ancestral land," Waweru had answered at last. "I think this is just a passing cloud which will soon dissipate."

The teacher had pleaded and cajoled the old man to think about the issue. But even after the meeting, Kimani had known that his father would not give the issue a second thought. And in truth, it was impossible to imagine that something close to what the teacher was prophesying would happen to the peaceful village.

These thoughts flashed in Kimani's mind as they entered the house, dropped their jembes and got down to eating. The food was served and for the next ten minutes or so, the only sounds heard were crunching noises as the two boys' jaws massacred the *githeri*. It was only when their stomachs began to fill that they resumed their talking. From across the room, Kimani's mother watched them trade jokes and jibes over each other's eating habits. She smiled pleasantly.

It's funny how life flies like a bee, she thought. Only the other day these boys were *tukere*, toddlers, and now they have started sporting moustaches!

By the time the boys finished the household chores and bathed in the small bathroom behind the kitchen, it was dark. Kimani came out of the room wearing a green sweater, ready to escort his friend and brother, Irungu, back to the shopping centre.

"Let's go, or do you want to extend your stay till supper?" he asked Irungu derisively. Kimani's mother simply smiled softly as the boys got into an argument at the door.

From the distance, loud shouts were heard rising above the village. Puzzled, the boys paused and looked in that direction and were soon joined by Kimani's mother. Then they saw the huge, orange-red flames that lit up the horizon.

"That surely is a burning house," declared Irungu. In one accord, the boys ran out into the night.

The area was called Nguirubi, though the locals called it Gwa Athuri or Kwa Wazee. When the boys got to the burning huts, the whole area looked like a battlefield. There were villagers huddled in the homestead, wondering loudly why two different houses should suddenly start burning at the same time.

The fire was too hot for the villagers to do anything about it. As some men tried unsuccessfully to douse the flames with small pails of water, one villager declared that it was not a normal fire. The fashion in which it raged was very similar to that of a petrol fire, he added. They all stood in a dazed, haphazard semi-circle and helplessly watched the flames swallow the two houses up.

Waweru, Kimani's father, spoke up. It was not a common occurrence for two houses to burn suddenly and at the same time. This was arson.

"So," he said, gesticulating wildly, "let us all 'take our legs' and go to the chief. He is our servant and the one in charge of our security!" Everyone nodded in agreement and the multitude moved towards the chief's place.

"Do you think it's the Kalenjins?" Irungu asked Kimani as they joined the procession.

"Nonsense!" someone nearby answered. "Why would they do this? We have co-existed for years, and they are like our brothers now."

"*Niguo*," another added. It is true. "We have even married their daughters, and their sons married ours. We can't do without each other."

*   *   *

Chief Ndegwa was equally puzzled at the oddity of the incident. "*Cifu*," someone said, "You are aware that we have been receiving eviction threats."

"Yes, yes," replied the administrator. "That is why I am treating this as a matter of urgency. In fact, I am now going to call the DO and the police OCS since they are the ones in charge of your security."

It was past eight thirty in the evening when the DO and the OCS arrived. The three leaders were engaged in deep conversation away from the multitude that had rapidly increased till it now numbered close to three hundred.

There was nothing that could be done at the time, the DO told the gathering from Nguirubi, Ndeffo, Banana, Kamwaura, and even some from as far as Sitoito. "What we will do is to go back to our homes. I'll call for a reconciliation meeting at Banana School tomorrow, Sunday.

I want all churches and all people to come together for a joint service. My security council will deal with the issue urgently." The Luo OCS also spoke, saying that he had detailed a heavy police presence in the area.

It was late in the night when the people settled in their houses to sleep. However, sleep seemed elusive, with the anxiety and apprehension that blew into the air more strongly than the Molo cold. What occupied everybody's mind was whether the burning of the two houses was a harbinger of worse things to come.

six

Nairobi, 2001

Bone knew that apart from the Keywest problem, another storm was brewing in his life. He had, in fact, been anticipating it ever since Nancy had come back to Ngando the second time, but when the encounter did materialize, he had let his guard down.

He had been escorting Nancy back to her car when they had run into Stella, just outside Nyang'anya's shop. Stella had been buying something from the shop and had come out at the very instant he and Nancy were passing by. Bone had hesitated when he saw her coming towards them. Nancy too, had stopped and glanced at him.

"*Niaje?*" he had greeted Stella feebly.

"*Poa*," Stella had replied as she shook both their hands, then she had looked at Nancy quizzically.

"Hi," Nancy had said to her, still shaking her hand. "You must be Stella. Glad to meet you. I am Nancy."

Bone had turned towards her and raised his eyebrows.

"You know her name?" he had asked.

Nancy's reply had been to flash him a smile. He had quickly looked away. He had known that the meeting was not coincidental. Somebody had obviously tipped Stella and she had come to confirm if it was true.

Not knowing how Stella would react bothered him. She was as

unpredictable as a lioness—lionesses were reputed to be serious predators, but then one of them had recently broken a rule of nature and befriended a baby oryx, causing ripples all over the country. Stella could either pounce on Nancy in front of all these people or act indifferently.

He had shuffled his legs uncomfortably. Luckily, Stella had chosen to play it cool – for the time.

"I have a customer to plait," she had said. "I'll see you later." She had then walked away into the row of houses that led to her salon.

"She's a nice girl," Nancy had commented as they walked away. He had not replied, knowing in his heart that he had just escaped from a major crisis.

What would he have done if Stella had chosen to follow her ghetto-instinct and assaulted Nancy? Whose side would he have taken? Many times in his life he had had to stop fights among his girls, but it had never happened with Stella. He had wiped the sweat off his brow and walked on, full of gratitude.

*   *   *

But if Bone thought the issue was settled, he was terribly wrong. Stella came to The Slaughterhouse early the next morning. Playing a game of draughts on the stool were Bafu and Rock. On the bed, Bone lay facing the ceiling with his hands under his head and a smile on his face. Bomu, whose *matatu* had gone in for servicing, was next to the wall, sleeping soundly. When Stella entered in haste and declined the offer of a seat, everybody realized that she was in a foul mood. As if on cue, the crowd stood up slowly and walked out, each one giving some small excuse.

"Okay, I want to know the truth," she started with arms akimbo. Her sharp tone woke up Bomu who surveyed the scene, dug into his pockets in search of something, then walked out to buy cigarettes.

"What truth?" Bone asked calmly.

"Something is definitely going on between you and that girl and I want to know the truth." Bone took some time to answer as he thought of the most appropriate words. She stood patiently, her pretty face contorting in pain and now taking on a murderous twist.

The long braids on her head making her look more dangerous. She was about his height, which did not improve matters. Stella was a pretty girl. Though she could not boast as much grace and elegance as Nancy, she too made heads turn. Bone decided to come clean this time, rather than try to feign innocence.

He knew Stella to be a fair person who never followed rumours blindly but made sure she first established the truth. He knew, therefore, that there was nothing about him and Nancy that she didn't know already.

Sparing the more erotic details, he explained how he'd met Nancy and everything that had transpired between them. She listened to him, as if very much in agreement with the story, but he knew better than to trust the tranquility that was pasted on her face.

"So you see, the girl seems to have a crush on me and is heavily loaded with cash," he concluded.

"Huh!" she retorted, "so you see, it's all about money."

"Not that I'm after money, but you know this is Kenya. Everybody is materialistic in their own way!"

"I hate listening to a grown-up feeding me with crap!" She was spoiling for a fight.

"Listen, Stella," he defended himself. "Just like me, you have been raised in the ghetto. You and I know the struggles we go through day in and out. The struggles that have prevented us from getting married up to now. It was you who told me the other day how you hate this life. Now, if you met a *mlami* – a white man – or a rich guy who was ready to take you out of here, would you stop to think about anything else?"

"Yes! I told you how I hate this life. Life that makes you stoop so low as to accept any passing harlot so long as she has money."

"Not that I love her!" he exclaimed. "It's you I love, and you know that."

"Have you ever thought of what kind of woman she is? Why is she interested in you with all these men available in Nairobi? This is the era of AIDS—how sure are you that she is not a walking time bomb?"

Bone was at a loss for words. Sometimes it was better to let a woman rave on until she was exhausted. Only then could you try to pump sense into her head.

"Have you thought about the life you will lead together? You, a ghetto thug, and she, a *babi?* What does she know about ghetto life? Has she ever been arrested? Has her mother ever sold *chang'aa* to educate her? Has she ever lived in a one-roomed house with a family of six, which room doubles up as the bedroom, sitting room, bathroom and kitchen? What does she know about eating ugali and *terere*, pigweed seven days a week?"

He was about to talk, when she angrily waved him to silence.

"And you! What do you know about Muthaiga, Runda and Lavington? Have you ever stepped inside a bungalow apart from standing at the gate and asking for work? What are you going to talk during dinner with her parents or with her fellow business people when you don't know a thing about golf, market prices and the fuel consumption of the Mercedes compared to the BMW? And how are you going to act when you lie in a bed with a real mattress on it, not this straw one here? How are you going to carry yourself on those bow-tie nights at the Hilton? You two are worlds apart, Bone."

He looked down, flushing. If Stella had been any other ordinary girl, he would have struck her down before she even started this tantrum. But he knew that if he dared touch her, there would be such a war that even Kamjesh and Mungiki gangs would stop their own wars to stare.

"Aw! Come on, be a lady and . . ."

"I've been born and raised in the gutter," she spat at him, "so I don't know about being a lady. Maybe you should go say that to that whore of yours! Isn't she the perfect lady?"

"Listen," he started once more, this time in a conciliatory tone.

"We've been together from the start. Do you think I would let an outsider ruin what we share? I care about you as much as you do about me, and I understand how you feel. I know you are fighting to see that our relationship goes on. There is no need to get worked up over . . ."

"Tell me," she cut him short, "would you be this worked up if it was the other way round, with me and some rich boy?"

He hesitated, knowing he'd probably kill the two of them.

"That is not the point," he finally said.

"Listen," she stated matter-of-factly. "I've invested too much in this relationship. Continue with your little infatuation as much as you like, but let me not see that woman here. I will not suffer any more humiliation. If she comes here again, I will do something that will make the whole of this place stink!"

She stormed out, leaving Bone with a dazed mind. He knew she would carry out the threat if made to. It was the idea of an outsider challenging her in her territory that made her so incensed. This was her own turf and she would protect it with all her might.

Stella never lived to carry out her threat, though, because that very day she was killed in a hit and run accident on the busy Ngong Road after she alighted from the bus, coming from buying hair pieces on River Road.

seven

Banana Primary School, Molo South, March 15, 1992

The school compound was filled to capacity that Sunday. The atmosphere was electric. Different religious denominations had come together on this day: Catholics, Protestants and even the Akorino. Chief Ndegwa called the everyone to attention and asked Mzee Joseph Mbure, one of the Akorino, to lead the congregation in prayer.

Mzee Mbure was a tall man. He stood towering above the crowd. Now, he raised his right hand and gave an emotional prayer. His long beard with patches of grey and the white turban on his head shook with the quivering timbre of his voice. The congregation was held, enthralled in the serene mood as the prayer went for the better part of half an hour. Finally, each person complemented the humble appeal for divine intervention with a sombre 'Amen'. The Catholics, as usual, tapped their foreheads and chests in honour of the Holy Trinity.

The ceremony would stick into the minds of many as a strong reminder of the people's strength and togetherness in the face of fear and uncertainty. The hundreds who witnessed the events of the day will never forget that Sunday, the fifteenth of March, 1992. Events which can never be explained in writing without losing the intensity of the moment.

*   *   *

It was about four or five in the late afternoon when it happened. People were going back to their houses when the air was rent with shouts and cries for help. The villages of Nguirubi and Mang'ara sounded like one huge, prolonged wail. Leaving the women, children and invalids behind, all able-bodied men rushed to the area. They collected any crude weapons they could lay their hands on as they went along. You don't answer a call of distress without a *njora*, someone had said.

Kimani found himself between Irungu on one side and Mzee Mbure on the other. His heart thundered in his ribcage as he contemplated the unexpected twist of events. In the distance he could see scores of houses aflame and others being torched.

They hurried round a corner and bumped into the attackers. Each group gasped with surprise at the unexpected meeting. The attackers were dressed only in their undergarments, small shorts that exposed their thighs. Around each of their heads was a red headband and on each hand was strung a bow with large quivers on their backs. They seemed to recover from the surprise encounter quicker than the villagers, because suddenly one of them gave a yelp like that of a dog which was immediately picked up by the others as they surged forward.

Those who lived to tell this story will always stop here, trying to conjure in their minds the correct words to explain the calamity appropriately. The audience is caught enchanted in suspense as the narrator unsuccessfully tries to describe the bloodbath scene that was Molo South that day, 15th March, 1992.

The two warring sides were too close for any missiles to be thrown. The bows and arrows, stones and spears became useless. A hand-to-hand, man-to-man fight ensued. Those with *njoras, pangas* and knives were a lot luckier.

Irungu dodged a *panga* slash and grabbed its owner with both his hands. Suddenly, he identified the face as that of one of his neighbours. Despite the face painting and bizarre dress, Tarus arap Sogomo was recognizable!

"*Leo hakuna ndugu ama rafiki!*" Today there is no brotherhood or friendship, Tarus declared as he pulled out of Irungu's hold and swung out again. Irungu lashed out with his bent knee, catching him full in the stomach. The man gasped and doubled up in pain. Irungu grabbed his panga and swung out to finish him off, but suddenly, a wave of feelings assailed him. To immobilize him, he turned the weapon the other way in his hand and smashed his lead with the handle. The man went limp with unconsciousness.

More of the villagers rushed in and the attackers were pushed back slowly. The villagers lunged after them angrily until they ran back the same way they had come.

Mzee Joseph Mbure was bent on one knee, supporting a fallen man. He called out for help and a few villagers came to his aid. The man had a deep cut right across his stomach, and his shirt was soaking in fresh blood. Mzee Mbure ripped the wounded man's bloodstained shirt apart and helped him push back the intestines into his bowels. The sight was painful to bear – the man's stomach had literally been torn open.

The wounded man, Peter Ngundo Njoroge who was also a *mukorino*, lay his turbaned head on Mzee Mbure's lap, sweating profusely and breathing labouriously. Mzee Mbure knew this man well. In fact, he was one of his close friends. Tears welled in his eyes as he saw the severity of Njoroge's injuries and knew he was not going to survive. Indeed, Peter Ngundo Njoroge passed on two days later at the Nakuru General Hospital. His last words from his parched lips being, "But we are neighbours!"

The fighting would have gone on and on had the Administration Police not intervened. As soon as the law enforcers shot in the air, the characteristic barking, similar to a dog's, was made and the attackers retreated. They were chased back across Thathumwo River and into Ndoinet forest.

But they were not to be defeated easily. They emerged four kilometres away, at Kamwaura, and burnt almost half the village down. At Boron, they did the most horrendous damage, burning over two hundred houses and killing four men.

The tribal clashes had started. For months, the situation would boil and overflow, and degenerate into a national crisis.

eight
Nairobi, 2001

Different couples walking hand in hand, dressed in their Sunday best, littered the well-tended lawn leading all the way to Ngong Road. In one corner, at the place where the long gravel road ended in a parking bay at the Commonwealth War Cemetery, a battered pick-up was parked. Beside it a couple was enjoying a picnic on the grass. Children ran around the whole area, criss-crossing over the many clusters of people whiling away the Sunday in the best way they knew.

Ndung'u, the short, bearded photographer was as usual walking from group to group, taking photographs. He was sporting his trademark half-coat with uncountable pockets, here and there stuffed with extra film and packets of developed photographs. He saw the figure hunched on the stairs leading to the graves and waved on recognizing him. When the figure did not respond and only stared blankly at him, Ndung'u was surprised. It was unlike Bone to ignore a greeting.

Bone sat on the stairs and gazed at the quarry chips that stretched out to Ngong Road. Ngong Road, the monster that had swallowed his girl. The news of her tragic demise had hit him like a sledgehammer, and he was still smarting from the shock. The feeling that he was solely to blame for the death of Stella kept on haunting him.

He had come here because he could not stand The Slaughterhouse, the last place he had been with Stella and the venue of his last confrontation with her. The accusing glances from the neighbours could not hide their feelings about what they thought of him following the tragedy.

He took another sip of the spirit he was drinking, and stared into the open space.

The area around the grave held only vivid memories of Stella. It was here that the two of them spent most of the days when Stella could escape from Smart-Look Salon. Right from the start when they had met for the first time, this had become their hideout. They would steal away day or night and come here. He had first taken her here, right on the well-manicured lawn, under a starry sky. They would walk hand in hand, each one in deep thought, in silence because no words could explain what they felt for each other.

Sometimes they would walk right into the well-tended graves of the soldiers who had died in the war. These war graves were a source of intrigue for most people who visited them. It was almost impossible to imagine that under the well-manicured grass whose edges were so expertly trimmed were human remains. The lush pasture complemented well the white tombstones where European, Indian and African soldiers reposed side by side.

"Why would they not be buried together, now that they all died for the same cause?" Stella would ask with her hand round his waist and her head on his chest.

"But did they ever live together?" he would challenge her. Then he would answer himself, "No! In normal circumstances that did not call for sacrificing life, they were fences apart. But then, life's like that. You have to live it to know it," he would finish as he tenderly looked at her. And Ndung'u the photographer would capture the moment without their knowledge. Bone would cherish the photographs all his life.

It would be difficult to forget Stella. She had been the only girl who loved him when he was among the lowest of the low, living with his friends in a makeshift room that was flooded half a metre high during the El-Nino rains. She helped him not only to get acquainted with Ngando, but also uplifted his financial status. Had she not sacrificed her weekly earnings for him to go for showtime sessions at Florida 2000, his musical talent would not have been known.

Even though he enjoyed a near celebrity status in Ngando and could get any girl he wanted, the couple had remained fiercely loyal to each other. Until Nancy and fate had struck.

Sighing, he took another swig of the spirit, the acrid taste filling his mouth. He felt it go all the way to his intestines, searing his body every inch of the way. And even then, the spirit could not dull the pin pricks of the thoughts piercing his mind.

He did not see the Toyota Corolla come slowly towards the graves, although it drew the attention of every other person in the area. His brain did not register its presence even as it stopped a metre away, and it was only when the car door slammed shut that he was jolted awake.

Nancy stood for a whole minute staring intently at him, then crossed over and sat next to him on the step.

"Hi," he said weakly.

"Hi," she answered.

There was a loud silence.

"I was passing by and decided to pop in. Your friends told me what happened."

"Thanks," he said, without looking at her.

"I'm really sorry about this," she started. "I know how sad it must be for you."

He did not answer. His hand mechanically unscrewed the bottle of spirit as he prepared for another swig. She grabbed it in mid-air.

"I don't think you can solve anything by drinking," she said, a quiver in her voice.

"I'm from the ghetto, this is how I shed my tears," he replied shortly, though he let her take away the bottle. "Besides, you don't understand what I am going through."

She sat still for a minute or so, surveying thoughtfully the surroundings. Her hand rested on the long, black velvet dress she was wearing. Bone was thinking he had said something bad when she looked up. There was a film of tears in her eyes.

"It's unfair of you to say I don't understand what you are going through. You don't know about me," she said, wiping the tears on the back of her hand. "I too, know death!" she said, almost viciously.

"You see, I am an orphan. I lost my parents years ago, so I know what death means," she added, almost composed once more.

Bone dryly reflected upon what she had said, then muttered, "Sorry to hear about that. What happened?" .

"I'd rather not talk about it," Nancy answered. From somewhere in her dress she removed a crisp white handkerchief and dabbed at her eyes, taking care not to wipe off the eye shadow.

They then kept quiet for a whole ten minutes.

"It's amazing how you don't realize how much you loved someone until they are gone," he finally said to break the silence.

She moved closer and put her arm round his shoulder. He could smell the rich fragrance of her perfume. Somehow, it reassured him so much that he started talking without realizing he was doing so. He poured out his heart without knowing.

"Today, I went to Stella's place. Her mother chased me away, calling me a greedy pig who is so enchanted by the attractive glitter of a stranger that I let her daughter go mad and drive herself to death. Causing a huge scene, she nearly tore my clothes off, saying that had her daughter not been thinking about my cheating habits, she would have been more careful while crossing the road . . . she would have seen the construction lorry."

"Everyone knows you are not to blame for this," Nancy said reassuringly.

"Yes, everyone except those who matter. The neighbours who heard my argument with Stella are actually calling me a murderer. The whole of Ngando does not trust me, I can't help feeling guilty myself."

He looked at her, searching for more reassurance and suddenly realized how beautiful she looked even with that pained expression on her face. Her hair was made neatly into a knot at the back of her head, leaving two long curls to fall on her face. Her face had been expertly made-up and it enhanced her features with superb precision. Their eyes met and locked for a second, then they both looked away hastily. There was a long silence as they watched the afternoon unfold ahead of them.

A small toddler threw his plastic ball towards them. Bone stood up, picked the ball and threw it back gently.

"On normal days the whole graveyard is filled with people coming to fetch water," he said to change the subject. "But this weekend nobody has come because the shortage of water has abated. Anyway, at this time the grave attendants don't sell the water because they fear their superiors may show up anytime."

"What do the attendants use the water for?" she ask innocently.

"To water the lawn," he explained. "That's why the grass here is so green," he added. "We make sure that the dead have enough water to green their dwelling place, while the living traverse the whole neighbourhood with empty buckets on their heads, Stella used to say."

"What causes the water shortage?"

"We don't have a water supply system. We always buy water from vendors or landlords who have boreholes in their plots. Sometimes, there is an artificial shortage when water is cut off so that we buy it at exorbitant prices from the numerous vendors employed by the City Council lords. In September, all the water is diverted from the slums to the agricultural show. Then even the vendors themselves have none and people from Kibera, Kawangware, Riruta Satellite and Ngando have to buy it at twenty shillings a jerrycan."
She kept quiet, the story seeming to intrigue her.

They sat in silence for another half hour. Finally, Nancy looked at her gold watch and up at him.

"Let's go," she said.

"No!" he almost shouted. "I can't face Ngando again! I will have to wait until dark. You leave me here."

"No. I'm saying we go to my place. You need to stay away from here for some time."

He thought about it for a while, then shrugged and stood up. People looked up from their engagements as the wheels of the car crunched on the gravel. Ndung'u, the photographer, was speechless.

Bone looked at the 'CAR RENT LTD' sticker on the dashboard. Her eyes followed his.

"I have rented it for an indefinite period. That is, until I finish a project I'm working on," she explained as she turned on the radio and some soft music started playing from somewhere in the car. Bone slid further into the comfortable velvet seat as they drove out onto Ngong Road and headed towards the city centre.

"By the way, that's a nice bracelet you have," he commended her.

"Oh thanks. It was a present from my uncle on my twentieth birthday."

"You are twenty?" he asked. With these 'dot-com' girls, there was no guessing the age. She looked young enough to be even nineteen, but he had to make sure.

"Twenty two to be exact," she replied.

She was a good driver. She manoeuvred through the Sunday evening traffic like someone who had been born with a steering wheel in her hand.

"How come you talk like that. . . with that drawl?" he asked, now that they were discussing her.

"When my family were. . . er . . . died, I was picked up by an uncle who is based in the United States. I lived with him for almost twelve years. Actually, I came back only two months ago to embark on . . . the project I was telling you about."

In that case, she was doing a great job speaking all that Kiswahili, he concluded. It was rare to find someone who had stayed in the United States for more than a year still remembering their mother-tongue. They always came back pretending they could not speak vernacular. He rested his hand behind his head, and only then remembered he had not buckled up the safety belt. He was actually sitting on it.

The cassette player in the car belted out a popular song and the pair was charmed by the vocalist's smooth voice:

"I keep on falling... in love with you, Oh, I never loved someone... the way that I love you."

Bone ventured, "Has anyone ever told you that you are a beautiful woman?"

She smiled shyly. "Of course you're just flattering me."

"No, I mean it! I tell you, when you smile, I feel like looking at you the whole day." She laughed at this.

Town Centre was as deserted as it could be on a Sunday evening. At the Haile Selassie Avenue roundabout, a bus had broken down and the frustrated passengers were alighting. Nancy turned right towards Mombasa Road. They passed the huge billboards installed by different advertising agencies and Bone wondered exactly where they were headed to.

"I stay at Imara Daima Estate," she explained as they passed the General Motors compound where several gleaming heavy-duty trucks were parked outside, awaiting buyers. After a moment, she turned into the dirt road that led to the middle class estate. At the entrance, she waited patiently while the driver in front of her stopped, walked to the shops, bought bread and milk and walked casually back to his car.

A real lady, Bone thought. A typical Nairobi driver would have stood on the horn, made horrid gestures and unleashed expletives that would shock even the devil. Nancy instead smiled tolerantly.

"I'm finding it very difficult to drive in Kenya," she said as she waited for the car ahead to start moving again. "Nobody here seems to have respect for traffic rules. It's even harder for me because I have had to learn to drive on the left side of the street. What is more, I can't afford to get involved in an accident because I don't have a Kenyan driving licence."

They parked in the small parking area in front of a beautiful maisonette. Bone took care not to step on the well-trimmed patch of lawn. The huge security lights hung on the roof flung their strong beams of light all over the modest compound in the darkening evening.

She tapped once on a white doorbell and he heard a faint chink echo inside the house. A second later, the door was opened by a woman in a spotless white uniform who stood smiling at them.

"Hallo, Martha," Nancy greeted. "How was your day?"

"Fine thank you, Madam," she replied, then turned to Bone.

"Good evening, Sir."

"Er . . .Good evening," Bone replied. He had never been called 'Sir' in his life.

The furnishing was exquisite. Around a stained glass table was a set of velvet sofas. The entertainment unit facing him boasted of a small television set, a video cassette recorder and a hi-fi system. Beside it a refrigerator hummed softly.

"Do sit down, darling," Nancy said. "Feel at home. No, don't mind the carpet. Have a seat."

He sank into the sofa feeling a bit ashamed of his well-worn sports shoes and afraid of messing the milk-white carpet. Though fashionable in Ngando, his sneakers now looked out of place on the tiled floor. 'Just like a street boy at the Hilton,' Bone thought as his mind recalled Stella's words. He shrugged her out of his mind and looked around the room.   All the furniture smelt new. It couldn't have been used more than a month. The wall boasted of no decorations, save for a large glossy calendar hung over the television set, with some dates highlighted in bright Indian ink. The curtains were exactly the same colour as the sofas.

Bone could not help thinking that the house had been somehow hurriedly furnished. He understood—after all, wasn't this just a temporary dwelling place while she completed her project?

She walked back in and used a remote controlled switch to turn on the TV and immediately, a documentary full of frightening statistics about HIV/AIDS popped on the screen. Bone recalled their encounter with the young peer counsellor at Ngando and chuckled. Nancy opened a sideboard in which were arranged many bottles and pulled out a half-full wine bottle. She placed it carefully on the table, then went to the kitchen and came back with two wine glasses.

"Let's make a toast," she suggested as she handed him a glass. She poured small amounts of the wine. "To a happy future".

Bone could only say 'Yes' in reply. Where he came from, you didn't need a ritual to partake of alcohol. And why did she keep that whole amount of drinks only to drink small mouthfuls? In Ngando, you did not put down the bottle until it was empty, or until you blacked out – which ever came first.

"You have a very beautiful place," he said aloud.

"Thanks," she snuggled closer. "It's yours as well if you so wish, darling."

He could only nod, dumbfounded.

nine

Molo Town, 1992

Peterson Lihanda lived alone near Kimotho Mbembe Hotel, a kilometre away from the Molo Post Office on the way to Mau Summit. He had left his family in Mumias years earlier in search of greener pastures in the fast growing town. Life in the village had become weary and monotonous. Besides, he had always wanted a white collar job where he would wear a suit and carry important files under his armpit.

His greatest shortcoming was that he had not received much education – he had dropped out of school in Standard One due to lack of school fees. His father had a sizeable amount of land where he grew sugar cane, but there was hardly any time they benefitted from the crop. The old man was almost always up to this neck in debt. He always used his earnings for his own enjoyments which, of course, added to his debts.

He had left his native Mumias through Kakamega to Kapsabet, spent a year in Eldoret and Kabarnet before landing in Molo. The situation he had met in Molo town had not been very pleasant at all. With hardly any education, his childhood dreams of success clouded when he failed to get any employment. He had to settle for small menial jobs here and there. Over the five years he had been there, he became famous as *kijana wa mkono* – an unskilled labourer.

What he prided himself for most was his excellent command of many languages. Apart from his native Luhya, he could speak Kikuyu and Kalenjin with native like fluency. It was only English which proved a bit difficult, and Kiswahili which he spoke with a heavy mother tongue intonation, that he didn't like speaking. He spoke Kikuyu with such finesse that the residents called him Waithaka, and indeed in some areas nobody knew his real name.

In fact, it was his multilingual prowess that helped him earn a friend in Mwalimu Kipruto, the teacher who lived two plots away from him in one of the nicer, self-contained houses.

During Lihanda's formative years, his mother had taught him the virtue of making friends.

"Plant a tree wherever you go: make a new friend everyday of your life," she would tell him as they worked on the sugar cane farm.

"At the end of the year you will have 365 friends. Surely, one of them will help you one day. In life, friends will help you even more than your own relatives." With this kind of upbringing, Lihanda boasted of friends from all walks of life.

With Kipruto, it had started with the respectful greeting each time the teacher passed by on his way to work.

"*Chamige*?" How are you?

"*Mising,*" the teacher would reply.

"*Iwendi boisyett?*" Going to work?

"*Weei,*" Yes.

"*Abwathi ale kararan betungung.*" I hope you have a nice day.

"*Angenye, ngetuya koskoling.*" You too, see you in the evening.

With time, Mwalimu Kipruto had stopped to enquire how the rugged boy came to learn such flawless Kalenjin. The friendship had blossomed into a deep trust. It became symbiotic – Kipruto relied on the teenager to fetch water for him while he was away. Lihanda on the other hand benefitted greatly from the financial support he received from the teacher. Despite the obvious intellectual gap between the two, they found that they had a lot to discuss. Of particular interest to the two was the local geography of Kenya which Lihanda knew from his travels with what Kipruto could only describe as an 'atlas accuracy'.

As it happened, when the teacher had gone to visit his family in Molo South two weeks earlier, he had left Lihanda taking care of his house. The teenager had deserted his own house, arguing that there was nothing worth stealing there, and moved to his friend's place, guarding it like his own.

Kipruto had come back to Molo a disturbed man. A few months earlier, he had thought his father's statements about the Kikuyu were mere overstretched prejudices from a senile old man. It was when more details emerged of the cleansing and oathing that was taking place that Kipruto had realized the immensity of the issue. He had hastened to warn his best friend among the Kikuyu, Mzee Waweru. He now only hoped the man had listened to his warning and would move away. The news coming in from his home area was not pleasant at all.

Indeed, two days earlier there had been a report that a confrontation had taken place at Nguirubi in Molo South. Molo town had become tense as thousands of families flocked in from the clash-torn areas. Looking at the human exodus, you would have thought that a third world war was in progress. There were stories of the hundreds who had camped at St. John as well as St. Paul's Catholic churches with their remaining livestock and whatever little they could salvage.

Suddenly, Molo became one strange town. When a crowd shouting anti-government and anti-KANU slogans had demonstrated in the town earlier in the day, Lihanda had suggested to Kipruto that he leave the area for a while until things returned to normal. Kipruto had to agree. He had seen the fear in the eyes of his tribesmen and consultation with another fellow Kalenjin elder had convinced him that it was better to move away.

And so it happened that on the 18th of March, 1992, Kipruto asked for leave of absence from his school. In the middle of the night, he took what was extremely necessary and climbed into a taxi that a friend had offered. Of course, his trusted friend, Peterson Lihanda, was left to take care of his house.

In one sudden show of emotions, the two friends hugged before

Kipruto tearfully entered the car.

"*Memamegi, ki agetugul ko kararanitu,*" Lihanda whispered, a huge lump in his throat. Don't worry, everything will be alright.

He watched the taxi's taillights as it made its way out of the residential plot and joined the tarmac road.

"*Vuta nimie,*" he prayed. Nice journey. Suddenly, he realized the emptiness in his heart. He now, was all alone .

Kamwaura Farm, April, 1992

It is amazing how in just one month, things can fall apart with the horrendous collapse they did in Molo. Every passing day was met with the grim reality of the situation on the ground, which could hardly be adequately reflected by the huge newspaper headlines it earned. Every day was an uncertainty.

At night, most of the families who had not joined the exodus spent their time in the *shamba* for fear of being attacked. The Waweru family was in one of the plots on their farm.

The *rwamba* of the napier grass ate at Kimani as he gazed at the ominous clouds in the sky. He had many unanswered questions on his mind. Would things ever go back to the way they were before the clashes? Would the two warring tribes ever see eye to eye again? What about the now broken marriages between their sons and daughters? Would they ever reform?

Kimani listened to the subdued sounds of his small sister sleeping beside him and his parents in the shamba. Her mouth had been gagged to ensure she did not make a sound that would alert anybody of their presence.

Waweru, Kimani's father, had adamantly refused to join the flight of people leaving Kamwaura even though he had ample time to do so even before the clashes started. "Why should I leave my inheritance – my only link with my forefathers – for the Kalenjin cattle to graze?" he would ask the family when his wife begged him to take the family away from the danger zone.

The attackers were puzzling everybody with the fervor with

which they carried out their mayhem. From the well-orchestrated pattern of raids – always excluding settlements that had a sizeable presence of their own tribesmen – the locals had speculated that these were not ordinary men but highly trained soldiers. Although these rumours were never substantiated, it was said that the arrows pulled out of the victim's bodies were 'Made in Korea.'

It was, therefore, ironical that they looted anything of value they came across. Before mortally injuring one man, it was said, they had angrily demanded a *sanduku la maneno* – a box of words – and it had taken a lot of beating for the unfortunate man to realize that they wanted his radio. At another place, they first sat down to eat from the pot of *githeri* simmering on the fire before burning down the house.

Kimani had suddenly been thrown into a role he had not anticipated. He had to join his father in ensuring that their family was not harmed. At night in the *shamba*, he and his father took turns to watch out for raiders. It was frightening to be so suddenly thrust into adulthood at his age.

*   *   *

In another *shamba*, a few hundred metres away, Irungu was also looking at the same foreboding sky from beneath a banana plant. The uncertainty over life and the future had never been this much.

All the schools had been closed down indefinitely, and the prospects of the situation returning to normal in time for him to sit for his Kenya Certificate of Primary Education examinations were very bleak. The future was not important for now. What mattered was living each day at a time.

In the last month, horrifying experiences had occurred. Hardly two days after the attack on Nguirubi, angry villagers had burnt down a substantial part of Ndoinet Forest to flush out the raiders who were reportedly holed up in there. By the end of March, over 30,000 hectares of forest had been burnt down.

About the same time, a contigent of armed villagers had attacked the house of one Captain Belsoi and burnt him alive in his house.

Rumour had it that thereafter they had unearthed an underground tunnel dug underneath the house where warriors used to hide. Serious reprisals were expected.

At a *baraza* held by the DC in Kamwaura, one plausible chain of events explaining the clashes was given. One theory explaining the cause of the clashes was that elders appointed by the community to help retrieve property stolen in the area had approached one suspect. The Kalenjin suspect, however, let out a war cry that attracted over a hundred of his tribesmen who then attacked the elders. In fact, the locals forwarded the names of those involved to the DC. The administrator urged for restraint, but there was no respite in the clashes.

In less than a week, seven people had been killed in Boron and Kamwaura, and many more admitted in Molo and Nakuru hospitals. The DC had hardly left the scene when the air was rent with screams and shouts. A bloodbath had started again. His security men had to fire in the air to scare the attackers. They had retreated, but in a systematic turn, re-emerged from the forest and attacked several villages further down.

Irungu was more perplexed when the sequence of raids suggested that the raiders were heading towards Karirikania farm. Here, he thought, there would be the fiercest battle. The farm belonged to the NDEFFO, a collection of ex-freedom fighters and their offspring, and it was expected that they would strongly challenge the raiders.

Another raging rumour involved the missions of the regular helicopter patrols in the area. Villagers speculated that they were providing arms and logistics to the raiders. Irungu, like his fellow villagers, watched the helicopters warily.

It had been many days since he had seen his friend, Kimani. After three weeks, the two friends had met when Irungu went to bid Kimani farewell. Irungu's father had finally seen the light and decided to leave. It had, however, taken the torching of his shop for him to agree to move to Molo town until things quietened down. A lorry which had been donated by one of the wealthier and kinder businessmen in Molo town would be transporting the people from

Molo South. Irungu turned over uncomfortably. He could not wait for morning.

*   *   *

Kirui was a frustrated man. Since the clashes had started, life had changed for him and his family. He had had to close down his shop near the forest for fear of an attack and looting. If he had continued operating the business, it would have been the target of attacks either by the Kikuyus or by his own people who derided him for sitting on the fence rather than joining them in the war. Now he had no source of income.

He also had had to pull his children out of the local Banana Primary School. Their safety was not guaranteed due to the fact that in that school their tribe was a minority.

He had spent sleepless nights thinking about the future of his family as well as the society at large. He wished everybody was like him – he had nothing to do with the clashes. In fact, he loathed the fact that the tranquility that had previously prevailed in his home area had suddenly evaporated to be replaced by the squall of war.
He now had to sleep with a weapon at hand. Every night, he prayed that sanity would return to his clash-torn area.

Mama Cherotich, his wife, stirred in bed beside him. Unable to sleep, Kirui listened to her subdued breathing. Behind the wall he could hear the children snoring softly. He envied them. Knowing they had a protector, they could get snatches of sleep. But the question was, would he really protect them?

For a millionth time, he wished dawn would break immediately. The cold nights were getting longer, the waiting unbearable. Suddenly, he heard quick footsteps outside his main door. He heard a loud crack and his heart missed a beat. The next crack was louder. He heard the door come down with a mighty crash. His wife sprang up, frightened out of sleep. She grabbed him and he could hear her heart beating like a drum.

"*Nituoka!* " We have come! Came the shout from the sitting room.

They heard the fast footsteps approach the bedroom. Kirui heard his wife gasp. Then she let out a scream. He had never felt so powerless in his life.

Powerful torches picked them out, blinding them. There must have been over fifty men armed with crude weapons.

She screamed again. "Taret!" Help!

"*Kiria kanua!*" Shut your mouth! They ordered the woman and followed it with a slap. Kirui was paralyzed. He could not move. Then he heard a scream from the children's room.

"God! Don't let them kill my children. Please!" he prayed.

The attackers pulled him unceremoniously out of his matrimonial bed and onto the floor. Then over ten men pinned him down. He felt his body go numb with all the weight placed on him.

"Please don't kill us!" he pleaded with the men, some of whom he recognised even in the darkness. "*Haki Njoroge, tuonee huruma!*" Have mercy on us, Njoroge!

Njoroge, the bearded leader of the gang, shone his torch on him.

"*Pole rafiki, lakini hii ni vita.*" Sorry friend, but this is war.

"Friendship does not mean anything. We are not going to kill you. We are going to do something worse."

Kirui's heart skipped a beat. His children were shepherded into the room, shivering with fear.

"Baba, *taretech!* Help us," one of them pleaded. He was slapped and went quiet.

The helplessness drove Kirui crazy. He could not move. Someone pressed a large knife against his throat.

"If you move, even slightly, you will die!" he was warned. He kept quiet. What did they want to do? Three men approached the bed.

"*Taret!*" Mama Cherotich screamed again. "*Kakebarech!*" Murderers!

They fished her out of bed, roughly blocking off her desperate blows. Two of them pinned her to the ground and the third one cut her night-cloth into two with his large knife. Suddenly, Kirui realized what they wanted to do.

"Oh, no!" he moaned. With renewed vigour, he tried to free himself. He was easily subdued and even pinned down more firmly.

"Keep still and watch this!" a man ordered him in a gruff voice. As the men formed a line and dropped their trousers, the frightened children wailed loudly. Kirui wailed even louder, almost like a ghostly howl.

"Help! They are soiling my wife!"

But nobody came to help. The whole family watched as their mother was raped in turns. Kirui was propped up to see it all; the agonized voice of his wife, her anguished face, the bloody mess on the floor, the frightened faces of the children, everything! He saw the sardonic grins on the attacker's faces as they humiliated him.

After what seemed like an eternity, it came to an end. Satiated, the attackers left, some of them laughing. The children at once ran to their mother's still form. Kirui did not move an inch. He sat at the same corner, still propped against the wall, crying like a baby. He did not bother to wipe the tears off his face.

Kirui is now a village madman, his case having defeated even the most qualified specialists at Mathare Mental Hospital. He is usually seen on market days running furiously from one end to the other screaming, "*Taret!*"

Molo Town, 1992

Early one morning, all the *matatus* in Molo were grounded, the drivers and touts having striked in protest against the skirmishes in the interior. Commuters planning to go to Nakuru, Njoro and Nairobi were stranded at the terminus, helplessly watching the irate transporters demonstrating in defiance.

Lihanda was busy buying tomatoes at the market the day after the strike commenced. That market, once a hub of activity drawing traders from as far as Kericho, was now subdued and quiet. The clashes had halted the supply of vegetables. Today, only a few of the stalls were open. Lihanda was perturbed – at this rate the town would starve.

A loud cry suddenly split the air. Everyone looked up to see a small, plump woman bolt through the scattered stalls, upsetting a few bucketfuls of potatoes. A split second after, two other women followed her shouting. "*Ua! Ua!*" Kill! Kill! as they waved sticks in the air.

"*Kari ki?*" What is it? asked one of the vendors. She spread out her hands to salvage her own commodities from the approaching women.

"*Reke tumakahure matu,*" one of her friends replied without looking back. "*Nio maroraga andu aitu.*" Let us chop off their ears; they are the ones who are killing our people.

That was when Lihanda understood it now. The clashes had broken all known boundaries. He did not wait to see what happened to the unfortunate woman whose crime was being a member of the wrong tribe in the wrong place and at the wrong time. He quickly put his tomatoes in the crook of his arm and made a silent exit back home.

At the police station, he stopped for a while to see the huge gathering camped there – local Kalenjins who feared the wrath of the residents. He stopped at the bar near Agip Petrol Station where a larger group of Kikuyus were squeezed in. The owner had converted the premises into a refugee camp. Another landowner up ahead had also let the incoming families camp in his compound.

It had reached a point where one just watched as a hapless family walked into one's house unannounced, settled on the floor and slept – getting only a roof over their heads was fortune enough.

Most Molo residents who now own large flocks of livestock got them during that period. Rather than watch their animals die of starvation in the town, the incomers opted to sell their valuable animals at throwaway prices. A bull was going for less than two thousand shillings instead of ten, and goats and sheep for a thousand shillings or less. Poultry was not sold – hens were exchanged for a single meal or an overnight stay. Those lucky ones with ready money bought many animals and carted them away to their farms.

In apparent solidarity with the striking *matatu* operators, all the Molo traders closed their shops in protest. Not even appeals from Mr. Mungai, the local Member of Parliament and the District Commissioner could make them rescind their decision.

"Stop the killings first!" somebody shouted at the leaders. The MP played a big role in making Parliament and the whole country aware of the horror of the clashes. His popularity grew with every meeting he held to condemn the clashes.

Reports came in of more attacks in Molo South and the businesses remained closed. The number of refugees swelled. The stadium was filled to the brim with people and their herds of livestock. Others camped at Molo Secondary School and yet others at Mugumo School. Starvation was imminent as the thousands of people depleted their food reserves and started depending on handouts from sympathizers. The town was filled with street families, some of which still live on the streets to this day.

Security was heightened, sparking off speculation that the President would be visiting the area at the end of the month. There was a sudden lull in the fighting. Lihanda could not comprehend what was happening to his country.

The effects of the clashes were felt all over the country. In Nakuru, approximately forty kilometres away from the battle zone, the touts and drivers at the bus station ran amok. A *matatu* operated by two Kalenjins was stoned by the irate mob and the two men escaped death by a whisker. Only a day earlier, a suspect had been arrested with two bows and thirty arrows at Kwa Rhoda, a suburb of the town. He had cowed at the back of the police Land Rover as the residents bayed like hounds for his blood. Luckily, he had been smuggled away alive.

It became so chaotic such that in early April the President himself urged people not to take the law into their own hands. The plea was disregarded twenty days later when a man was stopped at the Molo–Njoro Stage in Nakuru. The crowd demanded he produce the arrows he was carrying. He did not have any, but they killed him all the same. Another unfortunate fellow was pulled out of a moving matatu and almost killed. In Nairobi, at the infamous Nyamakima Stage, a Kalenjin couple was roughed up and almost lynched just days after the lynching of another man in the streets.

Molo-Sitoito Road, April 24 – 5:05 a.m.

Irungu sat huddled at the back of the Fuso lorry together with a few dozen families. Next to him sat his two little siblings and his mother. His father, being a respected person in the area, sat in the driver's cabin.

The lorry ambled on, stopping now and then to pick up more escapees who had braved the early morning cold to flee to safety. It was full to capacity and some of the people literally hung on the sides. Irungu respectfully stood up to let one of the women, who was expectant, to have his place.

Nobody spoke. It was painful to leave your home behind not knowing whether you would ever come back. The pain was so great that any attempts at striking a conversation were met with expressionless faces. Everybody looked ahead, anxiously waiting to reach the destination.

They rounded a bend lined with tall gum trees and instantly the lorry braked. After the inertia jolted them forward they stood up to see what was happening in front. Ahead of them a huge log was placed right across the road. With apprehension, they looked around the small cluster of trees as the lorry started reversing.

A loud war cry broke the early morning silence. The travellers peered at the surroundings, frantically trying to ascertain the source of the commotion. The dawn light showed them the hundreds of men emerging from the bushes. A scream shot out from the lorry.

A huge rock brought the windscreen down in one huge shattering crash as the driver unsuccessfully tried to manoeuvre the lorry round the log. Arrows flew in the air like sparrows. One plunged into the driver's shoulder and made him howl in anguish. He was unable to drive any further. Dozens of armed men jumped into the back of the lorry and slashed at the travellers with their *pangas*, cutting up everyone in sight. The driver made some effort to reverse, his teeth clenched in pain, then he gave up completely, apparently resigned to his fate.

Caught by surprise, most of the escapees only cowered in the lorry. Those who were luckier jumped out and ran for their lives, the attackers in hot pursuit.

Irungu was one of the lucky ones. He looked up and saw a man with a *panga* raised in the air, and sprang up. He bumped into the raider and they fell onto the ground together. He ran on as the lorry which had miraculously started reversing again rolled over the unfortunate attacker.

His lungs were almost ripping apart, and his heart was beating so loud that he could hear it. He heard the man running behind him give a cry of pain and fall down flat. Frantically, he looked behind and saw him lying down with an arrow sticking in his back. He also saw a dozen or so men charging at him. He increased his speed tenfold.

"*Barr!*" Kill! Came the shouts. Half of the men at Irungu's heels fell back to finish off the fallen man. The others kept on with the chase.

An arrow hit him in the thigh. He screamed in pain as he flew in the air and landed with a mighty thud five metres away. Having lost any hope of survival, he shut his eyes painfully and waited for death as the attackers noisily approached.

He did not get to finish his prayer.

Molo Town, April 27, 1992

Lihanda had had a very busy day. All morning he had been handling one of the numerous chores given to him by a neighbour. He hated these demeaning jobs of course, but he knew he had to survive somehow. Man must live, he thought. He had taken some bales of *mitumba* towards Transport House on the opposite side of town and seen the heavy security presence in the area. There were hundreds of heavily armed General Service Unit as well as regular police officers all over.

At the *matatu* terminus, he heard in hushed tones the story that a number of victims had been brought in two days earlier from the south after an ambush. Curiosity got the better of him and he took the murram road to the District Hospital. He was not prepared for what he saw.

The wards were overflowing with injured and maimed people. It was said that most of the other patients recovered miraculously on seeing the maimed clash victims. They willingly left their beds and moved to the floor for these new arrivals. Lihanda cringed on seeing the wounded; fresh bandages on their limbs, their blank eyes staring back at his surprised face. When he saw a woman with an arrow still lodged in her groin, he walked out. He could not take it any more. Why this inhumanity? That was all he could ask.

A crowd was gathered outside the theatre, peering at the hospital Land Rover which also doubled up as an ambulance. He edged closer, wondering what they were looking at. Somebody moved aside for Lihanda and he noticed that there lay a man with an arrow lodged in the head. From the crowd, he gathered that the previous night the man had heard his neighbour scream for help. When he dashed out to assist him, he had not seen the raiders waiting outside and had been shot in the head.

It was whispered that the doctors at the hospital were undecided on whether to remove the arrow since the X-ray pictures showed that the arrow had touched a major blood vessel and the patient was likely to die from bleeding if it was ruptured. Since the arrow was barbed, it also meant that it would come out with parts of the man's brain. So he had been referred to Nakuru Provincial Hospital. Perplexed, Lihanda looked at the small under-equipped building that was the mortuary. It was said to be so full that if you came to collect a body, the attendants would have to pull out tens of other bodies first.

A few hours later, on his way to yet another errand, Lihanda was informed by one of the nurses that the victim with the arrow in his head had not made it to Nakuru. He had died on the way. With a heavy heart, Lihanda was now walking to Kaloleni to collect some money for another of his neighbours.

It was then that he saw the President. It happened by sheer coincidence. He had just turned the corner when he saw a convoy of sleek cars emerge from Olenguruone Road, and stop at Keep Left. He jumped over the hedges in people's shambas as he ran on towards the cars. He stopped in his tracks when he saw that something was amiss. Instead of crowding round the convoy, the opposite was happening. The crowd was running away from the convoy.

"*Muuaji!*" Killer! The defiant shouts from the disintegrating crowd reached him. Some of the women even stripped their clothes off their bodies.

A security cordon surrounded one of the cars and the tall confident President Moi stepped out and calmly surveyed the scene. Lihanda edged closer when a few of the people began to walk back.

In spite of the tepid welcome he had received, the President, as usual, looked calm and composed as he addressed the small crowd. He spoke on the current crisis at hand, saying he had made a tour of the Olenguruone area and promising that the government would provide security for all residents regardless of tribe or political affiliation. He added that the clashes were politically instigated by non-patriotic self-seekers who wanted to see innocent wananchi spill their blood. Then he took issue with the striking touts whom he said were also being used by the same politicians for their own selfish interests. The crisis had been blown out of proportion by the press and the international community, he said.

The residents, on the other hand, reiterated the fact that the feuding ethnic communities had lived together in harmony for decades and it was unfortunate that this was happening. Somebody called for the immediate transfer of the Provincial Commissioner who was accused of fueling the conflict. The crowd unanimously agreed to this, and the president responded: "*Taangalia hiyo*". We'll look into that. Someone else mumbled something about the military helicopters that were alleged to be overflying the clash area and dropping weapons for the attackers.

The head of state reiterated his point about national security, urging the *wananchi* not to flee from their homes since security would be enhanced. He asked those who had run away to return to their homes.

"*Lakini, Mzee,*" someone interrupted, "*hatuna nyumba za kuishi. Zilichomwa!*" But *Mzee*, we don't have houses to live in. They were burnt down. The President looked at the man straight in the eye and the man looked down immediately. "Who will build for you houses where you are going? Do you want to go somewhere else?"

Then with his usual, "*Mkae na amani*", live in peace, farewell, the President stepped into his official car. His security cordon was impenetrable.

Lihanda walked back home. Later, he heard the now familiar story that the presidential motorcade had earlier been stopped at Olenguruone. The cars had rounded a corner only to halt at an unusual roadblock. Across the road, a barricade of human bodies, some with arrows sticking from them, were piled up to a metre high. It was said that the President himself had joined the security team in fighting off the dogs that were feasting on their flesh.

Whether this disturbing story was true or not has to date never been established.

ten

Kamwaura, April-May, 1992

The heavy rains had rendered the roads to the interior impassable. The government announced that helicopters would be used to monitor the security situation in Molo South since road transport was now impossible.

Villagers in Kamwaura heard about the pandemonium in the capital. Thousands of students from the University of Nairobi had taken to the streets to protest against the clashes and turned the streets into a battlefield. Apparently, they wanted to forcibly enter Parliament Buildings, but the anti-riot police would not let them.

Then, a record number of district officers – fifteen – were posted to Molo and Olenguruone. The government had acknowledged that this was a national crisis.

In Kamwaura, the onus of security was left to the vigilante groups. These groups patrolled the whole area in their dozens, and now it was relatively safer. The vigilante group members knew each other well. They had a rather interesting way of calling each other for the patrol. Rather than compromise the security by calling names, the patrollers hurled a huge rock in the air. Then young men would know what the missile meant and would come out. It was a crime for any able-bodied man not to join the vigilantes on their rounds.

Most of the villagers spent their days on their farms, and then went back to the refugee camps at night. One such camp was the one at the St. John and St. Paul's Catholic Churches. In the compound was a half-completed building where they sheltered amid rumours that they would be attacked. Their most valuable goods were stored inside the church. How this settlement came to acquire the nickname, Riboi, has never been known up-to-the-minute.

Kimani walked beside one of the most talkative men who was yapping despite his obvious disinterest. It was past midnight and Kimani was too tired to concentrate on anything.

When the report that the lorry ferrying people to Molo had been ambushed reached the village, Kimani had wept openly. Nothing was spoken about survivors, and he knew that it was highly likely that his best friend was among the dead. He could not bear those thoughts. He clenched his fist tighter as he remembered the day, a week earlier, when Irungu had come to inform him that they would be fleeing the area.

"*Mzee* has finally seen the light," Irungu had said, shivering from the early evening cold.

"You're lucky to be leaving this hell," Kimani had replied. "My father is stubborn. He refuses to budge because of the family shamba."

"Don't worry, he will see the light. My father was hesitant, but when our shop was burnt down, he was convinced we should leave. It is better to be alive and poor than to be dead."

"So when are you leaving?"

Irungu had told him about the lorry donated by some kind businessman which they would be boarding at dawn.

"I wish I could come along too," Kimani had said, "but there is the family to protect. My father is counting on me to help him ensure that my mother and sister are safe."

A long silence had ensued as both realized that this might be the last time they were seeing each other. A dog had passed by, stopped and looked at them devilishly. It had bared its teeth and snarled, then suddenly ran off. Both teenagers had looked at it, not at all amazed at the strange behaviour. They were aware that dogs had a field day, feeding on human bodies strewn all over the country. Now it was dangerous to play with the canines since they had already tasted human flesh. It was not only the dogs that behaved strangely – sometimes even poultry suddenly ran amok, fluttering in the air and clattering loudly without any apparent provocation. This was wartime and every creature was uneasy.

"Farewell, my friend," Irungu had whispered. Tearfully, the two pals had hugged each other. And now that Irungu was dead, a huge emptiness hung heavily on Kimani's heart.

Molo, mid-May, 1992

Molo had become a ghost town. A deathly and subdued gloom loomed over it like a mist. Only a handful of shops were open. Scattered groups of apprehensive men gathered every few metres.

A patrol of General Service Unit policemen marched up the road, the officers clutching their AK-47 rifles as if their whole lives depended on them. Mwalimu Kipruto grasped his letter tighter in his hand and increased his pace. He had to go back to Molo South and out of the ghostly town as soon as circumstances allowed.

The headmaster of his former school in Molo had finally agreed to give him a transfer letter. It had taken Kipruto much cajoling and pleading.

"Mr. Kipruto," the short, slightly overweight man had said, "you know very well that such a letter needs some backing from a higher authority in the ministry. I don't want to do something that will later be my undoing."

Kipruto had leaned forward. "But, Sir, you understand what the situation is like. The clashes have not abated as I had hoped. I want to teach – I still need a job. But I can't work here anymore because of who I am. Since I can't change my tribe, I can only teach in a school in my home area. Yet that obstinate headmaster has refused to let me teach unless I have a letter from you."

"What about me? What will I tell the ministry later?"

"Sir, everybody in the country knows what is happening. You can't be victimized because of something you did during this chaotic time."

A heavy load had been lifted off his chest when the reluctant headmaster had pulled open a drawer, selected a sheet of paper and written out a recommendation.

"I'm doing this as a friend," the educationist had reminded him.

As soon as he had walked out of the school, Kipruto had felt the urge to see his friend Lihanda on the other side of town. He had left the house so abruptly that he feared some of his things may not be in order. He didn't doubt Lihanda's capability to keep his place secure, though. Lihanda was probably the most trustworthy man on earth. Kipruto crossed the Molo River and to the other side of town, wondering at the town's transformation from its usual vibrant, genial atmosphere to its present ghostly state.

Just outside Caltex Petrol Station, a small crowd of about twenty men stood in a random circle. They raised their heads as he approached, then immediately looked away. They seemed to be discussing something in hushed tones. A wave of fear shot through Kipruto's body. It did not disappear even as he made to pass them.

"Hallo, *Mwalimu!*" somebody called behind him. "Aren't you going to say *habari?*"

He turned round to look at the men. The one who had spoken was a familiar face around town, Kipruto reflected, trying to remember his name. There was a friendly smile on his face.

"Come on! Come and say hello to old friends," he cajoled.

Kipruto moved closer, feeling the strength leave his legs. He shook each hand warmly, thinking that they must have felt his own trembling one.

"How is Molo South, *Mwalimu?* " asked another man, looking straight into Kipruto's eyes.

"As bad as it can get," Kipruto tried to joke, trying to smile off his fear.

"Aha, I see. Is that why you have come to spy on us?"

Kipruto laughed uneasily. "No! No! I'm not here as a. . ."

Suddenly one of them struck out, hitting Kipruto full in the face. He staggered back as the others closed in. Someone kicked him to the ground. He touched his forehead, felt blood and groaned.

"*Ua mkale!*" someone shouted. Kill the Kalenjin!

Kipruto saw an opening in the circle of men around him. Summoning all the energy in his body, he shot up and pushed through the gap like a rabbit. He heard a curse as he ran on, then the approaching thunder of footsteps. A stone flew past, only a centimetre from his head. He did not know where he was headed.

"Oh, God!" he gasped. His heart thumped in his chest.

A stone hit him on the leg and he momentarily lost his balance. He staggered a step, then regained his footing and ran on.

The KGGCU building near Agip Petrol Station was open. A few people had rushed out to see what the commotion was all about. Kipruto pushed them out of the way as he ran into the building. There was a stampede as the crowd surged after him to avoid the pursuing attackers. The door was slammed shut and bolted from inside.

The attackers were enraged. They pelted the building with stones but fortunately couldn't immediately gain entry.

"Someone call the police!" Kipruto gasped, hardly recognizing his own voice. A man crawled to a telephone at the counter. His trembling hands unsuccessfully tried to dial a number.

Kipruto peeped outside and saw that the crowd had swelled. His whole body shook with fear. The hushed people in the building were also trembling.

"Throw that man out or we burn the whole building down!" the men outside shouted as they banged their fists on the window panes. Others were trying to barge their way into the building using a large log. A woman screamed out in fear.

"They are going to kill us all!" she whimpered.

Kipruto stood up slowly. He saw the hinges of the double doors start to give way. Outside, some of the men were pouring some liquid out of jerricans round the building. He knew it was petrol. He looked at the fifty or so people behind him and saw their fear. The attackers were serious.

"Let me get out," he said resolutely.

Rather than cause the death of all these people, he would rather give himself up. The people gathered inside stared at him, perhaps wondering if he really meant what he was saying. Nobody tried to stop him, though.

Bravely, he pushed his way out and faced the mob. The Biblical crowd that is alleged to have so feverishly cried out for Jesus' blood instead of Barnabas' may not have been as bloodthirsty as the Molo one. Kipruto was hardly out of the building when he was dragged to the ground, amid blows.

"Mercy!" he pleaded, but his pleas fell on deaf ears. He was subjected to a slow and painful death. As he lay there, sprawled half-conscious in a pool of his own blood, someone produced a pair of shears and proceeded to snip off of his fingers one after the other.

"Each finger is for one Kikuyu your people have killed," said the man. Kipruto's clouded mind instantly recognized him as a former staff-mate. Why he feigned unfamiliarity was a mystery.

A worn out tyre was finally brought to burn him, but by then, *Mwalimu* Kipruto was already dead.

Molo, end-May, 1992

Lihanda passed the same spot where Kipruto, the only person in Molo who understood him and treated him as an equal, had been murdered. The scene was only a patch of dark ash now, with the rings of wire that had been in the tyre forlornly resting on top. He felt anger and frustration at the war that had turned friends against each other.

He was heading towards the small market aptly named Soko Mjinga on an errand for Mama Adhiambo, the fishmonger. In his right hand he carried a huge fish basket.

His mind wondered what would happen to Kipruto's property. He had never known any of the teacher's relatives, and the only person who could help him out was the taximan who had driven the teacher that night he had left for Molo South. But how could the stranger be reached?

Presently, he saw a huge crowd of people surrounding a big Ndovu lorry, amid shouts and cries of anti-KANU slogans. He edged nearer. Scores of men carrying various crude weapons were climbing onto the lorry. Lihanda recognized some faces already up on the truck. Other men were banging the sides of the lorry fiercely shouting obscenities.

He was about to pass when somebody grabbed his hand. He turned round to see Ruhiu wa Kamau, a famous personality in the town for whom he had once worked for.

"Waithaka! *Urathii ku?*" Where are you going? Ruhiu asked, looking intently into Lihanda's eyes. "Aren't you coming with us?"

"Going with you? Where?"

"Our people are being killed in Kamwaura!" Ngunjiri the bicycle fundi who was already in the lorry shouted. "We are going to help them out!"

"But . . ." Lihanda stammered.

"But what? Climb right in!" another man shouted. All eyes were on Lihanda.

"*Ucio ti mugikuyu,*" Ndung'u the barber said. He is not a Kikuyu.

"*Waluhya na wakikuyu ni ndugu,*" Ngunjiri retorted. The Luhya and Kikuyu are brothers.

"Listen, Waithaka," Ruhiu wa Kamau added, stressing on Lihanda's pseudonym, "you are either with us or with them. Nothing in between! Tell us whether you will come with us or not, so that we decide what to do with you right away."

That came out more like a threat than a simple statement.

Lihanda looked from the ground to the lorry. This was not his war! Why risk his life for something he knew so little about? He had never fought in a battle before. He saw the hostile faces up on the lorry and knew what they would do to him if he refused to join them. Then he remembered the basket he was holding and an excuse formed in his mind.

"Er. . . but Mzee, I'm on an important errand. . ."

"*Wacha ujinga!*" Don't be stupid, came the roar from the lorry. "Do you think we are idlers? We have also left our businesses to go fight alongside our brothers!"

Lihanda saw Ngunjiri waving his panga menacingly. His brain was filled with indecision. Atop the lorry were men of all ages, some of them his age and size, but this didn't encourage him. He had grown up respecting the sanctity of life. He could not even harm a fly and now these people were literally ordering him to go and attack fellow human beings? He tried another line of approach.

"But I have no weapon. . ."

"Aaah," the men chorused, "*kumbe ni hivyo tu!*" so its just that.

Lihanda instantly regretted his statement when an axe was thrust into his unwilling hands. Before he could say anything else, he was hoisted up the lorry. He was forced to resign to his fate as he saw somebody ferociously kick his fish basket away.

The crowd on the ground became less civil with other passersby. A man who was passing by with a female companion was suddenly pulled into the lorry amid his protests and the girl's cries. The girl was chased off by the mob.

Soon, the lorry was full. Lihanda estimated that there were over two hundred men in it. As it labouriously pulled away, he overheard someone say that there were more lorries making the rounds all over the town, collecting more men. He wondered who had donated the lorries for such a horrendous mission. And what of the fuel?

When the lorry sped towards Keep Left, he knew his fate was sealed. He heard the 'warriors' sing war songs, interspersed with slogans that were frighteningly anti-government. Silently, he prayed that the lorry would get a puncture or, even better, an engine knock.

During his sojourn in Molo, Lihanda had let his spiritual side lapse. But now he found himself looking skyward in silent supplication. "*Nyasaye wanje,*" he murmured, "*obulamu bwosi nobubwo.*" God, all life is yours. As always happens, time had come to revert to mother tongue.

Ndoinet, end-May, morning

Young Kiprop had listened to the bearer of the sad news with interminable sorrow. His brother, Kipruto dead? Killed in cold blood? His mother had fainted while his younger brother had given a harrowing wail. Kipruto was everybody's role model. A sombre mood hung over the compound as if it was a graveyard. Kiprop himself could have cried, but then he quickly observed his father's attitude towards the sudden death and hesitated.

Mzee Kipyegon looked as impassive as a statue. The old man had keenly listened to the messenger with no hint of sadness or shock on his face. As the whole family burst into sobs at the death of its most educated and promising member, *Mzee* Kipyegon spat onto the earthen floor, gathered his old bones and stood up as if to walk out. He stood at the doorway and addressed the astonished family.

"Serves him right!" he spluttered venomously. "Always arguing with me. I told him the Kikuyu were no good, he didn't listen. He had to go collect a mere letter, he said. Where were his Kikuyu friends to help him in his hour of need? Couldn't they have stopped their tribesmen from murdering him?"

"*Mzee*..." his wife started.

"I told him not to go but he wouldn't listen, always the arguing fool. Why die over a mere letter? Wherever he is, I'm sure he is cursing himself for trusting those fiends!"

With that, *Mzee* Kipyegon walked out.

The twelve year old was puzzled. He did not know whether to be equally disgusted or to cry. The war was awfully confusing everyone.

*   *   *

The worst mistake the unknown planners of the Kikuyu attack had made was to assume that the Kalenjin settlements stood out from the rest and could easily be identified. As the two lorries waded through the muddy stretch that was the Molo-Sitoito Road and had to divert to other more passable routes, it started becoming increasingly obvious that most of the men on the lorry did not know their exact destination. Some of the more travelled ones were busy explaining the route to the others. They named some of the areas they bypassed: Mona, Kiambiriria, Muchorwe, Wira, Langwenda, Nyakinyua . . . and so on. When they approached the forest, however, the 'guides' became markedly silent and took sudden interest in the burnt out shells of houses that they saw along the way. Another thing they overlooked was the fact that there was no motorable road into the forest. When it became clear that the lorries could not move another metre further, they stopped and the 'warriors' were told to alight.

"From here we will proceed by foot. There are bound to be Kalenjins holed up in here," the driver said and pointed to the forest as the 'warriors' jumped out and peered into the trees apprehensively.

Another problem arose instantly. Nobody had thought about the weapons. While there was an impressive heap of stones in the back of the lorry, you could not carry so many of them to the forest. There was a shortage of weapons, but the men shared what they had amongst them. Lihanda was lucky to have the axe. In addition, he stuffed stones into his pockets and carried two sizeable ones in his left hand. The procession moved on into the forest.

Ndoinet was surprisingly quiet even at this time of the day. Even the birds and the other creatures of the forest seemed to have fled from the raging war. From the distance, a long trail of smoke rose into the air. A small cow trail led them on.

Suddenly, the distinct 'moo' of a cow was heard. Everyone stopped and stood rooted to the spot. A silent command got them diving for the bushes.

Lihanda's heart skipped a beat. "*Nyasaye,*" Lord, he prayed. "If you help me out of this . . ."

The cling-clang of a cowbell became louder every minute. The 'warriors' pulled out their weapons and waited. Lihanda heard the man behind him breath heavily with fear.

It was a herd of about fifteen animals walking in a single file, with slow, leisurely movements. The man behind the livestock did not bother to guide them. It was evident that they were headed to some home. A boy of about eight was trailing behind the short thin man, almost running to keep up with him.

The warriors waited until the shepherd was about five metres away, then five men jumped at him.

The man was visibly startled, and the little boy leapt behind his legs and peered at the strangers with little, widened eyes. The shepherd was dark, with shaggy hair on his head. He had a long bamboo stick between his shoulder blades and his hands slid onto both sides of the stick in Maasai fashion. He looked at the strangers as if trying to figure out where he had seen them, then suddenly broke into a grin.

"Ah! Kari inyui!" So it is you! he exclaimed in perfect Kikuyu. "I was afraid it might be the enemy."

They all heaved simultaneous sighs of relief. So it was a tribesman after all. At least we won't have to fight yet, Lihanda thought.

"*Karibu,*" the shepherd said. Welcome.

"Who are you and what are you doing in this evil forest?" one of the warriors asked.

"Evil forest?" the shepherd was shocked.

"Isn't this the haven of the '*Lumbwa*', the Kalenjin?" asked another man.

"You are looking for Kalenjins here?" the shepherd asked. When the people nodded, he laughed heartily. "You are quite lost, brothers."

Realizing that everything was okay, the other warriors emerged from their hiding places and surrounded the man. "The whole of this area is Kikuyu land," he explained. "The Kalenjin area is further into the forest."

He touched the boy and ordered him to go inform the rest of the village that friends had arrived, and they should prepare a welcoming ceremony. The crowd made way for the small boy to pass through.

"Let's go this way to the village," the shepherd suggested, then led the way. "And thanks for coming to help us. These people are finishing us!"

"What about the cows?" Lihanda asked.

"Oh, them? They know their way around. I'm only taking them to the river because of the prevailing circumstances. I don't want to find my cows all slashed up."

They walked on, branching into a smaller path deeper into the forest. Their guide told them how the Kalenjins had attacked them a few weeks earlier. The crowd became more incensed as the horrifying tale unfolded.

"But now that you have come, our men will join you and we will attack the enemy," he said confidently as he sized up the team.

Once in a while, he cupped his mouth and let out a shrill whistle to let the villagers know that they were getting nearer. The group was very thankful for their guide. They would have been lost in the jungle on their own.

After a thirty-minute walk, they came to a large clearing. Their guide loudly wondered why the villagers had not come to meet them.

"I know my son must have reached the village by now," he said. "Or maybe the administration policemen there are intimidating them! Those fools are supposed to guard us, but all they do is harass us. Let me go and check them out."

Some warriors sat down on the grass in the clearing while others paced about listlessly. They happily discussed the latest developments. It would be helpful to get fighters to help them in attacking the Kalenjin. *Kidole kimoja hakivunji chawa*, one finger does not kill a louse, one man observed. After all, the locals were more familiar with the territory.

A sudden rush of approaching footsteps and shouts startled them out of their languor. They stood up, looking around in confusion as pandemonium homed in on them from all directions. At the very instant they realized they had been led into a trap, the half-clothed army with red headbands emerged from every side of the clearing and charged at them, bows at the ready.

An arrow passed a centimetre away from Lihanda's eye just as he was bending to pick up his axe. He heard a painful moan as the missile connected with the man beside him. In shock, he looked at the source of the arrow and saw a short man wearing a pair of shorts get ready to load three more arrows on the sophisticated bow. He threw a desperate stone at the man.

Everybody was running around now. It was obvious that they were surrounded. There was nothing to do but wait for death.

Kamwaura, end-May, afternoon

The honed panga gleamed in the sun, blinding Kimani's eye for a second as he held it towards the light. He resumed filing it, lost in his own thoughts.

Three months earlier, anybody telling him he would be doing this instead of being in a classroom would have been daydreaming. However, he had now gotten used to the attack and counter-attack routine that was now a daily routine. In three months, he had seen more bloodshed than most people live to see in a lifetime. Now, the question of whether the acrimony that pervaded the area would ever fade away was thrown into the subconscious. Each day became a struggle for survival and was taken as it came.

Some distant commotion broke into his thoughts. He stood up in the deserted compound – all the females had fled – and saw the approaching men. He breathed out when he recognized his fellow villagers, but was concerned that they looked so agitated. Something must be wrong somewhere.

The noise woke up his father who was sleeping in the sitting room, having had no sleep the previous night. Waweru stepped out of the house scratching his beard, already having slipped into his gumboots, and joined his son at the fence.

"What is it?" he asked in a voice that could only come from someone who had suffered so much to care any more. There were more grey hairs in his beard.

"I don't know," Kimani answered.

They watched as the swelling crowd came nearer. The crowd stopped at the gate and Waweru stepped out.

"What is it?" he asked.

Word had reached the village that some men from Molo town had been ambushed in the forest. A man who had emerged from the forest with serious injuries had told them about the war that was raging there, 'now, now . . . even as they spoke.'

As the man was whisked away to hospital, an impromptu meeting of all men from Banana, Kamwaura, Boron and many other farms was held. The villagers decided to go help their tribesmen. And so, the group went round collecting all able-bodied men.

Kimani and his father joined the procession without a second thought. You did not refuse to answer to a cry of distress – next time it might be your own. The crowd was swollen to almost a hundred in just twenty minutes.

Ndoinet Forest, end-May, evening

When the reinforcements arrived on the battlefield, things were completely out of hand. Taken by surprise and heavily out-numbered in terms of weapons, many of the men from Molo had fallen. The arrival of the new men greatly encouraged the remaining few, and they jumped into the fray with surprisingly renewed bravado.

The forest was a flurry of running battles. Heads and limbs were slashed. Stones, *pangas* and arrows flew dangerously in the air. A sudden whistle, like the one their guide had been constantly using, split the air. Suddenly, the half-clothed warriors with red headbands retreated in unison.

Kimani joined his fellow villagers who were running after the retreating men with maniacal zeal. The retreating army, however, co-ordinated their movement so well that before the villagers realized it, they were nowhere to be seen. There was a round of applause and jubilation as comrades came back to the clearing and re-assessed the situation.

On their side, there was a casualty list of forty wounded, ten dead and sixteen missing. Five Kalenjin warriors were dead, while a sixth was seriously wounded and now lay in a pool of blood under a tree.

Ngunjiri, as if irritated by the whimpering noises he was making, quickly did away with him. He wiped the blood off his *panga* on the convulsing chest and spat into the bushes the way a man might do after squashing a repugnant bug.

Now that the enemy had been repulsed, there came a heated discussion over what to do next.

"We can't leave now without destroying a few villages," said one man.

"Ten of our people have been killed. We must avenge their death!" another incensed man shouted. The cry was taken up by the others and suddenly, the crowd started forward with their weapons high in the air.

Kimani was disturbed about the frenzy with which his people took up the call of war. It is said that once a man has killed, his mind becomes intoxicated with the smell of blood.

The first village they came to was attacked with so much ferocity that it was literally flattened. It seemed most of the people had been evacuated, because only a handful were flushed out of the huts. The attackers razed the houses to the ground. Nothing was spared, even the livestock was not left alive. A cow's belly was slashed and the unfortunate animal sent galloping with her guts hanging out.

Kimani rushed into one of the houses, closely followed by another young man he had never seen. There was nobody inside the room. The two young men let their hands fall back as they surveyed the empty room. There was an uneasy presence in the house, and Kimani turned to leave.

Suddenly, the glint of a weapon caught his eye.

"Watch out!" he shouted, and in one swift movement pushed his colleague out of the way. The spear flew in between them and thudded into the wall just where his colleague had been standing. An avalanche of dried mud came down the plastered wall.

Even before he reached the ground, Kimani had already started to strike out with his machete. He regained his balance at the same moment the machete connected with their attacker. He felt a tremor in his hand as the weapon reached bone and his victim let out a guttural cry.

He rose to his feet and with his pulse racing surveyed the fruits of his labour. The man had sunk down in a heap. The machete had almost severed his neck. The man lay staring at the roof with rapidly fluttering eyelids and a grimace of pain. Blood was gushing out of his neck like water from a burst pipe. Kimani saw the body break into erratic spasms as life left it. There was the sudden realization that he had killed a man – a human being. He rose to leave without bothering about his weapon.

His colleague appreciatively touched him on the shoulder and their eyes locked.

"Thank you for saving my life," the dark young man said, then added after a second, "My name is Peterson Lihanda. Maybe we will meet again . . . maybe we won't, but I will not forget you."

It was then that they discovered the presence of the small girl. She was standing at the doorway to the inner room from where the slain man had fallen. She was thin and frail-looking, and her face was contorted with hatred, her hands clenched in two small fists.

Lihanda swung his axe to finish her off but was stopped in midair. He turned to Kimani in surprise.

"What are you doing?" Kimani asked, holding the axe up in the air.

"We are not to leave anybody alive, remember?" Lihanda asked.

"Oh, hell! Are we to kill a little girl for a crime she doesn't even know and in which she has not even participated?"

Lihanda looked from the small girl to Kimani and back to the small girl again. For a whole minute, the room was deathly quiet, only the mayhem outside being heard. The girl continued to stare unflinchingly at Kimani and he started to feel quite disconcerted.

"Let's go!" he told Lihanda.

As they walked out, he looked behind and saw the little girl down on her knees, one hand touching the slain man's forehead, but her eyes still looking at them venomously. A pang of conscience now assailed him.

"Get away from here!" he said to Lihanda.

Outside the hut, they almost bumped into two of their comrades.

"There is somebody in?" one of them asked.

"Yes. We've killed him," Kimani replied.

"Right! Now, burn down the house."

Inside the house the girl froze in her position in a moment of indecision. She stared at her father's still form in disbelief. Around the house, loud footsteps could be heard. Soon, she smelt the smoke as the roof caught fire. She remained numbed, unable to move or cry. Suddenly, someone grabbed her from behind.

*   *   *

The village was in total shambles. Three quarters of it was up in smoke. Cows were slashed to death and others had their limbs cut off. As granaries were set on fire, the smell of roast maize wafted into the air. The attackers would have done more damage had the helicopter not arrived.

The approaching drone of the aircraft stopped them in their tracks. Kimani and his new friend, Lihanda, crouched low in the bush as the large military air craft emerged from behind the trees and loomed large in the sky above them. For a full ten minutes, it hovered above without doing anything. Suddenly, like a huge bird, it twirled around in one movement and made for the trees from where it had come, its rotor blades cutting the air in rapid clatter.

The warriors emerged from the bushes and looked up at the disappearing aircraft. Everybody seemed to have lost the resolve for battle as they thought of the implications of the sudden visit by the helicopter. The sun was beginning to set and its rays shot through the trees. And now, a call rang out for them to regroup so that they could go back home.

Maybe the Kalenjin army was waiting for the sun to set. Or maybe they had gone for reinforcements. As it turned out, they were planning a suitable strategy for a retaliatory attack.

When they did strike, they did so with so much force that nobody understood what happened. In their hundreds, they emerged from nowhere and came at Kimani's group, angered by the destruction of their village. Most of the invaders had exhausted their supply of stones and lost their pangas in the earlier fight. Now they found themselves overwhelmed by the revived army and had to run for their dear lives.

Despite the fact that he was running at his fastest pace, Lihanda was at the rear of the retreating men. This meant that most of the missiles were directed at him. He began to lag behind as a stitch ate at his stomach – it is a pity that stitches always come at the most inappropriate times. Suddenly, an arrow streaked through his jacket at the collar, missing his shoulder by a millimetre. The stitch and weariness forgotten, he overtook everybody in his flight.

"*Nyasaye!* If you help me out of this . . ."

He heard the slosh, slosh similar to somebody running with water in his shoes as he turned around a hedge. There was a bearded man two metres ahead of him who had an arrow sticking in his thigh. Blood was spluttering from the wound and pouring into his gumboots. Lihanda looked on ahead, knowing the man would not make it even as he overtook him. The war cries of their pursuers sounded frighteningly closer.

Lihanda jumped over the barbed wire fence in one swift movement and landed on his knees. Before he quite touched the ground, he was again up and running. He heard an anguished cry behind him and knew immediately that it was the bearded man. He stopped and looked back.

The old man was caught in the barbed wire and now he lay there, trapped like an animal, releasing small piteous gasps. Lihanda bent over and wrenched him away from the wire, once glancing at the approaching men two hundred metres away. They were coming at a well synchronized pace, with some of them falling back to finish off the fallen enemies. They are hunting us like wild dogs, Lihanda thought, the way a pack chases the prey, then falls back behind and another pack takes over, leaving only the prey to exhaust itself.

Lihanda tried to lift the half-conscious man.

"No! You run," the man said laboriously, his eyes shut out in pain.

"There is nothing you can do for me."

Lihanda admitted this was true. The arrow had come out of the man's leg but he was losing too much blood. The gumboot was now filled with blood.

"I can't leave you here to die! We'll die together if we have to!" he declared.

"Go! Leave me alone!" panted the man. He was shivering uncontrollably. "I'm old . . . you are young. Maybe you can make a difference."

Lihanda looked at the army of warriors, now a hundred metres away. They were beginning to load their bows. He made another attempt at lifting the wounded man. Suddenly, the man took hold of his hand in a powerful howls. He was gazing at Lihanda intently.

"Go look for my son, Kimani son of Waweru. Tell him I could not make it. But he is young, maybe he will make a difference. . . now, go!"

Lihanda did not need any more convincing because an arrow hit the fence post above him, making a humming sound as it quivered in the air. He shot up and was soon panting away. He heard the painful cries of the bearded man mingled with the victorious war cries of the pursuers as they fell upon him. Lihanda tried to shut out the anguished pleas from his mind, unsuccessfully.

*   *   *

Kimani had twisted his ankle when he fell a kilometre behind. Limping painfully, he had long lost the leading position in the race for the main road. He now had the nagging fear that he would fail to make it past the two kilometre forest and onto safety. His right leg was paining so much that he could not move another metre, despite the approaching warriors. He could not bear it any longer.

He decided to hide somewhere and rest his leg for a while. And to his left, he saw a destroyed homestead and limped towards it. It was one of the homesteads that had fallen under their attack earlier on. The roofs of the three houses in the compound had long caved in. Smoke was smoldering above the ruins.

He walked past the burnt shells and into the muddy cattle pen. At least here, nobody would see him unless they were very observant. He jumped into the long wooden feeding trough, and onto a human body stretched out on the napier grass.

Both of them were so surprised that nobody spoke for the better part of a minute. Each appraised the other warily. The boy was hardly twelve years old, and his looks betrayed him as Kalenjin. He looked at Kimani in awe, and for a fleeting moment, Kimani thought he was going to call out for help.

"Who are you?" the small boy asked, taking short gasps of air. Kimani noticed the clotting blood on the napier grass.

"A *chorwet*," I'm a friend, he replied, thanking heaven for his knowledge of Kalenjin.

"I don't know you," the boy gave him an accusing look.

"I don't know you too, but I'm a friend."

There was the nagging fear that the boy would scream. Kimani feared if he did so, he would have to kill his second person that day.

*   *   *

It was becoming very annoying. While most of the victorious pursuers had fallen back, one youth about Lihanda's age kept to his heels like a leech. It was as if there was a price on his head, the way the chap kept at him. Even after exhausting his supply of arrows, the warrior still chased on, armed with only a *panga*. Lihanda was wondering what to do next when he saw the destroyed compound and a plan formed in his mind. He would lure the insistent youth into some trap, ambush him and get him off his back.

As he ran towards the compound, he slowed down a little to make sure that his pursuer saw him take the turning to the destroyed houses. Once there, he crouched low and picked up a large piece of what had once been the door frame to one of the burnt houses. He edged towards the far end of the homestead to wait for his pursuer.

*   *   *

"Ilenjin ager oh," Kimani told the smaller boy and gestured towards the wounded leg. Let me have a look at that. The boy hesitated a little but changed his mind when he saw the genuine look of sympathy on the stranger's face. He slowly extended his leg towards him.

One look at the vicious tear on the boy's leg and Kimani winced. The wound ran through almost the entire length of flesh at the back of the boy's shin. Kimani now understood why he had been unable to shout out when he came into the compound. The boy couldn't even stand. Kimani pulled off his shirt and tore it into shreds. With the rapidly diminishing light of the nearing evening, he wound it over the injury.

"*Kikurenin ng'o?*" What's your name? he asked the boy to distract his mind from the painful dressing. The boy grimaced as the strip of cloth was knotted tight. His body was taut as he whispered,

"Kiprop. Kiprop son of Kipyegon." Kimani nodded slowly. The boy's forehead was covered in sweat. "Somebody is coming," the boy whispered labouriously. Kimani froze. The approaching footsteps were unmistakable.

"You are right," he whispered back as he slid deeper into the trough. After an agonizing moment, he lifted his head an inch and saw the intruder. The young man was instantly recognizable – he was the one he had carried out an attack with; the one who had had an axe.

Kimani heaved a sigh of relief. He watched Lihanda crouch low, then pick up a big piece of wood. Kimani let out a soft whistle. Lihanda was startled out of his skin. He looked frantically towards the source of the sound, his hand tightly holding the piece of wood, ready for combat. Then he saw Kimani's face. He crept nearer on recognizing him.

"So it's you!" he whispered. Lihanda peered down the trough and saw the injured boy. Kimani turned back to his work.

"Who is he?" Lihanda whispered back.

"Kiprop son of Kipyegon," replied Kimani. "He is injured. I met him here when looking for a place to hide."

"But. . ." Lihanda started.

Kimani looked up. "I could not leave him here to bleed to death, Kalenjin or not, could I?"

Kiprop half opened his eyes and tried to concentrate on the two strange boys. He was sweating profusely and starting to mumble words incoherently.

"They killed my father as I watched," he whispered. "Killed my father...a... as I watched." The boy was obviously in shock. "I saw it all . . ."

Kimani touched the boy's forehead and said, "He is getting a fever."

"My brother. . . killed in . . . Molo . . . Kipruto . . . Mwalimu," the boy whispered again as he shuddered loudly.

"What did he say?" Lihanda almost shouted. Did he say *Mwalimu* Kipruto?"

"Yes. He is mentioning a brother and Molo," replied Kimani who was wondering what had gotten into his friend. Then suddenly, he too realised whom the boy was talking about. "Wait a minute! You are Kipruto's brother! The teacher who was teaching in Molo?" The boy only managed to nod his head.

Lihanda looked at the small boy in amazement. He, the brother of his best friend in Molo? It's a really small world, so they say!

Silence pervaded the cattle shed. To break it off, Lihanda asked for the name of his friend.

"My name is Kimani. Kimani wa Waweru."

"What is this?" Lihanda was now exasperated, and Kimani had to nudge him to remind him they were still in hiding. "Did you say Kimani wa Waweru?" Lihanda whispered incredulously.

When Kimani nodded, Lihanda wondered how he would break the news of his father's death to him.

Prospects of further discussion were, however, cut short by the sudden appearance of the Kalenjin warrior who had been stalking Lihanda.

All three at the trough sat still, watching the armed man sweep through the whole compound peering at the darkening scene, tightly holding his *panga*.

*   *   *

The warrior's name was Kibet. He was tall and supple in build and moved with the natural instinct of a hunter. He was quite athletic for his fifteen years and could pass for a much older youth. Kibet did not know what made him go after the young Kikuyu man with so much zeal.

It was as if he was possessed. The fact that all his tribesmen had fallen back and given up the pursuit did not deter him. Neither did the knowledge that he was risking his life. The way he was chasing his enemy, one would think he was possessed. It was as if a supernatural being was urging him on. As he entered the empty compound, he tightened his hold on the *panga*. With all the houses razed to the ground and still smoking, the homestead looked deathly.

The Kikuyu invaders had left a wave of destruction through this village. Fortunately, most of the villagers had been evacuated long before their arrival; thanks to the genius of Tanui, the shepherd. It was darkening too fast now, and Kibet realized there was no way he would find his quarry. The bastard had gotten away. He decided to go home.

But as he turned, he heard a noise from the cattle shed and immediately peered in that direction. Was that a moan? He moved closer to investigate, all his senses on the alert.

The three had crouched lower into the trough when the Kalenjin warrior had burst into the compound. With apprehension, Lihanda watched his pursuer carefully. The way the warrior was watching his back and stayed away from corners where an ambush could come from showed that he had had some training.

The warrior was dressed like the others – red band around the head and in shorts. He wore a pair of worn out DH rubber shoes on his feet. Lihanda wondered how the warrior withstood the cold, dressed that way in the evening chill.

Luckily for the hiding trio, the warrior did not spare as much as a glance towards their direction. When their pursuer turned to leave, they all relaxed.

But then, Lihanda attempted to change his position in the trough and accidentally pressed his hand onto young Kiprop's wound. The boy howled out in pain.

The three hiding boys sat on the napier grass horrified as they saw the warrior stop, look towards the cattle shed, and retrace his steps.

*　　　　*　　　　*

When the warrior moved towards the cattle shed, he did not expect to meet three people huddled together in the feeding trough. He stopped in the doorway and surveyed the scene with growing consternation.

The young man he was chasing was instantly recognizable, but his bare-chested colleague was unfamiliar. The smaller boy lying between the pair was from this village. What was he doing with these villains? He recovered a second later and postured to strike out with the *panga*. Lihanda halted him in mid air with an outstretched hand.

"Kanyo!" Wait! he quickly said. *"Kichoronok, ma bonik."* We are friends, not enemies.

"Haa! Friends indeed!" scoffed Kibet as he edged closer.

"This boy here is your tribesmate," Kimani said, also in Kalenjin. "We could have killed him if we were enemies, but we chose to risk our lives and attend to his wounds."

"He has nobody to look after him," Lihanda added quickly. "His father was killed and . . ."

"His father was killed by you!" Kibet shouted as he moved within striking range.

"Us?" Lihanda and Kimani asked at the same time.

"You Kikuyus! And you have to pay for his death . . . and many others." His mind seemed to wander for a while before he added, "I can't let you live. It's against the oath."

"What oath?" a now agitated Lihanda asked. "What's an oath? An oath to kill for something you don't even know . . . something they don't even tell you? Why have you joined the war; you don't have anything against the Kikuyu, do you? It is just that they fed you with stories, oathed you and gave you weapons, telling you to kill!" Lihanda paused for a moment before adding passionately, "If you kill us, our blood will haunt you forever," he swore. "And I am a Luhya, not a Kikuyu," he added indignantly.

Kibet stared at the smaller boy and hesitated. Lihanda's words had struck a chord in his befogged mind. Everything was true – he really did not have anything against the Kikuyu except what he had been told. He had grown up and gone to school with their children. During this conflict, he had been forced to kill some of his closest friends. And yes, it was already haunting him, so much that no amount of bhang smoking could help.

Slowly, he let his weapon tilt downwards.

eleven

Molo, early June, 1992

They stayed in Molo for a week, the longest possible time circumstances could allow them to. While Kimani and Lihanda went out each morning to look for something to eat, Kibet and Kiprop stayed locked in the late Mwalimu Kipruto's house. They could not risk anybody in town knowing the two Kalenjin boys were harboured there. In fact, Lihanda had had to buy drugs for Kiprop over the counter at pharmacies rather than take him to hospital. Now that their secret had leaked it was important they get out of Molo as soon as possible.

Kimani and Lihanda owed their lives to Kibet. Without the warrior-turned-rebel, they would not have made it out of Molo South alive. Kibet had housed them for two days and nights in an abandoned house, sheltering them from the other warriors who had ran amok and were everywhere looking for hidden Kikuyus. All that time, he was searching for a way out of the village.

The greatest hurdle had been how to move the younger Kiprop. The boy's wound had become unbearable. Lihanda had even suggested that they leave the boy behind to make their escape easy, but Kimani had adamantly refused. With his father dead and the fate of the rest of his family unknown, he had nobody to look after him. Sick as he was, he would just slide into death if he were left by himself.

They finally left the forest through a most interesting means. Word had reached Kibet that Kipng'eno, charcoal dealer, had been gravely injured and could not transport his charcoal to the neighbouring settlement three kilometres away. Kibet immediately had a brilliant idea.

Kimani, Lihanda and Kiprop slipped into half-full sacks and Kibet discreetly loaded them onto the cart. He had whipped the donkeys hard towards the destined village, then halfway there, turned eastwards towards Molo.

They had arrived in Molo town very late in the night because they had had to use alternative routes where the chances of being spotted were minimal. They had only stopped once near Nguirubi for Kibet's turn to slip into the sack while Kimani took control of the reins; for this was now Kikuyu country. At Keep Left in Molo, the rebels had abandoned the donkey and its load and walked the rest of the distance to Lihanda's place, with Kibet carrying Kiprop on his shoulder. It was by miracle that they were not stopped by the GSU officers on patrol or by inquisitive locals.

After three days and with medication, Kiprop was feeling much better. He could hobble around in the room without moaning. During this time, two significant things happened in Molo that were to change the history of the town forever. To start with, a sack containing arrows was allegedly found under a sofa in a house belonging to one of the famous businesswomen in the town, Angelina Chebet. The woman escaped death narrowly when an irate mob broke into her huge house in Maishani and removed all the furniture. They then burnt everything down right as she watched, but let her go away unharmed.

The second thing was more disastrous. It was speculated that one of the butchery owners in the area, Mutai, was hiding weapons in one of his stores. Without waiting to confirm the allegation, a mob waited for him to enter the store, then locked it from outside and set it ablaze.

Just when Lihanda and his group were beginning to feel at ease in Molo town, the worst thing happened. Early one morning, as Lihanda was walking out of the plot, he met a neighbour who seemed eager to talk more than was usual. Lihanda was puzzled when the hitherto unfriendly man warmly greeted him and let the handshake linger on.

"So you have visitors and you are not telling us?" the man asked Lihanda.

Quite shocked, Lihanda looked at him and saw a malicious glint in the man's eye.

"I don't know what you are talking about," he mumbled.

"You know very well what I am saying!" The man said and winked mischievously. "*Kai ukugeria gwitua mugi,* Waithaka?" Are you trying to be clever.

In the course of that day, Lihanda experienced too many unusual happenings. People he hardly talked to stopped him in the streets and asked him questions on how he was getting on of late. A group of his close friends suddenly stopped talking as he approached them.

He knew there was something wrong, and also knew that pretty soon somebody would come knocking at their place. He did not wait for the evening. The four of them had urgent consultation on the issue.

"We can't stay here anymore," Kimani said as he summed up what was on everyone's mind.

Then the next question on the tips of their tongues was, where would they go to? And the one clear answer was, they couldn't go back to what had been their homes. What they had done was totally against the expectations of their respective tribes. They all knew that should they be found there, death was certain. Besides, none of them had families to go back to – everyone of their families had suffered casualties and been displaced by the war, except for Lihanda; maybe his family in Mumias were alive. But was he still part of them? Not after what he had done in Molo.

"Let's go to a place where we can live together without our tribes getting in the way," Kibet suggested.

"Yes, that is what we should do," Lihanda concurred. "But where?"

Kiprop looked at all the others, settled round the small table as a long silence descended on the room. Then he ventured, "Nairobi?"

Nakuru, 1996

The huge dark man watched the barmaid packing her meagre belongings into a worn out bag. A smile crossed his face – she had been easy to recruit. He lit a cigarette and let the smoke billow out of his mouth to get rid of the acrid smell of sweat and decay that hung over the single room. It had been years since he had been in such a den. Even now, he wondered how he had convinced himself to come here. It had all happened like a joke.

He had travelled to Molo the previous week on a successful fact-finding mission. He had found the information he wanted about the group of people he had been trying to trace for years now.

On the journey back to Nairobi, near Rongai Centre, his car had, unfortunately, developed engine problems. He had to wait for hours before the *jua kali* mechanics declared it fit for the rest of the journey.

By then, it was dark and since he detested driving at night, he spent the night in Nakuru. He had entered the bar to have a few drinks before booking a room. The bar had only a handful of customers, being the middle of the week and a bad day of the month for business.

Out of all the barmaids in the bar, it was the large timid one that intrigued him most. He settled in a far corner and studied her closely as she went about her business. Finally, he motioned her to come over, ignoring the young, petite and more attractive one standing next to him and eyeing him coquettishly. The larger barmaid seemed to have something fascinating about her and he was eager to find out.

She walked awkwardly towards him.

"Can I help you?" she asked. Her eyes had rings around them, maybe from lack of sleep.

"Yes, three Tuskers," he ordered, then added," and get two for yourself."

He was not a generous man and only gave out gifts when he needed information or favours in return.

"Thank you," the barmaid said, quite surprised.

The petite barmaid looked at her colleague enviously as she came back with the beers. The big man noticed that she had not brought her own. He understood – she was going to exchange the beers for hard cash later. It was a perfect way of transacting business.

"Sit down," he ordered as she placed the bottles on the table. In his profession, giving orders was normal.

"Sir, I'm working. If you want to 'talk', we can do so after my shift is over."

He knew what she meant. Most barmaids engaged in extra activities to add to their income. She was mistaken if she thought he wanted sex.

"Sit down," he repeated his order.

The barmaid, probably intimidated by his commanding presence and level voice, sat down slowly.

"Get yourself a beer first. I want to see you drink it."

She smiled for the first time, revealing a set of badly arranged teeth, yet unbelievably bearing a beauty gap in the middle.

As he watched her move to the bar, he took another swig at his beer. He had been an investigator long enough to know that she had a story to tell.

The other barmaid tried to get his attention by pulling up her mini skirt slightly. He ignored her completely. You don't mix business with pleasure, he knew from his long experience in the job.

"Just know that I will rise to serve the other customers when they require me to," she cautioned him, smiling apologetically.

He nodded, then turned to his newspaper as if there was a very important item in it.

"What's your name?" he asked without looking at her.

"Why do you want to know?" she countered. "Who are you?"

"I just want to know your name," he said in the same level voice. She shrugged. It made no difference if she told him her name anyway.

"I'm Angelina Chebet."

He nodded, then ordered another beer. Two hours later, as he had suspected that what loosened a barmaid was a bottle of beer, Angelina Chebet became very talkative. She rambled on and on about life, the challenges of her work, and her experiences in Molo. As he listened intently, he knew that she had never come to terms with her new life as a barmaid and part-time prostitute.

He nodded constantly to urge her on, a serious look on his face. From what he gathered he knew that she had never met someone to pour her heart out to before. He smiled warmly – she was what he had been looking for. She was ripe for recruitment.

"Anyway," she brought him out of his reverie, "four years ago, I wouldn't have believed it if somebody had told me I would be doing this kind of work. Now, I don't have anything to live for."

He bent over the six empty bottles on her side of the table. It was time to drop his clincher.

"What would you do if you had the chance to get even with those who ruined your life?"

She sat transfixed and deep in thought, looking at the ceiling as if an answer lay there. He could tell she was drunk, but she had enough wits to comprehend the question. He wondered how many beers it would take to drop her down. Six beers and she was still up? He had not even finished his second!

Finally, she turned to him again, "What would I do?" she asked rhetorically. "I would kill them."

He nodded the way a psychiatrist refraining from showing his true feelings to the patient does. "Wouldn't that be too harsh?"

She waved her hand in the air. "I don't care. If I got the bastards, I would kill them all."

He lifted his beer bottle, blocking its mouth with his tongue and pretending to take a long swig. It was after a full five minutes before he spoke again.

"What would you do if I gave you a chance to do exactly that, and paid you for it?"

It took time for her to digest that. When she finally did, she frowned. "Exactly who are you?"

He shrugged, "Let's say I'm a man who wants to see justice done."

She took another gulp of beer in a moment of indecision. After a long silence she shrugged then laughed out loudly. The huge man maintained his stony face. Inwardly, he already knew her answer.

"Are you willing to sacrifice everything you have – your job and all?"

"Hell! I don't care about my job. This is no life to talk about. I would be glad to get out of here."

He nodded slowly again. "Why don't you pack right away, then?"

Her house, if it could be called that, was a few hundred metres away from the bar. Once there, she fell onto the bed like a log and immediately started to snore. He took a look at the room and decided he could not spend the night there. Slowly, he shut the door behind him and drove back to the bar.

Now as he watched her zip her bag, he wondered how she remembered all that they had talked about the previous night. In fact, when he had arrived at her room minutes earlier, he had found her already packed.

"That's all," she announced. All her belongings were stuffed into the small bag. "Now, let me go and tell them I'm leaving."

"No," he told her, "don't let anybody know you are leaving. If anybody asks, you have gone up-country on an urgent journey, understand?" She nodded, but appeared not to have understood. He was infuriated at her naivety. Where did she think they were going?

He led her out to the car, threw the bag onto the back seat and opened the passenger door for her. She looked subdued. He could tell she was mesmerized by the sheer size of his car.

All through their journey out of the Rift Valley, he replied to her many questions monosyllabically. It was too early to trust her with any details.

When they reached Westlands, he could not help smiling. Thanks to the engine problems, he had come from Nakuru with a gem, rough as it looked.

Nairobi, February, 1996

Marigiti Market is situated on the lower parts of Haile Selassie Avenue. The dirty, crowded market is a hub of activity each morning, opening business as early as three o'clock. The vegetable and fruit stocks are sold by retail and wholesale. Most of Nairobi's green grocers buy their requirements here.

This was the season for mangoes, and in the open air were lined sacks of the fruit in rows. Irungu stood amongst the group of *bebas* beside the first row, braving the early morning cold with only a vest on. He was hoping, just like his porter colleagues, that one of the buyers would single him out to carry their load. Hopefully, he approached a woman buyer, seeing that she was buying two sacks of the fruit.

"*Mathee, niko na mkokoteni,*" I have a cart, he ventured.
The woman keenly looked at him. The dirty vest left much muscle out in the open. The equally dirty and greasy overalls slid at his waist with the top parts drawn out. The worn out sneakers had non-matching laces, even then indistinguishable in the slush.

"Just stick around,"she finally said. "I'll go buy some carrots."

"*Sawa!*" he said happily. "Let me get the cart."
That was fifty shillings more. If the woman was new to the market, he would charge a hundred. It was more strategic not to negotiate the price at the onset because then you could demand any amount of money you wanted on reaching the destination.

Before the woman came back, her two sacks of mangoes were already on the cart.

The *mkokoteni* itself was made of timber and rusty mabati clung together miraculously, the wheels sporting countless patches. On her return, the woman gave it a long disapproving look.

"Don't worry," Irungu assured her. "The *mkokoteni* is brand new – it has a six-year guarantee!"

He wedged his way through the throng of sellers and buyers arguing over prices, as he shouted obscenities at those who din't scuttle out of the way fast enough. The woman meekly followed him.

Irungu was smiling to himself. The woman doubted the cart which provided his daily bread and which had saved him from the streets and crime!

It was strange that he chose this tiresome and ill-paying occupation while he could have finished school and probably gotten a better job. But then, he could not face any more humiliation. It was better to live here amongst the lowest of the low, without everybody trying to dig up your past, than to live in comfort haunted by a life of embarrassment.

*   *   *

He had survived the ambush on the Molo-Sitoito Road by a whisker, just when the arrow felled him and he lay in a ditch waiting for the warriors to slash him to death, the canine yelp had issued from somewhere and, as suddenly as they had come, the warriors had disappeared.

Luckily for Irungu, the arrow had just made a superficial cut on his leg and after three days' treatment at Molo Hospital, he was discharged. After all, there were many serious casualties that needed the hospital bed more than he did.

Scores of people had been injured in that ambush. The definite number of people killed was never known. Unfortunately, the dead included Irungu's father as well as his younger sister. His mother had escaped unscathed.

His mother had been the most significant factor in his healing. She had stayed by his bedside consoling him, and making sure that he never lacked food every mealtime. He asked her where she got the food from, but she never quite answered his question. She only smiled and said, "God provided." Now that he was leaving hospital, the one pressing question was where they would go to.

"We can't go back there," Irungu had stated as he ate the last meal in the ward. "There is nothing to go back to."

"I know. We'll get out of Molo for good. This is no place for us," she had said.

Irungu's mother was not old, she was hardly in her forties, and looked ten years younger. Still, this afternoon, lines of worry clouded her face and made her look older.

"But where can we go to? We have no money, nothing." "God will provide, son."
Irungu had shrugged sceptically and concentrated on his food.

"There is a camp for the displaced people at the PCEA Church in Nderi," she had said. "There is another at Limuru. We can settle there for the time being," she had added.

*   *   *

Life at the Limuru camp was not easy. Having hitherto lived a life where you determined when and what to eat, it was difficult to adjust. It was disheartening to depend on handouts from the church and other well-wishers, and even worse as you ate your meal, not knowing where the next would come from. Then you just thought about your full granary at home.

Together with other displaced families, they slept hunched up on thin blankets that did not quite keep out the Limuru cold. Irungu was there when a group of political leaders arrived at the camp amid much pomp. They reiterated their efforts to bring peace to the clash-torn area. One of them even suggested that now that the clashes were over, the internally displaced should go back home. The response was tumultuous.

"No! Where do you want us to go?" "We have no homes!" "We will be killed!" "Oh, no, no, no," the politician tried to pacify the audience.

"Of course we can't send you there knowing it's insecure! We will give you Administration Police to escort you . . ."

"APs?" shouted a man. "Who are they? We have lost confidence in the government. The APs are part of that government."

"Yes!"agreed another. "We won't leave this place until our own Member of Parliament together with the Provincial Commissioner himself visits us!"

The leader was not known for giving up easily. "I believe that if we forget our differences we will go back and live in peace without the need for APs."

"Ahem!" an old man cleared his throat to speak, and the furore died down as everyone waited to hear what he had to say.

"*Kijana*," he started, "can you trust a man who killed your son as you watched and is still walking free?" There were tears in his eyes and in the eyes of many others. But after a few weeks in the camp, it seemed inevitable that people would have to go back to their homes. Some had already left with the few belongings they had lugged with them. Irungu and his mother, however, had opted to stay away from the Molo that carried too many unpleasant memories. They had moved to a place near Limuru Town called Kwa Mbira. With the money his mother had borrowed from a church elder, they rented a one-roomed house.

Life had been hard for them in Kwa Mbira, but that was not the reason why he had fallen out with his mother.

*   *   *

Irungu was immersed in deep thought when a chokora jolted him out of his memories. He screeched to a halt, the *mkokoteni* an inch away from the boy. "Damn you!" he hissed. "Can't you watch where you are going?"

"*Ah! ishia!*" Get lost, the street boy shot back. Stung more by the frustration of work than the boy's contempt, Irungu slid under the long handle of the handcart and seized him by the collar, almost lifting him off his feet.

"*Ati unasema nini?* " he demanded. What are you saying?

A few people turned their heads towards them. Then, in the infamous disinterest of Nairobians, turned away. The woman for whom Irungu was carrying the load caught up with them as Irungu glared at the *chokora*.

The boy was about fifteen years old, though the hardened glare suggested otherwise. He was thin with half-closed, drugged eyes – red as blood. His hair was a tangled mess. He wore a tattered half-coat and dirty brown jeans cut roughly at the knees. In his left hand he held the trademark bottle of glue, and in his right, a more sinister container whose top he now covered. Irungu knew it was human waste in the container – what the urchins used to intimidate people into giving them money.

"Repeat what you just said!" Irungu ordered as he tightened his grip on the boy's neck. He was more infuriated when he saw the unconcerned look on the boy's face. Suddenly, another bigger and more aggressive *chokora* jumped in between the pair and elbowed Irungu.

"Nini mbaya na wewe, mbuyu? " What's wrong with you, man? The bigger urchin asked Irungu menacingly. But abruptly, he stopped short. For what seemed to be an eternity, the two looked at each other with mouths agape.

"Wa !" It was Irungu who first found his voice.

"No. It can't be you!" The bigger urchin replied. "You are dead!" The two threw themselves at each other in a big hug. The onlookers who had been anticipating a street fight were visibly disappointed.

The smaller *chokosh* looked at the unfolding scene in consternation. The woman drew closer.

"What is happening? Why have we stopped?" she asked.
Irungu tore himself from Kimani's embrace and turned towards her. His face was radiant though there were tears in his eyes.

"This is my brother," he told her. "My long lost brother! We have not seen each other for four years."

"Okay, let's hurry on," she replied curtly as she looked at her watch. "I'm getting late!"

Irungu looked at Kimani. The latter looked nothing like his former self. Though now much older and past his teenage, Kimani looked thin and unhealthy. Like his smaller friend, he held a bottle of glue in his hand.

"Come on. Let's deliver this woman's load then we will have time to talk," Irungu said as he bounced back behind his handcart. He expertly manouvered the contraption back onto Haile Selassie Avenue and raced towards the Railway Station, shouting loudly for people to get out of the way. The woman, Kimani and the smaller *chokora* all ran after him.

"Who's this boy you were protecting so fiercely?" Irungu asked Kimani as he sped on.

"He is a 'tight' friend. We started in Molo. We call him Bafu."

"Bafu?" Irungu laughed.

"Yes, short for *kupiga bafu*. The guy is well known on the streets for his money-making activities. He has the lightest fingers on the streets."

"What a name!" Irungu remarked. After a short silence, he added,

"Although even I, everybody calls me something else, not Irungu. When I came to Marigiti early last year, I was so eager to work for anything. I could do even the worst donkey work most people dared not touch. They started making fun of me, calling me: the Rock. It has stuck ever since."

They arrived at the Railway Station and Irungu – Rock – parked the *mkokoteni* at the *matatu* terminus.

"*Haya, Mama,*" he stated, "*mia mbili.*"

"Two hundred?" The woman gasped. "From Marigiti to the Railway Station! You must be joking!"

Rock looked at the woman menacingly. "Pay me my money or I load these things back and take them home. You think carrying two sacks of mangoes and one of carrots is child's play? Why didn't you carry them yourself?"

The woman beseeched him to reduce the price, almost falling to her knees. After much cajoling, Rock agreed to half of the money.

He dipped back into his cart handles and turned to leave, followed by Kimani and his 'tight' friend, Bafu.

"I can see you are in business!" Kimani remarked.

"That's life," Rock smiled back as he extracted a crumbled Roster cigarette from somewhere in his trousers. "That's life, eat or get eaten. The have-nots have to find a way of eating off the have-too much. Let's go in here and have some breakfast."

They entered Kaka Hotel and Rock ordered tea and *mandazi* for the three of them. A few of the customers in the hotel turned up their noses on seeing the two *chokoras* and the equally dirty *beba*. Rock took a huge bite of the *mandazi*, chewed slowly and swallowed.

"Tell me, what has been going on in your life all these years," he asked Kimani.

Kimani told him everything – from the attack the village mounted in Ndoinet in May, 1992 to the rescue of young Kiprop and how they finally decided to come to Nairobi.

"We came here hiding on a goods train. It was tedious, we almost got killed jumping off near every railway station and running after the train as it started off again. Bafu had been wounded and was almost crushed under the train."

"It must have been hard for you," Rock said sympathetically.

"What about the others? You said there were four of you."

"There was Kibet, the warrior who spared us and helped us get to Molo. Now we call him Bomu because of the herbs he smokes. He stays in Mashimoni, Kibera. He is a *makanga* on a route 8 *matatu*. As for Ngeta – his real name is Lihanda – he lives like the rest of us, only that his business is more advanced."

Rock kept silent, knowing that his friend did not want to give any more details. The smaller *chokora*, Kiprop, was looking at the empty plate ravenously. Taking the cue, Rock ordered for another round of breakfast.

"I too, never got the chance to finish school," he said after a short lull in their conversation. "But it was not a matter of school fees. It's just that I fell out with my mother."

"What happened?" Kimani asked. Fond recollections of Irungu's mother making him very concerned.

"When we first arrived at Kwa Mbira in Limuru, getting food on the table was a tall order. My mother struggled for the two of us, working in lodgings and hotels twenty-four hours a day. We lived in a single room, with me spreading rags on the floor each night. It was pathetic," he said, the recollection showing pain on his face.

"For two months, things were not too bad. We had gotten used to the neighbours, most of whom were sympathetic to us. I also did small jobs to chip in. My mother suggested that I go back to school and sit for my Standard Eight exams, and I enrolled at a small school in the area." Rock looked upwards as if visualizing the school.

"Man, I tell you, God does not forget his people," he declared. "I passed well. Mum got some money from somewhere and I joined a secondary school not far from home."

He gazed at the ceiling with emotion. "I tell you, Kimani, it is my experiences while at Kwa Mbira Secondary School that I will never forget in my life. Never, man . . ."

*   *   *

Irungu hated Kwa Mbira Secondary School as soon as he and his mother arrived there. The dusty compound boasted of three blocks. Small, roughly painted sign posts tried to label them as dormitories, classrooms and an administration block. They went to the latter, him in his uniform and his mother in an old frayed dress.

He clutched the metal box tightly while his mother carried the secondhand plastic water bucket as they entered the office whose door was written: MATRON. This is where the first dose of embarrassment was administered.

The matron made him remove everything from the box as she

inspected what he had brought. She was a large woman with a scornful face and a wig on her head. The crisp brown uniform she wore had the word MATRON hurriedly embroidered on it.

"I say! The letter clearly stated that you bring at least three shirts," she hissed out. "Why am I seeing only one?"

"Er . . ." Irungu's mother started. "I will bring him some more as soon as I get the money."

Yet the matron went on and on: Why do you have *mitumba* clothes and yet the letter clearly said that uniforms be bought from 'The Uniform Shop' only? Why do you have only one pair of shoes? Why no sandals? And what does he think he was going to dry himself with if he doesn't have a towel? By the time they left the office to go to the dormitory, Irungu felt totally destitute.

The worst was still to come. Irungu had heard that there was bullying in some schools but he hadn't imagined that it would be this bad. His mother had hardly left the compound when the other students descended on him like a swarm of bees.

"You *mono!* Come here!"

"What is your name?"

"Where do you come from?"

"Why have you come here?"

"Which school did you spring from?"

"Have you only one name, like a dog?"

All the questions were fired at him simultaneously. He received so many slaps that tears flowed out of his eyes. His pail was wrenched away from his hand and his box opened and ransacked. He never saw the pail again thereafter. Then someone pushed an armload of clothes into his hands.

"Go wash these!" he ordered.

"But I don't know where to wash from," Irungu protested.

"That is not my problem. I want them clean," he ordered.

Each day was a nightmare for Irungu. He had so many shoes to polish that his tin of polish was finished in the first week. One of the bigger boys decided that Irungu would be his donkey and so after every evening prep he was made to carry the bully to the dormitory.

It was dehumanizing. Irungu tolerated it just because he knew his mother was doing everything to educate him. He was the family's only hope, the man of the house.

Unfortunately for Irungu, there soon came another new student from his former primary school. It was a tragedy when the bullies learnt that he was a victim of ethnic clashes. It took him a whole year to shake off the nickname, 'Refugee'. And some even called him, 'Rwanda'.

The fact that he was poor made it even worse. He was the only one in tattered and patched clothes, the only one without stationery, and the only one with no money for outings. For a student whose desire had been to excel in his studies; Irungu now found that his grades were dropping at an alarming rate, probably because he was always out of school for lack of fees.

If there was anything Irungu hated with a passion was visiting days. There was one visiting day every month. To Irungu, this was a day of great humiliation because he was never visited. Visiting days always coincided with the days when his mother was most broke.

Rather than come empty-handed, she preferred to stay away and send whatever little money she had instead. He had to sit idle in the classroom while his schoolmates ran out in turns to hug their parents. In the evenings, he was the only one who availed himself for the tasteless supper served in the school dining hall.

One such visiting day when he was in Form Three, Irungu lay on his bed in the dormitory staring at the ceiling, his hands under his head. Food wrappings were strewn all over. Luckier students strode up and down the corridor with bottles of juice and pieces of chicken in hand. He had grown to abhor begging and no matter how severely the pangs of hunger hit him, he refrained from asking for any.

On the bed next to his, some students gathered discussing the day's events and exchanging different foods. The loudest of them was waving a *chapati* in the air as he gesticulated wildly. Irungu looked at the *chapati* longingly.

He must have dozed off for a while. He woke up with a start and saw the boy offering him a piece of *chapati*, not even looking at him. Without a pause, Irungu grabbed the *chapati* and bit into it ravenously.

Suddenly, the boy turned on him as if he was a thief.

"You fool! Can't you at least ask for food if you don't have any?" he bellowed. Irungu sank back in his bed, watched by various pairs of hostile eyes. The boy had not intended to give him the *chapati?*

"Sorry, I thought . . ."

"Damn what you thought, you son of a prostitute!"

The boy grabbed the *chapati* from Irungu's hand and flung it out of the window.

"These sons of whores never have any decency in them!" he complained.

Irungu ran out of the dormitory in shame. From the ablution block, he could hear the din made by jovial boys in the dormitory. He burst into tears.

If Irungu did not commit suicide then, he would never do it. The thought actually crossed his mind as he cried bitterly. What kept him from ending his life was the solemn vow he had made.

I will never, ever depend on another human being. Never! he swore.

He must have stayed in the ablution block for hours. The tap! tap! of sandals approaching broke into his thoughts. He hurriedly wiped the tears off his face and turned to the sink.

He saw the boy who had embarrassed him enter the toilet. He bent into the sink to wash his face and avoided eye contact. Everything would have been okay had the boy not quipped:

"What's up, *chapo-snatcher?* Planning to snatch some more food?"

Something snapped in Irungu's brain. Without a thought, he jumped at the boy and hit him on the head. The boy gasped as he lost his balance. He slid onto the wet, muddy floor and lay on his back, unconscious.

Irungu looked down at him in panic, not knowing what to do.

Then, he bent and ransacked the fallen boy's pockets. There was a diary, a handkerchief, some money and a handful of either bread or *chapati* crumbs. He counted the money. Six hundred shillings.

He did not go back to the dormitory. Neither did he go home again. He took the night bus to Nairobi, 'Son of a prostitute' ringing in his mind.

*   *   *

"That was the end of my schooling," Rock concluded. "After all, school is not underwear which you have to wear all the time. I came here and started from scratch." He leaned forward. "And you know what?" he asked Kimani, "I have never borrowed anything from anyone since. Never!" There was a strange glint in his eye.

"What about your mother?" Kimani asked.

"I have never met her again," Rock replied, looking at his now cold tea. "Recently, I met one of my former neighbours who told me that she was dying from AIDS. But I don't have the courage to go back there, to my past. I have shut out my past completely. Now, I only live for today. Tomorrow always takes care of itself. Yesterday is past."

He emptied the cup of tea in one gulp.

"Come on, let's go now."

They walked out of Kaka Hotel. The flies that had flown out in protest now came back. Rock decided he would not go to work again. So they sat in the handcart outside the market and talked all day. Bafu left them and strolled lazily away, most likely going on some money-making mission. Rock looked at his friend.

"Why don't you leave the streets and join me at Korogocho?" he asked genuinely.

"It's not easy. There is Bafu. I can't leave him."

"You seem to have a strong liking for that boy," Rock observed. "You protect him like your own blood."

"He is the only family I have left. Him, Bomu and Ngeta. We decided to stay together. What we have gone through has bonded us together. And now, I have found you."

As it turned out, Kimani quit street life much sooner than he expected. It was a chilly Friday evening. He had spent the early hours of the night on Koinange Street, his area of operation. When day life ends at the infamous street, nights become even more bizarre. After the usual eventful evening, he retired to the alley where he and Bafu spent the night together with another street family. Just as he was collecting together the rags that were his bedding, he heard agonized cries coming from behind a huge city council dustbin.

Puzzled, he approached the scene and was almost blinded by what he saw. Two guards were standing; one holding down a smaller figure's head between his legs and the other the waist, his own trousers down. Kimani stood stupefied for a full minute watching the heinous act.

Suddenly, the piteous voice of the boy being sodomised registered on his mind. "What the . . .!" he shouted as he jumped at the guards. The two guards instantly recovered from the sudden intrusion. One of them struck Kimani with his *rungu* while the other, still buttoning his trousers, attacked with the whip. Kimani fell down under the heavy blows.

He lay on the ground bleeding profusely from a cut on the head and his now broken hand trying to ward off the blows. His eyes suddenly caught something – a large bone, the size of a human hand. He picked it up and in one sudden movement struck out. He heard the weapon connect with the guard's mouth, and felt the teeth caving in. Bafu stared wide-eyed as his molester shrieked in pain.

Just as the guard sank down, Kimani lashed out again catching the other guard on the forehead. There was an audible crack as the skull broke. Even as the two men were down, Kimani continued to pulp them mercilessly.

The scene attracted more street boys and guards. Within moments, it had degenerated into one of the bloodiest confrontations in the history of Nairobi streets. For three days, street boys and guards engaged in running battles. Human waste and stones flew in the air, and certain areas of Nairobi became no-go zones.

Kimani became famous. Long after the confrontation, his heroic act was the talk of the month. The fact that he had used a bone as his defence weapon earned him the nickname, *Mfupa*. The name Kimani was forgotten. He became *Mfupa*, the liberator. However, despite the exaltation he enjoyed as a newly crowned hero, he knew that he had to leave the streets. He was now a marked man, hunted both by the *askaris* and the police. He actually survived two attempts by vengeful *askaris* on his life. He took Bafu and, together with Bomu, Ngeta and Rock, they looked for shelter at Ngando, off Ngong Road.

It was the only place nobody knew them or would care about their tumultuous past.

*   *   *

The first house they resided in would have made even a pig flinch. For one whole year of torrential rain, the five men braved the flooded room and the cold, chilly nights. Though life here was relatively better than it had been on the streets, it was not smooth.

Ngeta continuously got fired from the few casual jobs he managed to land. Though Bomu soon got confirmed as the official tout of a *matatu*, he complained daily of the challenges of being a *matatu* tout. Rock was always in problems with the city council since he did not have a licence for the kiosk he set up to sell greens. Bone was unable to land any job, while Bafu's football talent slowly went to waste.

With nothing better to do, the five friends idled their days away in the dark alleys of Ngando. There, they learned new rules of survival they had not known during their life on the streets.

Funny enough, they never talked about their past experiences in Molo. They shut their minds to that part of their life completely. Now they lived only for the present.

That was when the sex orgies, the binges and the fights started becoming a regular feature of The Slaughterhouse.

Things got better when Rock suddenly landed on a substantial amount of money after the bomb blast, and improved even more when Bone struck up a relationship with Stella.

Stella earned her living by plaiting people's hair at a fee. Many ladies were attracted to her because of the speed at which her fingers worked, and her affordable rates. She, therefore, earned some money on a daily basis, which helped The Slaughterhouse Five a lot.

Most of the Ngando youths whiled away their time at Thiong'o's place where pool and darts were played all day. Outside the establishment was a long bench where many of the idlers sat and made catcalls at every passing female. It was during one of the catcalling sessions that Bone saw Stella.

Unlike other girls who kept their eyes glued to the fence, away from the idlers, Stella did not flinch at all even when whistled at. Bone was curious about this brave girl, so he began to make enquiries.

Stella was one hard nut to crack, though. She remained unapproachable. Bone was enthralled by the way she put him off on one hand, then led him on, on the other. It took him six months before he realized the fruits of his labour. And as it turned out, she very well understood him; his wild ways and even sometimes violent temperament.

It was Stella, too, who helped him discover in himself a hitherto unknown talent. During many of their walks to the Commonwealth War Cemetery, the only decent place they could afford for a picnic, Bone would put a hand round her waist and recite a suitable rhyme. Kalamashaka's *Ata kaa* was his favourite.

Kuja tuka-dine	*Come, let us dine*
Ama unataka ma - Intercont	*Or do you want the*
	Intercontinental?
Doo sina	*Money I don't have*
Lakini tutajipata pale chini	*But we'll find ourselves there*
Order chochote	*Order anything*
Baadaye boo	*Later, love*
Tukiletwa juu	*When we are confronted*
Kuwa na mii	*Be with me*
Tukipeel waru	*As we peel the potatoes*

Me and you, na thick na thin	*Me and you, through thick and thin*
Tu pull through.	*We will pull through.*

"You know," she said as she pondered over the lyrics, "I think you can make a good rapper."

"No," he answered modestly, "I don't think I can do this professionally."

"I've been to many talent shows, and I'm sure you can do better than most of the guys I see there," she said with finality.

It was at Stella's insistence and expense that Bone found himself at Club Florida 2000, known by everyone as F2, registered as one of the performers on 'Showtime'.

The afternoon jam went on with a mixture of rap, slow jam, reggae, and dancehall. Everyone was up dancing most of the time. Bone was, however, rather unhappy. Having not planned to perform, he had no rhymes to render. When the time came for the MCs to showcase their talent, however, Bone realized it would be easier for him. Most of the rappers were only bragging about their lyrical prowess and 'power over the microphone'.

We have a lot of issues happening in the society. I don't think all this is relevant, he thought to himself as each of the MCs took to the stage.

When his turn came, Bone jumped into the centre of the ring. He was going to tell them about his life, about the clashes:

"I didn't choose to kill,
killing chose me!
So I had to let his blood flow,
like a nosebleed!"

Interestingly, however, the crowd did not appreciate his effort. Either they didn't like the newcomer, or the message of the song. As it happened, a few beer cans landed on the emotionally charged Bone as he decried the poverty, corruption and crime in the society. Finally, he handed the microphone back to the master of ceremony and came back into the crowd, unhappy and sweating profusely.

"One day they'll understand!" he swore.

Yes, it had been one uphill and arduous journey for Bone and his group. Finally, Ngando had come to accept them as some of their own, and slowly they had become so integrated into the lives of the residents such that it was impossible to remember when and from where they had come.

twelve

Nairobi, December, 2001

The Village Market is an ultra-modern shopping complex that boasts of everything – from the best fashion wear to immaculate fast food restaurants and glittering jewellery shops. There is plenty of entertainment too.

"After this, we go straight to Ngando. I'm really missing the chips *cia kobole*," Nancy said as Bone placed the steaming packets of chips and chicken on the table.

He picked up a piece of chicken and smiled. "A few months ago, I predicted that you would be eating ghetto food like a malnourished child. I now see that I'm a good seer."

She chuckled, "But still, there are things I won't touch, like that *mutura* you brought for me from Kawangware."

He remembered the look on her face when he had come with the *mutura* and laughed. "Still, one day you will ask me to bring it for you."

"Not me!" she swore.

They watched the hundreds of fun seekers around them enjoying the festive atmosphere. New Year was approaching and you could tell from the flurry of activity that everybody was busy getting ready for it. The gift shops in the complex were doing roaring business.

Nancy and Bone had come here purely to have fun. They had started at Tinman's Pool Parlour where a game cost sixty shillings – a far cry from Thiong'o's where a game went for ten. Then they had swam at the huge Hi-tide Waterpark before taking in a bowling game. Finally, they had settled down at the Southern Fried Chicken parlour for a late lunch.

"On a serious note," she now said, "I would like to thank you for the time we have spent together. It has taught me a lot, and I'm enjoying every minute of it."

Bone paused, a large piece of chicken held between his thumb and forefinger. "So am I, that is, except when you take me to the New Stanley and I embarrass everybody."

Nancy laughed at the recollection. They had dined at the five-star hotel and at the end Bone had taken one critical look at their bill, then asked the impeccably dressed waiter why he had brought them his pay slip. The waiter had not taken that comment lightly.

"Before you came into my life, I thought Nairobi had no life worth writing home about. Now, all those trips to Kibera, Laini Saba, Mashimoni, Mathare, Mukuru kwa Njenga and Kawangware, not forgetting the trips to the children's home, have helped me change my attitude completely."

"Don't remind me about the home!" he groaned.

They had taken time off entertainment to do some philanthropy, visiting homes for the destitute with gifts amounting to thousands. At Mji wa Wazee, they had spent three hours with the senior citizens.

It was at Nyumbani Children's Home that they had almost quarrelled. Nancy had had to be pulled away when it was time to leave.

"Such hope!" she had remarked tearfully. "Seeing those beautiful kids, you'd never believe they were AIDS orphans."

"Yes, I know," he had said impatiently, "but it's now time to leave." Still, he had had to literally carry her away.

Bone took another bite of the chicken, a challenging glint in his eye. Her face was serious.

"I'm glad I decided to come back home for my holiday instead of going to Seychelles with my colleagues. There is a strange vibrancy here," she said.

He shrugged. Those things he took for granted were the ones intriguing her most.

"I wish this would never end,"she added regretably.

"I too feel you've made a big change in me. I mean, I never thought I would live like this. I . . . feel more like a gentleman now," Bone said and laughed at himself.

"But you still have not changed!" she accused him. "You still go to The Slaughterhouse. You are more or less the Bone I met at The Los Angeles. I think the person who said that you can take a man out of the village but you can't take the village out of him was very right.

He smiled smugly. It was true that he had been dividing his time fifty-fifty between Imara Daima and Ngando. It was also true that he still engaged in typical Ngando activities, chewing *miraa* and making catcalls at passing girls. All the same he said, "That's where you are wrong. I go there simply because I don't want to look like I have forsaken my people."

From the Village Market, they left to watch a movie at the Fox Cineplex, Sarit Centre. Bone settled in the car seat and watched the city pass by. He couldn't believe all that had happened to him.

He looked at a yellow piece of paper sticking out of the glove compartment and curiosity got the better of him. He pulled it out. It was a Western Union Money Transfer receipt.

He frowned – she received money from overseas almost weekly. Once, he had accompanied her to Postbank and had been astounded to see that the transaction involved thousands of shillings.

"Your uncle must be very sound . . . financially, I mean," he now observed.

"What?" she saw him studying the receipt and involuntarily stepped on her brakes. "Oh that? It's for the education project I'm undertaking," she explained.

He kept quiet. Had she been shocked on seeing him with the document or was it his imagination? Interestingly, he thought, he had never seen her writing anything project-like. What was the project about?

"I was thinking of the perfect event to celebrate our love," she said quickly. "What do you say to a three-day visit to the Coast? Just the two of us."

"What!" he exclaimed. "I have never been to the Coast."

"We'll usher in the New Year there. I have booked a room at the Diani Beach Hotel."

"You have already booked a hotel? What if I refused to come?"

"I know you well enough now," she answered, looking carefully ahead to avoid a large pothole at the Sarit Centre roundabout. "I knew you would not decline the offer."

"I don't know," Bone said. "I hear those coast buses to Mombasa are very dangerously driven."

She flipped open the glove compartment, pulled out several documents and handed him an envelope. His face registered surprise, then he smiled broadly.

"We are leaving in the morning by flight," she told him as she pulled into the parking bay. Bone put the air tickets in his pocket and buttoned it carefully. He couldn't bear the thought of having them stolen.

Nairobi, January 1, 2002 – 10.02 a.m.

The aroma of frying chips that Luthuli Avenue is so famous for wafted slowly into Bomu's nostrils. Not that he was hungry – he had just eaten a sumptuous breakfast. In any case, you don't feel hungry when you have money in your pocket.

Who would have ever thought it would come to this? he mused as he dodged a speeding *matatu*. What was thought by many to be a 'one-night stand' between Bone and Nancy had turned out to be something else altogether. He smiled when he thought of all the things that had come out of his friend's relationship with the rich girl.

They were now wearing expensive clothes and, most importantly, never had to worry about their next meal.

As he dodged another *matatu* which had just swung into his

path, Bomu thought about the late Stella. He felt pity for the girl. No matter how good or financially stable Nancy was, she would never match the solidity of that girl. Up to now, the five friends had not recovered from the shock of Stella's sudden death. Once in a while, conversation at The Slaughterhouse would drift to Stella, then Bone's face would contort with rage and pain.

Ngeta once wondered aloud whether Stella had committed suicide, but that line of thought was refuted at once. Stella was not that soft; she would never kill herself because of a man. And anyway, anybody who had lived half her kind of life would suffer nothing more miserable to make them commit suicide.

It pained Bomu terribly that neither he nor his friends had attended Stella's funeral. They had not even gone for the *matanga*. There had been so much acrimony between them and her family that they had decided to stay away for their own safety. Even when the body was brought in from the City Mortuary for the overnight stay before burial the next day, and the air rent with screams, Bomu and his friends had silently stayed in The Slaughterhouse in tribute to the fallen woman.

It was when the screams had been interspersed with a cry for vengeance that the five had slipped away into the night. They knew well that Stella's family viewed Bone as the cause of their daughter's death. Details of Bone and Stella's last argument had been on everybody's lips.

Bomu now stood outside one of the many electronic shops that lined Luthuli Avenue and which seemed to compete viciously with the chips shops. On the huge window was written SONY in big lettering and under it the name Nancy had said, Al-Emir Electronics. Before Nancy came onto the scene, he would not have imagined making this trip. He would have only come here to buy something in a dream. He walked into the shop to prevent himself from smiling and looking stupid.

The small Asian behind the counter almost fell over himself coming to serve Bomu. His heart was however not in it. Countless times he saw many well dressed men who turned out to be mere poor window-shoppers with nothing on their minds but to disturb one.

The dreamers came in, spent precious hours asking myriads of questions about the various electronics in the shop, and walked out nodding like half-wits. What pained him most was the fact that he always had to run after them.

Bomu set his eyes on the metallic three CD changer.

"How much is that?"

"Sixteen. Sixteen thousand shillings," the Asian shopkeeper emphasized on the 'sixteen thousand' to scare him off if he was not a genuine buyer.

"What guarantees do you offer?" Bomu asked again in the ghetto drawl that set the Asian seething. He went over the same thing he repeated day in and day out. These people were funny, he thought as he smiled charmingly at Bomu. The poorer, the dreamier. You would find the poorest of them outside windows where the most expensive electronics and the dearest models of mobile phones were sold. Just go to any street and you will see for yourself. It always got into his nerves, but then he had to make a living.

"Three CD changer, auto reverse, CD to tape facility, full remote control mechanism, side sub-woofers . . ."

"Okay. Now tell me how much you will sell it to me for," Bomu said seriously.

"I told you!" the Asian almost snapped, "sixteen thousand, but I'll make it fourteen for you . . . New Year's gift, you know."

Bomu smiled, "There are many electronic shops on this street, *bwana*. Maybe I should try elsewhere?"

"This is one of the best music systems available," the shopkeeper tried to defend his pricing.

"I know, but I'm buying it for seven thousand, nothing more." Bomu was uncompromising. He was an experienced bargainer.

After much haggling and cajoling he had the system for nine thousand shillings. Fair enough, he thought.

After all, Nancy had given him sixteen thousand for the music system before she and Bone left for Mombasa. Apparently, she had been walking along the street with Bone when she saw it, and because of something Bone had said about how the guys in Ngando would love such a system, she had offered to buy it for them as New Year's gift.

It surprised him, though, that she had insisted on that particular shop while he knew that deeper into River Road, he would have bought the radio at a much lower price.

A plump woman in an ill-fitting yellow dress came into the shop and stood behind the counter, right beside Bomu. Her strong perfume hit his nostrils and he turned the other way. He watched her from the corner of his eye. She seemed unaware of her badly applied make-up as she looked up at the many electronics on the shelves.

He removed his wallet, pulled out nine crisp one thousand-shilling notes and handed them to the shopkeeper.

"Write out a permit too."

"That will be two hundred," the Asian said.

"Cool." Bomu handed him another note and smiled – he had just saved himself six thousand eight hundred shillings.

"Thank you," the shopkeeper said as he wrote out the permit, at the same time glancing greedily at the woman as if he was terribly excited at the prospect of another nine thousand shillings.

"Please, keep the radio for me while I go buy a CD or two," Bomu said to the Indian. Even as he finished the statement, he realized that some change must have come over him; words like 'please' had been nowhere in his vocabulary before Nancy came into their lives.

The shopkeeper gave him his change. He removed his wallet, once again exposing the balance of crisp notes remaining inside. He counted them once more and put them deep in his pocket. In the wallet, he placed the eight hundred shillings change. The woman stared at his receding figure for a long time.

"Can I help you, madam?" the shopkeeper intruded her thoughts. She turned to him quickly, "Oh, yes . . . not really. Just looking around."

The Asian groaned.

Mombasa, January 1, 2002 – 10.10 a.m.

He first opened one eye lazily, glanced at the empty side of the bed, then opened the other and started looking for her lithe body across the room. She was humming softly – some love song by a western musician. Now fully awake, he turned over and saw her at the balcony overlooking the blue expanse of ocean. He groaned as he stood up and approached her, dressed only in his boxer shorts.

She wore a blue bikini top and shorts with side pockets which hung well above her knees, revealing the legs that had caused a stir everywhere they went last night. Looking at her now, Bone could not help thinking that the group Kalamashaka had a girl like her in mind when they sang:

Hata siwezi aibika	*I cannot be ashamed*
Nikimpeleka kwetu ghetto	*to take her home to the ghetto*
Hizo miguu!	*Those legs!*
Chokora huangusha	*Parking boys drop their*
chupa ya glue akiziona!	*bottles of glue on seeing them!*

The ocean lay gently swaying below them, stretching out as far as the eye could see and reflecting the azure of the sky. He put out his hand and pulled her towards himself. In response, she coiled up to him and planted a kiss on his lips, sending a tremor through his bloodstream.

"You're late," she admonished. "You forgot your appointment with the barber."

He looked at his watch – the golden one she'd bought him for Christmas – and gasped when he saw it was already ten o'clock. How could he forget! But then, back home you did not need any appointment with the barber. You just went to Kax Kinyozi and stayed in line if there were other clients in the queue.

Months earlier, anybody telling him he would one day be fretting over an appointment at Cuts Hairdressers would have evoked a hearty laugh. Who would ever have thought that he would usher in the New Year at this five -star hotel?

Five months earlier, he was a nobody just like most of the Nairobians who only dreamt of owning phones while window-shopping on Kimathi Street. If you had told him he would one day wallow in such luxury, Bone would have told you solemnly, "Not in this lifetime, man. Maybe the next."

They had ushered in the New Year in style. After a whole day of playing golf – which had made Nancy laugh breathlessly, saying what he was playing was surely not golf but something else altogether – they had sat in the lounge with the hundreds of tourists from all over the world and watched the amazing display of fireworks light up the sky.

Mombasa had something more to celebrate about. It had just been elevated to city status, a few weeks after Kisumu had had the same honour bestowed on it. At the same time, however, a number of kiosks had been demolished in the town. Bone had argued vehemently against such merciless acts while in their hotel room, but Nancy didn't seem to understand the whole thing. Still, the spirit of jubilation was high in the air.

"We had better start packing if we are to catch the afternoon flight back to Nairobi," she said, jolting him out of his reverie.

He smiled, remembering how eventful and enjoyable the flight here had been. He longed for the return trip. She snuggled closer to him and tried to look up into his eyes. The morning breeze made her long hair rise up and fall down rather mystically.

"Expect a lot this year, Bone," she whispered. "You are not ready for what is coming your way," she added enigmatically.

He grinned. If what had happened to him so far was anything to go by, then he was not ready at all.

Nairobi, January 1, 2002 – 11.30 a.m.

Bomu bumped into a woman near Delicious Fish and Chips. He mumbled a quick apology and walked on. It was when a loud scream split the polluted air a minute later that his mind was jolted to the present.

"*Uuuu! Shika huyo mwizi!*" came the high-pitched cry.

Instinctively, Bomu turned round, looking for the thief and wondering who would be so stupid to snatch something on this street at this time of the day. When he saw nobody fleeing, he turned back to the woman and suddenly saw that she was coming straight for him, gesticulating frantically. He stood rooted to the spot until she reached him and held him by the collar.

"*Nini mbaya, wewe?*" What's wrong with you? he asked.

"*Mwizi!* Help! Help! thief!" she screamed louder and started pummeling his face with her large fists. He shielded the face with his right hand, and with the left pushed her away from him. She struggled to maintain her balance and landed on a parked Nissan matatu. A crowd was forming up. He realized that it was the same woman he had seen at the electronics shop. She looked strangely familiar.

"*Nini mbaya? Umechizi, nini?*" What's wrong with you? Are you mad, or what? He asked yet again, grabbing her by the front of her dress. He had surely seen her somewhere, but he could not tell where.

The crowd came nearer and people started demanding to be told what was happening. Bomu angrily told them how the woman had emerged from nowhere and was now calling him a thief.

"You have stolen my money!" she loudly asserted, holding tight onto his shirt. "He stole from me! Six thousand shillings! My whole salary for the month!"

"*Ati* six thousand?" Bomu countered. "You must be raving mad!" He removed the contents of his pocket to show the crowd and immediately realized the fatal mistake he had made. For he only had six thousand in his pocket. It was now impossible to explain the coincidence.

"*Na si ndizo hizo pesa!*" Isn't that the money? The woman now asked the swelling crowd.

"No! This is my money!" Bomu tried to explain, but the agitated woman shouted him down.

"Now that you have found the money, what are you men waiting for?" one man asked as he aimed a kick at Bomu. The other people closed in.

Bomu doubled over from the pain.

"Wait!" he shouted, pleading that they listen to his explanation.

"Let's go back to the shop where I have been given this money . . . " His heart was pounding now because he knew nobody would listen. He also knew that trying to dash off would only seal his fate.

Blows rained on him from all sides. He tried to shield his head as they pounded him. His wallet, shoes, jacket and phone were taken from him in seconds. His trousers were torn in two. Someone hit him from behind and he fell down. Someone else jumped up and landed on his groin. He screamed over and over as the stones landed on his body. In consternation, he realized the crowd was not letting up at all.

He heard the crack of bone as someone hit his leg with a metal bar. He was at that moment in too much pain to move, and now he let the blows land without trying to block them. His face became a bloody mess as he lay in his own pool of blood. The man with the metal bar was now working on his hands, making sure he broke every bone along the way.

He was fast losing consciousness. He opened one eye against the sunlight and saw the woman who had accused him standing over him with a huge rock in her hands. He heard and felt the impact as the boulder smashed into him. His face caved in with the force.

Fleeting images ran through his mind in a cloudy confusion. He tried to open his mouth but half his teeth and a lot of blood sloshed into his throat, choking him. He saw the woman take a hateful look at him before taking out a phone from her handbag. Even as he blacked out into oblivion, he was trying to remember where he had seen her. Then, with his final effort, he suddenly recalled seeing her in an old family photograph.

Bomu faded into oblivion.

"*Achomwe!*" Burn him! someone shouted.

The funny thing with lynchings in Nairobi is that you never know where the car tyre comes from. Neither can you tell who donates the petrol. Within a minute, the command had been echoed down the mob and from somewhere the right ingredients had materialised.

Nairobi, January 1, 2002 – 2.15 p.m.

The Kenya Airways flight to Nairobi had been uneventful but to Bone it had been quite entertaining. Once more, everything appeared novel to him: the smartly dressed stewardesses, the comfortable seats, and even the minute sandwich and glass of orange juice. The forty-five minute flight seemed just like twenty minutes.

All through the flight Bone had been engaged in 'serious' conversation with his girl, and she kept bursting out in laughter. He tried to sing:

"I might not always be talking money, but I'll keep you
with a smile, and walking funny . . ."

"You know," he had said loudly, "Me without you is like the Flying Squad without guns."

She giggled, "Get real!"

"Or better still," he said again romantically as he eyed the attendant walking past, "me without you is like Koinange Street without its sex workers."

"Bone! That's vulgar!" she whispered.

He reflected on her accusation for a while, then calmly countered: "If you live in a vulgar society, you have to become vulgar." He remained silent for some time, thinking of a quote he had heard somewhere: *When you exist in an environment that constantly keeps you on your toes, you have to be down to do whatever to survive.*

As soon as they landed at Jomo Kenyatta International Airport, they took a taxi to Nancy's place. Bone was feeling lethargic and stretched out on the sofa to relax.

But even with such unaccustomed pleasures, he found it hard to disregard a strange feeling of foreboding that started to creep up on him. He could not even concentrate on the television, although his favourite reggae programme was on. After a while, he took his cellphone and dialled Bomu's number. He could hear Nancy singing loudly in the shower.

There was a long pause, then someone said, "Hallo?"

At once, Bone knew it was not Bomu. Bomu always said, *"Niaje?"*

"Who is this?" Bone asked. "Is that you, Bomu?"

Nancy came from the bathroom, softly drying her hair with a white towel.

Another long pause at the other end of the line, then: "This is not Bomu or whoever. If the owner of this phone is the one you're calling Bomu, just know you'll not be talking to him anymore."

"What?" Bone asked, now suddenly alert. Had Bomu's phone been stolen? But nobody stole from Bomu and got to boast about it.

"Do you hear those noises in the background?" The voice now continued, "Well, I'm in the middle of Luthuli Avenue, and so is your Bomu. But he is past tense." And the line went dead.

"What?" Bone shouted. Nancy dropped the towel and came towards him.

Shivering, he hit the redial button. After five unanswered rings, the recorded message at the other end dutifully told him 'the mobile subscriber could not be reached.' He dropped the phone on the bed and stared at it as if it had suddenly grown a tail.

"What's happening?" Nancy asked. Bone was shivering feverishly. She came and sat next to him, concern showing on her face.

"Let's go," he said after a while. "I think Bomu is in trouble."

It took them a whole hour to find Bomu, or rather, what was left of him. The still smouldering remains of the car tyre emitted a swirl of black smoke that billowed over the crowd of *wananchi* standing beside the charred body on the ground. Bone instantly recognized the torn strip of shirt and the half-burnt shoe. The general form of the body was unmistakable even though it had been reduced to a blackened shell.

Nancy gave one long look at the scene, then leaned on Bone and started sobbing. Bone looked at the spectacle without flinching. He ignored the weeping woman and stared at what was left of his friend. The only thing that betrayed the turmoil in his head was the slight trembling that shook his frame.

A short dark man with a receding hairline approached the couple hesistantly. Only when he was standing in front of them did Bone notice his presence.

"Do you know the dead man?" he asked in a low voice.

Nancy nodded, but Bone continued staring blankly at the charred remains.

"I saw it all," the man added, as if announcing a major conspiracy.

"He was innocent. He did not even try to escape as the woman accosted him. I saw her frame him. I had been watching him for a while because of his fancy clothes. But I could not do anything at all. The crowd would have turned on me for being a sympathizer, or decided I was an accomplice."

Bone became instantly alert, but the man did not have anything more to add. And when he left them, Nancy looked at him all the way until he disappeared around the corner.

Nairobi, January 1, 2002 – 8:15 p.m.

He had had a busy day and was relaxing at his home. When the phone rang and woke him up from a drift of sleep, he was genuinely irritated. He cursed as he walked towards it. In his line of work, one never ignored a phone call no matter how tired one was.

"Yes?" In his hand he held a ball pen. Years in the profession had made it a habit to record what was said over the phone.

"Tell me it was not your work," the voice was hysterically unmistakable.

He paused a while. Hell! She was going to start another of the moral tirades that had been the cause of their recent disagreements.

"What do you think?" he asked.

"Did you have to do it that cruelly?" He could envision the

expression on her face even though he was not seeing her. He was beginning to get impatient.

"There was no better way," he said dryly.

"Hell! In the first place, did you really have to do it?"

"That's not a useful question!" he snapped, and slammed down the receiver.

He stared at the President's portrait hanging on the wall, deep in thought. Why she was now developing cold feet was a puzzle to him. If this went on, all their plans would be in jeopardy.

He picked up the receiver. It was time to call other people and ask for their opinion.

"Hallo, operator?" he started, "I would like to make an international call . . ."

thirteen

Nairobi, Friday, January 4, 2002

Ngando was waking up to another arduous day. Mothers could be seen in the early morning light walking to the shops for milk or sugar, and others coming from the water vendor with jerrycans of water on their heads, having 'caught the early worm' as they say. Most of the men who would have to walk all the way to town for work could be heard banging their doors as if to let the whole world know of their plight. Radios were switched on at full-blast, to the chagrin of the neighbours who were not endowed with music systems of their own. Therefore, there was quite a crowd to see the squad arrive at the slum.

They came in a convoy of two Peugeot saloon cars and two white Land Rovers. Petrified neighbours woke up when they heard the crunch of their boots on the dried mud and timidly peeped through windows to see the more than twenty armed men surrounding the whole plot in military fashion.

Six of the men formed a barricade at the entrance to the plot, and another six stood at the other side, effectively blocking every possible exit. More than ten of them stood with poised rifles at the door to The Slaughterhouse.

With a slight nod, one of them communicated a command and the door flew open with a single kick. It flew off its hinges and fell into the room, followed by two men, guns at the ready.

Bafu and the woman with him in bed woke up with a start at the loud noise, then fell back under a volley of slaps and kicks. Both were pulled out of bed, stark naked, and ordered to lie down. The woman was about to scream when she was told to shut up and given a sharp slap.

Lying on the new PVC carpet, Bafu looked up to see the attackers ransack the whole room in a well-coordinated fashion. The new mattress was slit in two, the new furniture overturned and utensils scattered on the floor. The new wall clock fell off the wall and came crashing onto the floor, breaking into pieces.

"Wapi bunduki?" one of the raiders asked Bafu, kicking him in the head. Where are the guns?

"*Sijui nini mnasema"* I don't know what you are talking about, he replied earnestly, fearing the worst. Blood was flowing out of his mouth.

"You will soon know!" another informed him menacingly. Both men trained their guns on the couple as two others entered and went through the room piece by piece.

Bafu had long ago realized who the men were – the dreaded Flying Squad! The knowledge did not soothe him at all. What were they doing here, and what guns were they talking about? he wondered.
Outside, a few courageous neighbours ventured close to see what the commotion was all about. They rushed back into their rooms after receiving hard-hitting slaps.

"Rudi ndani, mjinga wewe!" Go back inside, you fool, roared the officers. "Or you want to help out your colleagues? *Nyinyi ndio mnafuga majambazi hapa, eh?"* Are you the ones rearing gangsters here?

Bafu and the woman were made to hastily dress up and pushed outside where other officers waited. With slaps and kicks, they were ordered to squat with their heads tucked in between their knees. The woman started sobbing pitifully.

The PVC carpet was ripped to shreds. Bafu was still trying to make sense of all the hullabaloo. What would the Flying Squad be looking for in The Slaughterhouse? Though he knew there was nothing to warrant such a search, he was worried. There were stories of police planting evidence in suspects' houses. But then, none of The Slaughterhouse Five had any bad blood with the police to make the law enforcers attack them this way. Still, there was no knowing.

Suddenly, two of the officers emerged from the vandalized room.

"*Hakuna kitu ndani,*" one of them said. They had found nothing. Bafu heaved a sigh of relief and thanked his guardian angel.

Still, both of them were handcuffed, hoisted up and pushed out of the compound. Bafu did not protest at all as he was bundled into the boot of one of the Peugeots, and the woman into a Land Rover – you don't argue with the Flying Squad. Then, in unison, the officers climbed into the cars and they sped off. The operation had lasted only twenty minutes.

In the darkness of the boot, Bafu felt the presence of another human being. As he got more used to the darkness, he saw the unconscious man with a bloodied face. The car was driving dangerously and he felt pain in his ribs as he was jolted like a stick in a matchbox. It then braked suddenly and his hazy mind told him that it had got onto Ngong Road. He was starting to relax with the improved ride when the car braked again and took a right turn.

Cemetery Road! he thought as the car sped through the road between Kaburini and Telkom Sports Ground and which led to Jamhuri Park. He frowned again when only a hundred metres down, they stopped. There was an eerie silence for almost an eternity, then he heard other car doors bang shut, followed by approaching footsteps.

The boot door was raised unceremoniously. Blinking from the sudden light, Bafu saw five mean faces looking down at him.

"*Tokeni nje!*" came the sharp order. Get out!

*   *   *

Bone had had a very busy day. Apart from the driving lessons, he was busy running all over the city mortuaries. The authorities had collected Bomu's remains and taken them to a place only they knew. Bone had been furious – the mob justice incident had not been investigated even after he had given out 'something small' to the detectives and received their assurance that the truth would be unearthed. The police officers at the scene had just entered the incident as 'mob violence with no available witnesses' in their Occurence Book.

Three days had passed without any trace of his friend's remains, and Bone was beginning to feel that they had been dumped somewhere. It infuriated him. Now that he had the money, his wish was to give his friend a decent send off.

When he entered the house, he made a mental note to call Rock and Ngeta. He felt guilty at not having been to Ngando since Tuesday when Bomu was killed. He now lay on the bed and tried to get a minute's rest before going for his evening bath. He was drifting off to sleep when suddenly somebody jumped onto him. "Wake up, lazybones!"

"Go away!" he moaned, trying to cover his head with a pillow, but the girl was not one to be deterred. She pulled at him playfully.

"Ah!" he grumbled. *"Wewe ni kama ka-siafu!"* You are like safari ants! "You always come when you are not wanted."

"Wake up!" Nancy said. "It's going to nine."
She turned on the small 14 inch television set they had for watching late-night movies. Most channels were showing the prime time news. She increased the volume to irk him, and giggled when he tossed in bed.

"Do me a favour and run off to hell!" he said.

" . . . and in another incident, three men were shot dead in a dramatic shoot-out with police early this morning . . ." came the newscaster's voice. Bone looked up to see the latest unfortunate victims of police brutality and realized that the footage was showing very familiar surroundings. He tried to jog his mind to recall where the place was.

"Hey, that's Cemetery Road!" he declared, drawing Nancy's attention to the news item.

The police boss was showing off the guns recovered from the slain gangsters. The speech was the same old, well-rehearsed monotone that every police boss used in such circumstances.

"*My men* ordered them to stop, but they opened fire at *my men*, so *my men* gave chase all the way from town. They shot at *my men* again and my men returned fire, killing three of them on the spot. *my men* recovered five Beretta pistols, an AK-47 rifle, and rounds of ammunition . . ."

"The fool!" he swore. "*Ati,* 'my men'! The way he is talking, you'd think he was in the thick of the battle. Who is he kidding? Doesn't he realize that we all know that the regular police are never involved in these shootouts, and are only called in to clean up the mess and deal with the media when the executions have already been carried out and the Flying Squad has gone? This fool here . . ."

His voice trailed off as he saw the fallen victims. The footage showed a close-up of the dead men, each of them in a pool of blood. The man in the middle still had a pistol in his hand. A small bullet wound stood out in the centre of his forehead. The face was splashed in blood, but there was no mistaking it.

"Bafu!" Bone and Nancy shouted at the same time.

"Oh my God!" Nancy whispered as they listened to the presenter summarise the whole story. Bone's hands were trembling heavily as he dialled Rock's number, all the weariness having left him.

"Hallo?" he said into the phone when there was a connection.

"Bone," came Rock's anguished voice. "Where are you? I've been trying to reach you since morning!"

"My phone was off all day," Bone explained. "Where is Bafu?" he asked quickly.

The hesitation at the other end of the line was long enough to confirm his fears.

"That's why I've been trying to reach you all day," Rock finally said in a low voice. Bone found himself trembling worse than when he had faced Bomu's corpse.

"What happened?" He asked in a tremulous voice.

"Nobody knows for sure. It's said that he was picked up by a heavily armed contingent of police. A half hour later, gunshots were heard at Kaburini, and he was there among the two other men. Nobody knows what happened."

Bone tried hard to contain himself. "I'm coming there right away."

They drove through the town like lunatics. Nancy almost crashed into a bus on Kenyatta Avenue. She ignored every traffic light and flouted every traffic rule in the book. They reached Ngando in a record twenty-five minutes.

The Toyota Corolla was hurriedly parked outside Nyang'anya's shop. The couple rushed into The Slaughterhouse, this time neither of them worrying about losing the side mirrors.

The room was illuminated by only one candle, its weak light wavering such that half the room was in darkness. Ngeta was sitting alone on the upturned bed, his head in his hands. He did not try to hide the tears that ran down his face as he looked up. Bone looked away – it was a pity to see Ngeta crying.

The Slaughterhouse was in total shambles. You would think City Council *askaris* and street hawkers had been battling it out in the room. Everything was in disarray.

"This is pure murder!" Ngeta spat out. There was a disheartening tremor in his voice which unsettled Nancy. Ngeta was so hardened it was impossible to imagine him so emotionally devastated.

Bone sank onto the bed. "How can they claim he was in a gang that robbed a bank in the opposite side of town when it's a fact he was taken from here?" he asked.

"That's why I'm saying it's murder. Maybe the gangsters escaped and the *karaus* had to find somebody to show to their superiors." Ngeta was so deflated.

Nancy took one fallen stool, turned it the right way up and sat on it. "What happened to the room?" she asked.

"The police ransacked it. When they left, the crowd of onlookers came in to loot what remained. It was when Rock arrived that they took off."

Bone shook his head sadly, then buried his face in his hands.

"Why would the police think of killing Bafu, for God's sake?"

"*Labda mtu alimseti.*" Maybe somebody set him up, Ngeta ventured.

"Who?"

It was true that there were people who thought them enemies – people Bafu conned, or some whose girlfriends he snatched. But who had the ability to use the Flying Squad to revenge?

"That's what is on everybody's lips," Ngeta replied.

Bone gave the room another glance. Even in its jumbled state, one could tell that a great deal of things had been stolen. The worldspace receiver Nancy had bought them was gone, as well as the corn popper and a some clothes.

"What a society!" he said.

Nairobi, Friday, January 4 – Midnight

The telephone conversation was becoming fairly tense.

"Why are you, of all people, getting so jittery about this?" he asked.

"I don't know," she answered. Her voice had lost all confidence. He could tell that she had been crying previously. I don't like what is happening. I mean, is it really necessary? I don't like it, at all, at all."

"The same with many of us," he tried to pump sense into her head.

"We don't like it, but circumstances force us to proceed. If we don't do it, nobody else will."

"It's getting harder to do this."

He sighed to avoid bursting out in anger. "It's not easy for us too, but we have to go on with it. You know that many people have invested their time, money and even staked their future to get this project going. I wouldn't want to be the one to sabotage the project.

Would you?"

She remained silent.

"Would you want to derail the project?" he repeated his question.

"No," she answered reluctantly.

"Good. Then please do your part. Right?"

"Alright." Her voice was resigned.

He was angry at himself for forcing it on her, but really, he had no choice. What had to be done, had to be done. There was no other way out.

"We must not betray our cause," he said more gently before he hung up.

Nairobi, January 14, 2002

Bafu was buried like a national hero. In solidarity, the whole of Ngando was there for the *matanga*. It was difficult for The Slaughterhouse neighbours, for they did not sleep a wink as the unruly crowds belted out their versions of popular elegies each night.

The day before the burial, people came from all the neighbouring villages: Kawangware, Kangemi, Riruta Satellite and Kibera, and as far as Mathare and Eastleigh. There was a sudden and unplanned show of protest – the coffin bearing Bafu's remains was carried by a multitude of people and taken to Ngando Police Post where it was dumped amid loud shouts of 'murderers! murderers!' Then the protesters sat down and waited for audience with the officer in-charge.

The situation, though tense, was under control until the panicking police officers holed up in the small police post called in reinforcements. Three lorry-loads of anti-riot police officers in full combat gear came and settled at a distance.

"*Fisi!*" the people shouted. "*Fisi ndio hao!*" It seemed some of the protesters were eagerly waiting for some way of venting their anger.

A hail of stones descended on the unfortunate law enforcers as they jumped out of the lorries and charged at the mob like angry rhinos whose calves the crowd was snatching. Each officer held a shield and truncheon.

Tear gas canisters were unleashed, however, the crowd seemed to have learnt a few things about this kind of combat from university students because they calmly collected the billowing canisters and hurled them right back at the police. The war raged on for hours.

The next day, the crowd reorganised and walked all the way to the City Mortuary where the body had been taken by the police. It was as if the slain man was a political hero, thought Rock, as the chanting crowd surged forward right in the centre of the busy Ngong Road, bringing all traffic to a halt. From the mortuary, they branched onto Mbagathi Way, carrying the coffin shoulder–high and loudly shouting anti-police and anti-government slogans.

A traffic policeman walking up the hill was almost lynched as people poured out their anger on him. It took the kind intervention of a group of TV reporters to save the man whose shirt was already soaked in blood. Nancy clung onto Bone as she watched the policeman being helped away. He smiled at her inexperience, and exchanged glances with Rock and Ngeta.

The burial at Langata Cemetery was charged and emotional. Each speaker asked for vengeance. Though most politicians had shied away from the event fearing that it would degenerate into chaos, one of them famous for his confrontational nature was there.

He animatedly promised the mourners that the matter would be brought to Parliament's attention. Nevertheless, the burial went on smoothly. It only turned a bit rowdy when the pastor extended the prayers by one word too many and the mob forced him to stop.

"Destiny! I wonna rule my destiny!" They sang instead of following the written dirges. After all, they said, there should be no pretence: the slain man had probably never seen the inside of a church.

*   *   *

What bothered most of the mourners was the fact that the organisers of the burial – Bone, Ngeta and Rock – adamantly refused to disclose Bafu's real name. On the wooden cross only the name 'BAFU' and the date of birth were inscribed.

When some people inquired on Bafu's real name and place of origin, Bone calmly told them that names were immaterial. Was it the man who made the name or the name which made the man? They had known him only as Bafu, so why change his name in death?

They kept quiet but knew there was a deeper, underlying reason for this . . . a reason that the remaining friends wanted to keep secret at all cost.

Another thing that bothered people was the large turnout of *chokora* and street families at the burial. In fact, they came with a special wreath which they placed on the freshly covered grave. And to everybody's surprise, Bone took countless photographs with them and seemed to be completely at ease in their presence. It left the Ngando residents totally baffled.

*   *   *

The young, beautiful woman was seated on the sofa, her legs folded on the comfortable cushion. She was drinking from a bottle of Guinness. Another bottle stood, unopened, on the expensive coffee table in front of her.

Behind the sofa, the dark, burly man paced angrily, and on the other sofa the ungainly, heavy woman lay sipping from a bottle of cane liquor. "I don't like this one little bit!" the man finally grunted. For a long time nobody spoke.

"Listen, dear," the well endowed woman said with a slur to her words, "we have reached a point of no return. It is now that we need to be even more united. Our plans will fail miserably if we disagree at this point." The girl remained silent. She stared at the muted television set, oblivious of what was happening on the screen. Then she looked up at the ceiling and sighed.

"In any case, what do you have to lose? Remember, you are repaying an injustice done to you. Blood must be paid with blood," the woman added. The girl sighed again. When she spoke, it was in a subdued, unconvincing voice, as if she knew that they would not hear her out, that she might as well be talking to the air.

"I think that what we have done so far is punishment enough," she said.

"No amount of punishment can justify what was done to us," the woman spoke. She reeked of alcohol, and the bitterness in her voice was quite clear. The man chuckled, perhaps to conceal his anger. Then he moved closer to her.

"We have gone too deep into this. We can't stop now. With or without your support, we are going ahead with our plans. Justice must be done," he said with finality.

The girl sighed again. Then she stood up and hurried into the bedroom. The burly man and the heavily built woman looked at her retreating figure, then at each other. The burly man shrugged his broad shoulders and held up his hand to the drunk woman.

"Come," he said. "She will do it."

fourteen

Nairobi, January 18, 2002

Nairobi looked like one forlorn, God-forsaken city. Though the Friday afternoon human and motor traffic was as usual very hectic, Bone was oblivious of it all. He ploughed through the mass of humanity on Tom Mboya Street like an automaton. It was as if his life had come to a standstill.

He had come to town to escape the reality of Ngando. For four days, he and his friends had locked themselves in The Slaughterhouse, drinking heavily and chain-smoking. The floor was littered with crushed, empty beer cans and broken bottles of spirits. Nobody had spoken to the other. Bafu's death had left a gaping hole in their lives. The fact that they could not avenge his death, let alone protest against the authorities, left them even more frustrated.

"Damn! First it was Bomu, then Bafu – within half a month!" Ngeta moaned as he angrily chewed on some *miraa*.

"We have stayed together all these years . . ." Rock began. "Why does everything seem to be falling apart now?"

"We have lived from hand to mouth for all these years, and when the future starts to look brighter, we begin to lose our colleagues. I can't understand this."

Bone had taken another swig at the spirit, then verbalised what had been forming in their minds: "It's as if a curse has fallen upon us!"

"Yes, it's as if we are in the presence of some evil," Ngeta concurred.

"But why now, when our lives have dramatically improved?" Rock asked once more.

To say their lives had dramatically improved would have been an understatement. Thanks to Nancy, Rock had revitalised his grocery shop and it was fast becoming a major business in Ngando. He was the first kiosk owner to instal electricity. Ngeta, on the other hand, had enrolled at the local driving school.

Bone had proved, to the surprise of most Ngando inhabitants, that he and his friends could give something back to society. It happened that one day as he was playing pool at Thiongo's, the East African Church of the Holy Ghost, Kenya Chapter was being closed because of nonpayment of rent. The pool players were all showing signs of happiness – the church, after all, had been a source of noise and discomfort to them. And in any case, it reminded them of their sinful world, pricking their conscience when they saw that other people were going to church while they played pool. But the faces of the distraught worshippers who stood watching as their prized church furniture was thrown out had touched Bone.

Something was not right, Bone had thought. Everyone always complained of the church, yet it was so much a part of Ngando. Slowly, he had made his way to the well-endowed landlord who was busy supervising the eviction. Beside him stood a man, presumably the church leader, pleading with him.

"Don't talk to me!" the landlord growled. "I didn't bring you to Nairobi, did I?"

"How much money does he owe you?" Bone asked.
The landlord gave him one look, ignored him for a while, then said, "I don't know what business of yours that is."

"I want to pay for them," Bone declared.
There immediately arose a murmur from his colleagues at the pool table. He also heard a few whispers from the worshippers. The landlord raised an eyebrow, then laughed out loudly.

"How could you possibly raise ten months' rent?"

"Tell me how much these people owe you. How I will raise it is entirely my own worry," Bone retorted.

When the well-endowed man had told him, Bone had surprised everyone by fishing out his wallet, removing a wad of notes and handing them over.

"This should clear the arrears, as well as cover the next ten months' rent. That, I presume, is enough to stop you pestering the poor worshippers."

*　　　*　　　*

Nancy catered for their every need. This, however, had brought about its own problems as Ngeta had stated candidly one night.

"Man!" he had lamented. "Months ago, getting a girl to come home with me was an uphill task. Now that my wallet is full, I find myself with hordes of girlfriends. I'm getting tired of having to stop them from fighting over me."

Bone had laughed. "Do you mean to say you are not happy with all the attention?"

"I'm not complaining," Ngeta had clarified. "Of course, it's nice to have ladies all over one. What bothers me is the fact that they are only after my money."

"How do you know that?" Rock had asked.

"Can't you see, man? I've been looking at my photographs taken before Nancy's arrival. I swear, I look the same. I haven't changed, have I?"

They had all laughed, especially when just then Ngeta's phone had rang and he had said: "Damn! What does this Eva want now?"

The future looked promising. Very promising. But then, the sudden death of their two colleagues worried everyone. Why now? Bone asked himself. Was there indeed some evil following them? Had their guardian angel, the one who had seen them through the perils of Molo, and the streets of Nairobi, finally fallen asleep?

The loud screeching of brakes jolted him out of his thoughts. A Kenya Bus Service truck came to a halt inches away from him. He recoiled in shock. People turned to look at the source of the commotion.

"*Mbwa, mang'aa wewe!*" Dog, vagabond! The driver shouted at him through the window.

Bone shouted obscenities at him and walked on. His heart was beating rapidly, though. Then someone held his hand. He turned round to see a short man who looked vaguely familiar.

"Remember me?" asked the stranger. They were standing on the veranda, being jostled about by the passing crowds. Bone shook his head – he could not quite place him.

"You remember two weeks ago, when your friend was lynched on Luthuli Avenue? I told you he had been framed. You still don't remember me?" Bone, now recalled the man, but thinking he was about to be touched for a favour, he pretended he didn't.

"I'm sorry, but you understand that I was very confused that time. I can't remember anything much of what happened."

"I understand," replied the man. "Up to now, I believe your friend was innocent."

"Thanks for your support," Bone said. "If it were another country, justice would have been upheld. Unfortunately . . ." He shrugged his shoulders to show his helplessness.

"Alright,"the stranger said as he shook Bone's hand. "See you again some day." Bone watched him turn to leave, and then stiffen as if he had seen a ghost in the crowd. He seemed shocked as he turned back to Bone and clutched his hand once more.

"What a coincidence!" he remarked, his eyes riveted on the crowd. Bone frowned, not comprehending the reason for this behaviour. He followed the man's gaze but could not see anybody he knew in the crowd.

"You see that woman?" the man said in a strange voice. "She is the one who framed your friend – the one who claimed that he had stolen her money." He animatedly pointed at a heavily built woman who was walking down the street.

"Are you sure?" Bone asked, quite shocked at the turn of events. But he recovered quickly and saw that, unless the man was a seasoned actor, he was telling the truth.

"Haki!" the man exclaimed. For real "I would never forget a killer!"

Bone pushed his way through the crowd without thinking. He only stopped when he reached the woman. She was looking into a shoe shop, apparently in no hurry. Grabbing her arm roughly, he spun her round and glared at her.

Her reaction left him totally flabbergasted. She was petrified to see him, and so startled she almost lost her balance. Bone looked at her calmly, maliciously enjoying her discomfiture.

"I've heard that you are the one who set up my best friend and got him lynched," he told her. Her surprised look had long given her away, and Bone knew she wouldn't try to deny the accusation.

She was well over in her late forties, if not into her early fifties. Her skin showed signs of care once upon a time, but at the moment was beginning to wrinkle. She wore an overgrown, distateful hairstyle. Bone disliked her right away.

"Your friend?" she stammered. "But he . . . he . . . stole from me!" Her words, heavily laced with a Kalenjin accent, confirmed her guilt.

"Nonsense!" Bone shot back. "My friend was not a thief. You think he would steal money from you on Luthuli Avenue, in broad daylight?"

"It's true," she stammered. She was shaking as if she was about to have an epileptic fit. "He stole six thousand . . ."

"Listen!" Bone told her menacingly, "I don't know what your motive was, but I intend to find out soon. Where I come from, we don't let murderers get off that easily." The idea of smashing her into the display glass of the shoe shop crossed his mind, but he suppressed it.

"You are very lucky we are in a busy street, otherwise I would have done something very nasty to you. But know that if we meet in other circumstances, you'll know who I am!"

Bone walked away. The woman was too shaken to move for a whole three minutes. When her energy returned, she ran like a hen that had seen a mongoose and dived into a restaurant.

Bone walked along the street, wishing there was something he could do about the woman. The whole encounter with her had brought his spirits down even further. Her discomfiture proved beyond doubt that there was more to Bomu's death than he had suspected. The realisation that there was nothing he could do about it sickened him. He no longer felt the need to walk around town. He boarded the next Metro Shuttle bus home.

As if to irk him more, the bus developed a mechanical problem along the way. It took almost a whole hour for the driver to realise that the problem could not be fixed and send for another bus. He arrived home almost at eight o'clock.

As he alighted at Kenol Stage, Bone could not help noticing the irony – six months earlier, nobody would have guessed he would be riding the expensive bus home. Him in a Metro Shuttle? Not in this lifetime!

But then, six months earlier he had been with Bomu and Bafu. He mechanically crossed the road. Some metres down the dirt road, he saw Chomelea walking briskly and whistling loudly. The plastics repair man was braving the early night cold with his characteristic energy. In one hand he carried the charcoal burner, an old halved *debe* from which dry sticks smoked, and in the other the tools of his trade. On his back was a tattered bag in which he carried the pieces of plastics he used in repairing the containers. His bearded face broke into a smile the moment he saw Bone.

"*Niaje*, Bone? How are you, You are so lost!"

"No, I'm not lost." The two shook hands vigorously.

"Man, when one climbs up a ladder, he should remember those he was with in the lower ranks."

"*Usiwe hivyo*," Bone defended himself. Don't be like that. "*Sema*, how is business?"

The self-proclaimed plastic *makanika* placed the *jiko* down. His forehead was wrinkled by years of hardship.

"Business is okay. We are still pushing on."

Bone liked Chomelea. Of all his neighbours, Chomelea was the only one who never bothered about what went on outside his door. If one went to Chomelea for gossip, the *makanika* would only respond

with a few nods and short grunts of 'Oh, really' and 'Isn't that bad?'
Finally, the frustrated gossiper would walk away. Bone knew that
Chomelea was the only neighbour who genuinely felt the loss of his
friends.

"Here's some money for the rent," he said as he handed him a few
notes.

Chomelea was bewildered. He licked his lower lip in one swift
movement.

"No, Bone. You don't have to . . ."

"Take it," Bone urged. "Whenever we were both down, did
either of us decline cigarettes offered by the other?" He patted the
repairman's back encouragingly.

Chomelea shook his head, smiled lamely and took the proffered
money. He dug his hand into the tattered waist of his dirty overalls to
reach into the pocket of the equally dirty jeans he wore underneath.

"Thanks, man," he said genuinely.

Bone walked further up the road. At the corner towards
Nyang'anya's shop, he bumped into Njogu the kerosene dealer.

"Sema!" he greeted. How are you!

Njogu looked distraught. He returned the greeting with a nod.
Instantly, Bone knew that something was wrong.

"Is something the matter?" he asked.

Njogu replied with another nod. The frightened look in his eyes
gave Bone a feeling of deep premonition that whatever was wrong
had to do with himself. His heart missed a beat when he saw the
kerosene dealer's hands trembling.

"What's the matter, Njogu?" Bone asked impatiently.

"Have you seen Rock?" Njogu replied with a question.

"No, why?"

"I have heard news from Keywest," Njogu started with a
stammer.

"And . . .?" Bone was impatient.

"And . . . something has happened to Ngeta."

"What?"

"Something awful has happened to Ngeta," he emphasised.

"Ngeta and Rock came to my shop on their way to Thiong'o's for a duel . . . I understand Thiong'o bought a new pool table and invited them over. Then Rock came again ten minutes later to ask if I had seen Ngeta. I told him, 'No, you were together the last time I saw you.' He explained that he had stayed behind, buying roasted maize at the kiosk. Ahead of him he had seen some commotion and a van speeding off, and although he had hurried up to see what it was about, everything had quietened when he reached there. Nobody knew what had happened. He could not trace Ngeta – not even at Thiong'o's."

"When was this?" Bone was bewildered by this strange story.

"About forty minutes ago," the kerosene dealer replied. "Then, Rock came back after another ten minutes, quite shocked, and said that Ngeta had been kidnapped."

"Kidnapped?"

"That's what he said, then he added that he was going to find out more about it."

"Nobody can kidnap Ngeta at this time!" Bone declared, chuckling softly to convince himself that it was not happening. "This is a joke."

"No, it's not," Njogu said with all the seriousness he could muster.

"Somebody has done something worse." The tremor in his voice was now more evident.

"What do you mean?" Bone's whole body was tense as he asked. After a long silence, Njogu said hoarsely, "Charlie has been to my place. He tells me that Ngeta is lying in a pool of blood in Keywest. He has been murdered!"

"Murdered by whom?" Bone almost shrieked out.

"Who knows?" Njogu shot back defensively. Then he added, "But according to Charlie, Ngeta is *kaputt! Finito!*"

Bone left him standing there by the roadside and walked hurriedly towards The Slaughterhouse.

Ngeta? No! This was too much, he thought. There was no way

this could be real. Who would have the audacity to kidnap Ngeta in Ngando, then go murder him in Keywest, at such an hour? And why, in the first place, would anybody want to do something like that? Or was the attack a result of the bad blood between Ngando and Keywest? Was the enmity that bad? Bone's mind suddenly went back to a few months ago, to the boy he had clobbered for stealing the side mirror from Nancy's car. He trembled at the recollection.

Before he got to The Slaughterhouse, he retraced his steps and headed towards Rock's single-room.

Word spread fast in Ngando. From the number of curious visitors at his friend's place, he knew that word had already reached Rock's woman.

The poor girl was in tears because she did not know the fate of her lover. She feared the worst, especially after he told her about Ngeta. Unable to answer the myriad questions she posed, Bone left her and proceeded to The Slaughterhouse. A number of people followed him, trying to find out what was happening. But Bone din't want to talk to anybody. He felt suddenly afraid and wanted to be alone to think through this whole madness.

He walked on and found himself at Revellers, one of the popular bars in Ngando. He ordered six bottles of Tusker and gulped down the first three in rapid succession. He belched loudly, and his mind returned to the grim reality of the moment.

He'd better go check on things, he thought. He stood up and hurried out of the pub, leaving the rest of his beer on the table. He went back to Rock's place and found the wife surrounded by women sympathizers. Rock had not resurfaced. Bone left instructions that he was at The Slaughterhouse and walked out.

Rock's disappearance was now a neighbourhood mystery. Bone met many of their friends all searching for him. He bought them cigarettes and urged them on.

He rounded the first row of houses and was going to enter his own row when he stopped short. A cigarette smoker lit up the area around The Slaughterhouse using a gas lighter and the flame illuminated the faces of the four or more men at the door. Instinctively, Bone crouched, then instantly retraced his steps. Nobody could mistake the long overcoats and crowned caps of the men. Bone was puzzled. What would the police be doing outside his house?

He hurried back to Revellers and approached one of the small, decrepit taxis outside. The taxi driver was sound asleep, having reclined his seat backwards. He woke up with a start as Bone loudly rapped on the window.

"How much to Imara Daima?"

"Imara Daima?" The taxi man had not completely woken up. He wiped off the drool from his jaw and regarded Bone with a pair of sleepy eyes. "That will be fifteen hundred shillings."

"Fifteen hundred! *Unadhani mimi ni fala, nini?*" exclaimed Bone. The man must have mistaken him for a fool.

"Imara Daima is on the other side of town, man."

"*Mimi ni msee wa mtaani.*" I'm a local chap, Bone argued. "I'll give you three hundred."

After much bargaining and cajoling, they settled at four hundred shillings. The taxi man slowly pulled up his seat and ignited the ramshackle of a car.

Bone's mind was whirling. Why was he running away?

Ngando, January 18 – 11:00 p.m.

The hunter was dressed in a combat jacket and denim trousers. Despite the darkness, he wore dark glasses which covered his face incongruously.

He walked carefully – he had been premonished that the place was very insecure. He gripped the small metal bar in his hand and kept checking to ensure that the Somali knife was still under his belt. Tucked in his jacket pocket was a loaded pistol with the silencer screwed on.

A few metres ahead of him a cigarette lit up the darkness. In that moment of light he saw the silhouette of a lone man. The hunter walked to him, the corners of his eyes wary of any movement from the dark vegetable stalls.

"Hello."

"Yeah," came the gruff reply.

"I'm looking for a friend of mine who lives around here. His name is Rock. Do you know where I can find him?"

The lone man calmly pulled at the cigarette. He exhaled slowly, to the chagrin of the hunter. "Check him in that room over there. Door number fifteen."

The hunter looked at the derelict block. "Thank you," he said. Then he checked to see if the pistol was still there. He took out a flashlight from his pocket but did not switch it on. He tightened his grip on the metal bar and walked up to the den.

The scout took another long pull at the cigarette. He exhaled in his characteristic slow manner. His eyes moved up and down the alley carefully. Satisfied that nobody else was approaching, he turned and slipped back into the shadows. Then he blew a shrill whistle.

The row of single rooms was so run down such that a visitor would mistake it for a collection of pigsties. There was intense silence in the area. Only an occasional cough or the creaking of a bed gave away signs of life. It seemed as if the inhabitants used the front of their houses as rubbish dumps. The hunter stepped into some slush and cursed.

He was one of the most wanted criminals around town, wanted for scores of hijackings and kidnaps. His name, Danger, struck fear in many hearts in Nairobi's underworld. He was known to go to any lengths to get money – from pick-pocketing to mugging pedestrians and robbing banks. Maybe that was why he had taken on this simple assignment.

At number fifteen he stopped and shone the flashlight on the door. He stepped forward and listened. There was no sign of life inside. He thought about going back to call his colleagues, but the temptation of getting all the credit for nabbing Rock to himself overcame him.

He knocked softly.

He heard a bed creak, then approaching footsteps. The door was opened a foot. His trained eye saw that the room was lit by a small tin lamp. On the wall were three shadows – there were three more men inside. He tried to look casual.

"Yes?" the heavily muscled man at the door prompted him.

"Is Rock here?"

The hunter looked behind him and said: "Someone wants to see you, Rock."

"*Ni manzi?*" Is it a girl? came the brusque reply.

Danger breathed a sigh of relief. So Rock was in, after all. This was going to be easier than he expected.

"No. It's a man."

"Then tell him to get in!" Rock commanded. The man opened the door another foot and moved back. Danger stepped inside.

Suddenly, the door was slammed shut behind him. The same instant, the tin lamp was blown out. Before he knew what was happening, somebody jumped on him from above. He heard the bed creak as the three men attacked simultaneously.

They fell on him like jackals. As he fell down, he reached for his gun but somebody grabbed his hand and slammed it onto the floor. Someone else hit him on the head with a metal bar.

A powerful battery torch was switched on, almost blinding him as he lay stretched out on the floor with three men pinning him down. Blood oozed from a deep cut on his forehead. He was helpless. Somebody slammed a boot into his face.

"Guys! Guys!" Danger heard the man who had spoken as Rock say, "don't finish him off. We need him alive."

"Tie him up quickly," the man ordered. He held Danger's gun in his hand.

A long piece of telephone wire was used to trounce Danger up. The three men effortlessly lifted him onto the edge of the bed. When he tried to force himself out of their tight grip, he was punched hard in the stomach. He doubled over in pain. He did not resist as they tied him to the bed, so tightly that he felt instantly numb.

"Good! Let me call Rock now." One of them went out.

Though Danger had been immobilized, the three men hovered over him like buzzards. He wished he had called the others as soon as he had established Rock's whereabouts. How have I been fooled? he asked himself as he turned his tongue in his mouth to feel whether any of his teeth had come out. One of his molars was very loose. Damn! And to think Rock was not even here! It was so uncharacteristic of Danger to get into such a fix. He was not known to make such blunders. But then, nobody had told him that he would be dealing with professional muggers.

The door opened and the fellow who had gone out returned, followed by another smartly dressed man.

"Thank you, guys," the smartly dressed one said. He took a stool and placed it close to the bed. Lighting a cigarette with a silver lighter, he picked up Danger's gun peered at it, then shoved it into his own pocket and sat down. Now, he turned to the bloody face of the hunter.

"Hello," he said calmly. "I'm sorry about my welcoming committee. You see, they are not trained in customer service. I'm terribly sorry." The others broke into laughter. "My name is Rock. I understand you have been looking for me?"

Danger stared back at him with contempt. Rock looked at his comrades. "Our guest does not want to talk to me!" he said, causing another ripple of laughter.

"Why are you people looking for me?"
Danger opted to keep mum.

"Listen," Rock bent closer, "it would be better for everyone if you talked immediately. In case you can't see, around me are four of Ngando's most dreaded people. I don't want to have to set them on you."

"They can go to hell!" Danger growled.

Rock laughed softly. He looked unperturbed at his captive. He rose up from the stool calmly, took a pack of cigarettes from his pocket and passed it to his colleagues, each of whom took one.

"Gosti," he said softly.

The big man who had opened the door for Danger moved in so quickly, it was unbelievable. His big fist crashed into the captive's skull like a sledgehammer. Danger grunted. Gosti kneed him hard in the groin. Rock held up his hand and stepped forward again.

"Why are you looking for me?" he asked once more.

Danger opened his mouth to curse him again but instead a stream of blood spluttered out together with the loose molar.

"I'm telling you nothing."
Rock laughed again.

"*Bongo Lala,*" he said. "Your turn now."
A stout, dark man came forward. He lifted Danger's head up and turned it at an angle, then slapped him so hard that the sound resonated in his ears. Rock winced when Bongo Lala jumped high in the air and landed on Danger's chest. There was an audible expulsion of air from the man's chest. Then he gasped painfully. His pride would not let him cry.

"Don't finish him off yet," Rock said. "We have the whole night to work on him. You don't want to spoil the fun, do you?" Bongo smiled. He tapped Danger on the neck with an outstretched finger. The captive felt pain shoot through his whole body.

"What do you want to know?" he growled.
Rock smiled, "Sorry guys," he told his other friends. "He has decided to talk. Pity you won't have your turn. Not just yet."

He turned to Danger. "Who sent you here?"

"I don't know his name," Danger answered reluctantly.

"That's not good enough." Rock lit another cigarette. "You have to remember something. Should I call one of my friends?" He lifted up his hand to give the order. Bongo grinned and moved a step forward. When Danger opened his mouth again he talked rapidly.

"It's true! I swear, I don't know his name. He just approached us and hired us to kidnap you and your friend Ngeta and drop you off at Keywest where other people would be waiting. He didn't tell us his name. All I know is that, he is a senior police officer."

"A police officer?"

"Yes. A *mkale*. A Kalenjin. I have had several brushes with him in the past, but I have never known his name. Actually, when he came to me, I thought he had come to arrest me, but I soon learnt he wanted something different this time."

"How much did he offer you?"

"Ten thousand before the operation, twenty thousand after. That was good money for simply kidnapping someone and dropping them a kilometre away. It was the lady who gave me the money."

"The lady?"

"Yes . . . he came with a girl . . . a beautiful girl. I can't remember her name."

"Please do. I don't want to have Gosti here jogging your memory."

Danger saw Gosti smile devilishly as he slammed his right fist into his left palm.

"I think he . . . he called her *Manzi* or Nancy. . . or something."

"Nancy?" Rock asked. His colleagues exchanged worried glances. "Tell me more. What else can you remember?"

"They had two cars, a brown Pajero and a white Toyota Corolla."

The car Nancy used everyday, Rock thought. Nancy? He could not believe his ears.

"So, what exactly were you hired to do?"

"I told you," Danger said. "To kidnap you and take you to the other slum. You slipped away and we only got Ngeta. That's all I know. I swear!" he added sincerely.

"And where is Ngeta?" Rock asked.

"In Keywest," Danger said. "We handed him to the guys there and returned to look for you."

Rock looked at the sweaty face with disbelief. There was now no doubt in his mind that what the gangster was saying was true. Nancy!

He could not imagine the implications of it all. It all felt like a bad dream. Then suddenly, he remembered that Bone had gone to town and would probably be with Nancy even now. If that was the case, then Bone was in grave danger.

He tried calling Bone on his cellphone, but some irritating voice informed him that he had insufficient funds to make the call. He turned to Gosti.

"I'm going to Imara Daima. Please deal with things here. And find out ways of getting Ngeta out of Keywest."

"Let us come with you," Bongo Lala offered.

"No. I can't get you into this mess. I will handle it alone. Thanks though." And he walked bravely towards Revellers to re-load his phone and hire a taxi.

fifteen
Imara Daima, January 18 – 11:00 p.m.

The journey to Nancy's place took twenty minutes only. From Ngando, the taxi was going against the traffic since most people were moving out of town. There were also fewer cars now that it was past ten o'clock. Coast-bound buses flew past them at breakneck speed. The taxi driver started to comment on the dangerous driving but quickly realized Bone was not listening.

When they reached the estate, Bone gave him a five hundred shilling note and stepped out without waiting for his change.

There was a brown Mitsubishi Pajero parked beside Nancy's Toyota on which was a sticker: '*Protected by* SHARK CAR SECURITY SYSTEMS.' That must belong to a wealthy person, he concluded. That security system cost thousands, Bone had heard.

He stood on the white-painted porch and pressed the doorbell softly. There was a brief lapse before Nancy opened the door. She was dressed in a leather outfit that clung to her body like a mermaid's skin.

Bone noticed two odd things. One, it was unusual for her to open the door herself. Usually, it was Martha the househelp who answered the door. Two, she did not welcome him with the usual kiss and hug. Maybe it was the ungodly hour he had come in, he thought casually. All in all, it was clear that she was not expecting him.

"Oh, hi," she tried to smile, "Do get in. There are some visitors . . ."

"Visitors?" he asked as he walked in. She was left at the door, and only followed him in after locking it and pocketing the key.

He grabbed a can of Red Bull energy drink from a shelf in the kitchen and then walked into the sitting room. He almost collided with a huge dark man, nearly upsetting the glass of red wine in his hand.

"Oh, sorry," he mumbled a quick apology.

Slowly, he opened the can in his hand and took a large swig. Then he saw the woman sitting on the settee at the far end of the room and froze. There was no mistaking that woman. The can remained suspended in his hand as he looked at her.

Nancy entered the room. He turned to her, a quizzical look on his face.

"What's this murderer doing in your house?" he hissed.

"Murderer?" she asked, her eyebrows raised innocently.

"Precisely," he repeated curtly." That woman over there is the one who framed Bomu and got a mad crowd to beat him to death."

His outburst didn't seem to shock Nancy at all. He turned to the unwelcome visitor, his voice rising. " *Wee, mama!* I think you should be leaving now. I'm sorry, but you're in the wrong house." Turning to Nancy, he asked: "Or do you know her?"

"As far as I'm concerned, you are the only murderer here," she said in a clear, deliberate voice.

In complete stupefaction, Bone realized that she was addressing him. "What?" he exclaimed.

And it was then that the burly man struck out with his huge fist. The blow took Bone by surprise. Too late to duck, it caught him straight on the jaw and dropped him down like a sack of potatoes. Always a willing fighter, he sprang up immediately. But then, he felt the cold touch of something metallic on his neck. He froze.

"Stand still and shut up, else I won't hesitate to pull the trigger."

Bone was astounded. That could not be Nancy's voice. It sounded too harsh and menacing. He turned round slowly and saw the weapon. He had watched enough movies at the local Miami Video to tell a pistol from a distance. His eyes widened as Nancy casually fingered the safety catch and it produced a loud click.

"My God! Nancy! What has gotten into your head?" he cried out.

"Oh, nothing, sweetheart," she replied in the strange new voice. There was an evil glint in her eyes. "It's just that your day of reckoning has come, Kimani."

That shocked him even more.

"Kimani? What . . . what are you talking about?" he whispered, suddenly scared. Nobody had called him by that name for years, and he knew that nobody, least of all Nancy, was aware of it.

Nobody answered back. Nancy kept the gun trained on him, as if she feared he would bolt off. She was mistaken, he thought. He was so shocked at the way things had happened that escape was the last thing on his mind. The burly man removed a pair of handcuffs from somewhere in his suit and cuffed his hand to one of the metal bars on the window.

"Can somebody tell me what the hell is happening?" Bone demanded. The answer was another mighty blow from the huge man, this time directed at his stomach, that made him sink to his knees.

The man spoke a second later. "I'm Senior Superintendent Rotich, and I head the . . ."

"I honestly don't care who you are or what you head," Bone retorted defiantly as he massaged the jaw that had almost been disconnected from the face with his free hand. "Just tell me what is happening."

For that effort, he earned himself a slap that made his head reel. He could taste blood in his mouth. Nancy bent nearer. Now the gun was held down her waist where it looked very much out of place.

"You don't know what is happening? Well, let me tell you. The long hunt for one Kimani wa Waweru has finally come to fruition." That name again! Bone wondered how much more she knew about his past and its many dark skeletons. Were all the recent happenings to do with his past?

"If this is all about my past, let me say that all I did was unintended. My actions were meant to protect my family, my village and myself," he offered.

Suddenly, he began wondering who exactly Nancy was, and how she had come to know his real names. What was her relationship with the fat woman and this burly policeman? Was it the policeman who had informed her that her boyfriend was not a saint? Then it dawned on him that he knew next to nothing about Nancy.

"Exactly who are you, Nancy?" he asked, looking up at her. She smiled sardonically.

"In full, my name is Nancy Chelangat, Kalenjin by tribe . . ."

"I don't want to know about your tribe," he broke in. "To me, tribes are nothing but tags used by the rich politicians to divide the poor! We have been together for months without bothering about each other's tribes. Why does it matter all of a sudden?"

"It matters a lot, Bone-Kimani," she told him, "because ten years ago, my whole family was wiped out for being Kalenjin. I was orphaned just because of my tribe!"

Bone pondered over this new revelation with wonder.

"And what does that have to do with me?"

"It has everything to do with you," she looked him straight in the eye, and he could see a trace of fire in her pupils. She was trying very hard to control herself, "Because you are the one who killed my father, and right in front of my eyes." She paused, panting with emotion, then added, "I have been looking for you for all these years . . ."

"What? Me? You must be truly mad . . ."

"I know what I'm saying, Kimani," she said, sounding like a teacher being patient with an impertinent child. "Do you, by any chance remember a man you killed in Ndoinet Forest? There was a small girl in the house, and you told your colleague Ngeta-Lihanda not to kill her. Do you recall?"

He frowned in deep thought. The incidents of that fateful evening many years back still lingered in his brain, and now revealed themselves more vividly. Surely, that small, snotty village girl with baleful eyes could not be the same smart, rich lady in front of him?

"No! It can't be!" he declared.

"Huh! So you remember now! It's really me. I'm that small girl." He kept quiet for a long time. Events were developing too fast, too suddenly. The police officer had sat down on the nearest sofa, and like the woman, was watching the exchange most keenly. Bone wondered if the cop was here to arrest him.

"Then this must be a really small world," he declared. "They say that it's only mountains that don't meet!"

"Damn you!" Nancy cried out in anger. "I've lived a wretched life without parents because of you, and all you can do is grin at me and crack jokes?"

"*Ha!*" he scoffed. "You don't look like you've suffered at all. *Wewe ni babi.* You are rich. You are the ones who are milking the economy dry at the expense of the poor. You can't pretend to be that small girl. No!"

Nancy looked at him contemptuously, and for a fleeting moment Bone thought she was going to empty the gun into him. The police officer must have thought so too, because he suddenly shook his head. As an afterthought, Nancy walked to the fridge and pulled out another Guinness. Bone now knew that anything was bound to happen. She only drank Guinness when she was in a foul mood. Everyone in the room had their eyes on her as she took a large swig of the stout.

"When you killed my parents," she explained, pacing up and down the room "my uncle in the USA picked me up. He is the one who has been funding this project – my manhunt for you. That search for you has cost me so much time and money that even my university . . ."

"And how do these two come in?" Bone interrupted. He was not interested in unnecessary details.

As if waiting for that cue, the police superintendent stood up and walked closer. Then he spoke to him in a voice that carried so much malevolence that Bone was shocked.

"I happen to be Nancy's uncle. The man you killed was our youngest brother. His death was very painful to us, and the family decided we would not rest until we found the people who were responsible. We have been trailing you for the last five years, and it's only when we were sure we had all of you that we invited Nancy over. If we had had our own way, you would have died ages ago. Fortunately for you, she insisted on eliminating you herself."

"Uncle Rotich was very helpful," Nancy added, taking another swig at the beer. "He used the resources at his disposal, being a police officer, to trace you. He could have gone on to finish the work, but I had to be here to . . . experience what it feels like to kill a man."

Her face looked so angelic that the words coming out of the sensuous mouth were grossly incongruous. Even now, Bone could not believe what he was hearing was real. He would have thought it a bad dream were it not for the pain he felt as the handcuff cut into his wrist. The gravity of the words was beginning to eat at his defiance, and fear was now creeping into his heart.

"What about that woman?" he asked, to buy time.

He had talked himself out of countless dangerous situations while on the streets, and he knew that all hope was not lost. The first rule of survival was to always keep your head high and not show fear. Keep them talking, he told himself. That should delay any action until he thought of something. He had seen such a scene in a movie. Keep them talking!

"My name is Angelina Chebet," the heavily built woman now said in strong, accent-laden English. She walked towards him and Bone guessed she was drunk. "I used to be a rich businesswoman in Molo until you Kikuyus reduced it to ashes. Very rich, I tell you. I could buy whatever I wanted . . . anybody in Molo or Nakuru." She stopped and pointed at him, "Then you torched my premises. Now see what I look like, you stupid Kikuyu!"

"Those clashes had nothing to do with business! We were incited. It was all about politics," Bone shouted.

"It doesn't matter to me. I have my personal reasons. They took my business, they burnt my property to ashes and reduced me to a pauper," she shouted back.

She was standing at an awkward angle, and looked more like a habitual drunk than a once successful businesswoman. "So, my job has been to follow you around and ensure you don't vanish into thin air. We figured you would not notice a woman walking behind you.

That's what I have been doing for the last five years. Tracking you, you dirty *ng'ombe!*" She spat at him, then added: "By the way, I also happen to be a distant aunt to your late friend, Kibet."

"Bomu? But you are the one who set him up!" Bone exclaimed. The whole story was getting more bizarre.

"Yes," she replied simply, as if admitting to a very minor misdemeanour.

"I had to see him finished. *Teta! Hata yeye ng'ombe!*" she swore.

"But why, if he was your own blood?" Bone cried out, reliving the pain his departed friend must have felt as he was stoned to death.

"Bomu betrayed the whole tribe and he deserved to die," she said with finality. "He and Bafu had the chance to kill the enemies of the tribe, but they chose to side with them, hide them and then run away. There was no way they were going to escape our wrath.

You can't escape the long hand of the tribe, I tell you! *Huwezi!*" she swore. "*Magoi!*" she added.

"Even Bafu?" Bone was dumbfounded. "You planned Bafu's death as well?"

"Actually," the superintendent cleared his throat, "for Bafu's case, I was directly in charge. The idea was to kill you one by one without any of you knowing who would be next. For Bafu, it was a simple matter of tipping the Flying Squad. Show them any 'most wanted' criminal and they do the rest. And all controversy quietly fizzles out – it always does in Kenya." He laughed heartily at his ingenious summation.

"For Ngeta and Rock, the job entailed getting hold of them and taking them off to Keywest this evening. The rivalry between Ngando and Keywest has done the rest for us. Nobody will ask any questions when their mutilated bodies are discovered in Keywest," he said, talking about the whole thing as casually as a farmer discussing his heifers.

"And now . . . that you are here, we will finish everything tonight. The sages say killing two birds with one stone? Ha! Ha! Ha!" he laughed heartily at the joke.

Bone looked at Nancy. "But you . . . you had countless chances to kill me. Why didn't you do so earlier?"

"We wanted you to die knowing why you were dying. It was also a pleasure to watch you lose your pals, one by one."

"Okay," Bone said wearily. "That explains why you and I were together all the times my friends died."

"Yes, we didn't want to raise eyebrows you know? I was the perfect distraction, wasn't I?" she asked sweetly.

"I find it hard to imagine that someone can go to such an extent. Is this the project you always referred to?"

"Precisely!" Nancy answered. "We have gone to that extent in order to repay all the suffering we went through."

"What do you know about suffering?" he scoffed. "You were adopted by your rich uncle who shipped you off overseas for you to enjoy the full benefits of the United Nations High Commission for Refugees. You don't know anything about suffering. We do – we form part of the clash victims who had to pick up the pieces the hard way."

The fat woman spoke up. "I hate it when you Kikuyus talk about the clashes as if it was only you who were affected," she declared.

"We don't get to think about the others. What about the many Kalenjins who were killed? What do you say about the Kalenjins who were pulled out of *matatus* in Nakuru and Nairobi and lynched?"

"Yes," concurred Rotich. "Thousands of Kalenjins who were murdered simply because they were Kipsigis, Keiyo, or Nandi!"
He paused briefly then added, "It's for them that we swore to exterminate you vermins. *Gasia!*"
Bone realized that they were all fanatics. His fear grew with this realization.

"You won't get away with this," he told them. "God will make sure you pay. If He won't, I will. The society I've grown up in does not embrace forgiveness."

"We have gotten away already!" Angelina Chebet laughed at him.

"After all this, I will start a business, Nancy will go back to America, and Rotich here will go on with his life. Imagine you invoking the name of the Lord now! Your past deeds leave no room for heavenly pardon."

"Look. Let's stop this nonsense about revenge," Bone said appeasingly. "Hundreds of people lost their relatives in the clashes, I lost my father, just like you. My mother and my sister, I don't know what happened to them. But I have learnt to put it all in the past. That's what we should all do – forgive each other."

Rotich smiled at him the way a fisherman smiles at a handsome catch. "What would you do if you suddenly met your father's killer? Would you let him get away?"

Bone replied, "I would let him go because I know the clashes were fuelled by other people who are now untouchable. What do you think would happen if everyone started thinking about revenge? There would be a civil war just like what happened in Rwanda. I lost my family in the clashes. Rock, Bomu and Bafu too. Will revenge bring your family back?"

"You are only saying that to save yourself because you are finally on the receiving end. I wonder if you would feel the same way if you were in my shoes," Rotich dismissively told him.

It was evident that nothing would change their minds. Trying to make them see logic was as difficult as appealing to an incensed mob.

The inspector looked at his watch, and as if on cue, his phone rang out. He dipped his hand into his pocket and took it. He glanced once at the screen, then switched it on and pressed it against his ear.

"Yeah?" he said gruffly, then his face contorted into a frown as he listened to the caller.

"What are you saying?" he asked. He listened carefully before erupting again. "What do you mean you can't find him?"

The person on the other end of the line explained something. Angrily, Rotich switched off the phone and shoved it back into his pocket. His eyes were almost bulging out of their sockets when he looked at Nancy.

"Those fools have bungled," he announced, the veins on his neck throbbing with anger. "First of all, they failed to capture one of the villains, and now my man has been trapped."

"That is disastrous!" Nancy said. "It can bring the whole operation down."

"I've got to get back there and straighten things out, otherwise we'll not conclude tonight," he said as he started to leave.

"Let me come with you," Angelina Chebet said as she picked up her handbag. She stared at Bone venomously. "Should we kill this one first?" Bone's heart skipped a beat. Rotich looked at him. "No, we will delay that. He has to come last as planned."

He gave one long look at his captive, then told Nancy: "If this thug tries anything, don't hesitate to shoot him." There was enough malice in his voice to tell Bone he meant every word. He walked out, followed closely by Chebet.

Nancy gave Bone a long, distasteful look. He could not believe that all that hatred now reflected on Nancy's face had been concealed in her heart all the while. Was this the same girl who had laughed with him, paid for his clothes and shoes, and made love to him? Could it be the same Nancy who had almost succeeded in making him human once more?

"Now, I can see everything clearly," he declared without looking at her. "I can see how you 'accidentally' came into my life. I'm beginning to understand everything – the numerous money transfers. There were many glaring signs I should have seen, but I was blind."

She did not answer. Instead she took a swig at the Guinness, her right hand firmly gripping the pistol and her finger on the trigger.

Bone's mind drifted to his departed friends: Bafu with his loyalty and youthful zest, Bomu with his ingenious touch, Ngeta the Luhya who had become a Kenyan, and Rock, his dependable childhood friend – all dead because of his blindness. He felt more sad than annoyed.

Then he remembered what Rotich had said before he left: "*They failed to capture one of the villains . . .*" Maybe Rock was still alive . . . maybe Ngeta. Bone prayed to God for divine intervention. Please, God, whoever it is, please save them. After that, he came back to himself. The realization that their love had simply been part of a project bit at him like a stubborn ant. Damn! he swore. He should have seen it all.

"Why did I fall for you like a moth attracted to a light?" he asked her. "Was I so desperate for your money? I hate myself more than ever before!"

Nancy kept quiet. She stood up slowly, and strode majestically up to the window. Then she folded her arms and stared outside. A long silence ensued.

Bone felt the handcuff eat into his flesh. It was painful. However, the real pain was in the waiting, the suspense caused by not knowing when she would turn to him and pull the trigger.

"Why don't you kill me now?"

Silence.

"Kill me now and end this misery!" he shouted like a wounded animal as tears flowed down his cheeks.

"Shut up!" Nancy suddenly cried out, pivoting towards him with the gun pointed straight at his chest. The sheer spitefulness of her tone shocked him. In her fit of anger, she hurled the bottle of Guinness onto the wall with such force that it smashed into smithereens, the beer staining the white wall like blood on a white sheet. She watched the spectacle for a while, then went to her bag and took out a vial of pills. She extracted one and popped it into her mouth, then went again to the fridge, got another Guinness and drank some more to chase the drug down.

"So you want to die now?" she asked as she came to him, her eyes blazing. "You think it would pain me to see you lying there with a bullet lodged in your head? Well, watch this." His eyes widened as he saw her finger move to the trigger. This is it, he thought, the end!

He shut his eyes and waited for the impact. A whole minute elapsed. His eyes fluttering, he looked up slowly. She was still steadily pointing the gun at him, still fingering the trigger.

"Do it!" he told her firmly. "Go ahead and pull the trigger if it will make right every wrong done to you. If it will bring back your father and make you live a normal life once again, do it."

Her face was expressionless, her right hand firm on the gun, her finger still on the trigger.

"Go ahead, Nancy!" he now shouted. "Justice is only a squeeze away. A little more pressure on the trigger will make things right. After all, it's what you've wanted for years, isn't it?"

"Shut up!" She commanded, then walked slowly backwards and sunk on the sofa. It was as if she had been suddenly assailed by an attack of dizziness.

She sat staring at him but not quite seeing him for a whole ten minutes, then her hazy eyes began to clear and brighten as she stood up and came towards him once more. Her voice was harsh and even more menacing than before.

"You think I can't kill you, Kimani?"

"Nancy," Bone began softly, "I know that what I will tell you will not change what you have decided to do. Judgment has already been passed, and I know that death awaits me. Nevertheless, I must tell you something to think about in your life after this."

He studied her face for a sign that his words were having any effect on her. He might as well have been talking to the air. There was only a glazed expression on her face.

"The last one year has had a very profound effect on my life. I never knew I could do some things I have done since I met you. You have given me a life, made my heart learn what goodness means. When you appeared in my life, I was not very different from an animal. Yes . . . living like an animal, eating like an animal, even reacting to things like an animal" he paused. "You taught me to be a human being and I thank you. You did this knowing that I'm the person who ended your father's life – it must have been very painful for you. Please know that I feel no malice towards you, and go ahead and shoot me."

She flinched. A small, almost imperceptible flinch which Bone totally missed.

He continued, "I now know that you loathe me. I would feel the same way if you had killed my father. But do you realise that the person you hate so much is no longer I? That the monster they told you about is not this Bone you see before you?"

"Nobody told me you were a monster. Nobody had to. With my own two eyes, I saw you kill my father."

"No, Nancy. You are lying to me and to yourself, and you know it. I can tell you that since you came of age, they told you over and over how your father was killed and how you must avenge his death. I'm certain your uncles made you believe that if you killed me and my friends, everything would be okay . . . you would have exorcised the demons of the clashes."

An idea came to Bone and he decided to try it out. After all, he had nothing to lose. "They have even given you drugs to give you courage," he said. "Let me tell you, Nancy, the effect of those drugs will wear off and you'll come back to yourself, and live with the demons for the rest of your life."

Silence.

Bone knew he had been right.

"And let me disappoint you a little more, Nancy. You have awoken the demons. By killing Bafu and Bomu – the trusting idiots who adored the ground you walked on, Nancy, you have become just like me . . . a monster!"

"I did not kill Bomu and Bafu, and you know it!" she retorted.

"Sure, you did," Bone said calmly. "As surely as you will kill me when you pull that trigger."

She flinched again. This time it was quite visible.

"Allow me to repeat my questions," he continued. "Is this extermination a solution to the nightmares that haunt us all because of what we experienced during the clashes? Will we heal the deep wounds that Molo brought to each of us by taking arms and going after each other's throats? That, my dear, will be the beginning of another Rwanda . . . another Burundi."

Nancy did not say a word, so Bone continued: "Your uncle calls us villains; vermin to be exterminated. I know his intention is to take me back to the dark days when actually, I was a vermin. But I will not go back. And neither will Bomu, or Bafu, or Ngeta, or Rock. I can assure you that the association we have had with you, though not so intended, has given us our humaness back. Yes. Now you can call me Kimani, or speak of the others by their given names."

He paused once more. "But, you are not exterminating villains. You are killing people. Go ahead," he told her again, "kill me and experience the sweetness of killing a human being!"

Her hand shook slightly. Eager that he should not see it, she raised her other hand to steady her grip on the gun. He looked away. A lump formed in his throat.

He smiled without any happiness when he remembered some incident at the entrance to the church opposite Thiong'o's.

"Did you know that Bafu was paying school fees for an orphaned child in Ngando?"

Her finger was off the trigger, but the gun was still levelled at him.

"Bafu was paying school fees for this little girl whose parents died in Likoni in 1997. Bafu had never been to Mombasa, never met her parents. But when he heard about the destitute child who had come to Ngando from Likoni, he offered to pay fees for Akinyi." He wet his lips, then continued: "The other day I met the little girl, Nancy, and she asked me: 'Now that Bafu is gone, who will pay my fees?' he paused. "Shoot me and then go and tell Akinyi that there will be no one to pay school fees for her."

She now shook her head, then she sighed.

"Bone, I wish I could, but I can't let you go," she finally said. "We have invested so much in this. It will be the ultimate betrayal to my people."

"Ha!" he scoffed. "Your people! Your people have never kissed me. They have never been with me. It's you, Nancy, who has been with me for a year. Do you honestly think I deserve to die?"

She kept quiet. Their eyes locked. He saw tears well up in hers. After what seemed like an eternity, she shook her head as if to clear it, then raised the gun with renewed resolve.

"No! You must die, Bone," she said loudly, as if to convince herself. Her hand shook terribly. Now tears rolled down her cheeks. He waited for the final blast. But it did not come. She let her hand drop. Her head bowed down for a long time. When she sniffled, he realized she was crying.

"You are right," she sobbed softly. "And I hate myself for being unable to shoot you."

He could not find words. He too, was crying openly. "Don't hate yourself," he blurted out. "I'm glad that finally you've been hit by the truth."

She dropped the gun on the sofa and sobbed freely now. She dug into her pocket and took out a crisp white handkerchief which she used to dab her eyes.

"You are right," she repeated. "All my life, I had been brought up to hate my father's killer. I longed for the day I would see you, watch you writhing in pain. When I came to Kenya, my mind was all prepared for that project."

His eyes darted towards her. She was not looking at him. Her whole body was trembling involuntarily, like someone suffering the first throes of a malarial attack.

"When I met you, however, you were very different from the murderer I had conjured up in my mind. What I saw was someone who was disturbed by life, unable to control his behaviour. The more I learnt about you and your friends: group sex, the orgies, the alcohol binges and the fights . . . the more I learnt, the more I wanted to really get into your heart. It was like something in your heart was crying to be touched . . . pulling me towards you. I couldn't help liking you."
She paused as if the effort of recalling those early days of their relationship was in itself painful to her.

"You were an enigma to me. That day we arranged for our 'accidental' meeting at the Los Angeles, you came to rescue me from that boy we had hired. That was noble of you. But then, you were much too violent. Yet, after being with you for a while, it was as if you had two alter egos – the violent, uncaring outer being and the inner emotional, caring being. I felt a duty to pull out the best in you."

Her voice filled up the room with emotion. Bone was silent.

"I started asking myself if killing you would be of any benefit. When I tried to tell them that it would not solve anything, they started mistrusting me. They didn't let me in on their deeper secrets. All I was told was to give out money to your friends to buy something from a particular shop, then get you out of town," she paused for a while. "And when I tried to stop them . . . I mean, after Bafu and Bomu, they threatened me. Uncle Rotich said he would get Uncle Sang to withdraw my sponsorship, and one of my aunties to curse me." She wiped her eyes. "Then he brought me these pills and assured me that they would give me the courage to kill you – but I can't!" she whimpered.

"Now, I do not know what next. They will probably kill us both."

"No," Bone said softly. "If you are on my side, we will face them together. This is a battle between evil and good. We shall overcome."

He had hardly finished the words when there was a loud crack. The door splintered into two as a huge stone rolled on the ground followed by the figure of an inflamed Rock, gun in hand. Nancy dived for her gun.

"Don't even think about it!" came Rock's warning voice. He pointed his gun at her. She froze.

"No!" Bone shouted at Rock.

"Are you okay?" Rock asked him. He raised his eyebrows when he saw him cuffed to the window grill. "Is she the one who did this to you?"

"Don't shoot," Bone told him urgently.

"Why not?" Rock's cold eyes never left the girl. "This beautiful lady of yours is the cause of all our troubles, Bone."

"She is not," Bone said quickly. "Listen to me, Rock. Put that gun down and listen to me."

Rock did not obey him.

"I have talked to Nancy. She is with us now," he added, anxious to avoid a catastrophe.

"Oh?" Rock was not moved at all. "And I suppose that makes everything okay? The fact that she has crossed over makes Ngeta's death okay?" He lifted the gun higher to aim between Nancy's eyes.

"Don't do it, Rock!" Bone commanded his friend, his voice almost a wail.

Rock laughed. "You got us into this mess, Bone. You befriended this woman and she damaged our lives, killed our brothers . . . our blood brothers, Bone," his voice broke. "And yet she still has a hold on you, handcuffed to the window as you are?"

"Just don't do it, Irungu," Bone pleaded desperately.

And it was as if Bone's use of his real name rocked Rock back to his senses.

"Listen to me," Bone added quickly, "Nancy, too, has been used. Having her on our side gives us the strength to face the real assassins."

"How do you know this is not another trap?" Rock asked at last.

"I know it's not a trap," Bone said. He felt it. It was something he could not explain.

Rock chuckled, "I have come all the way here, have had to almost kill a man, only for you to stop me from killing this woman?"

"Put that gun down and listen, man."

Rock shrugged. "If you say so." He let his hand fall to his side, His eyes still fixed on Nancy. "I have my eyes on you, Nancy," he warned.

"You don't have to worry about me," she told him boldly. "Worry about my uncle. He will stop at nothing to do what he set out to. And worry about your friend here whom we have to set free before they come back," she added, attempting to smile at Bone.

*   *   *

All attention was turned to the handcuffs. There were deep bruises on Bone's hand where the iron had cut into his flesh.

"Can you get a piece of metal anywhere?" Rock asked Nancy. She ran past the kitchen into the store. Rock moved close to Bone.

"Are you sure we can trust her?" he whispered.

"Sure. She had a chance to kill me, but she didn't."

"Still I'm keeping an eye on her."

They did not have time to say more because at that moment she returned with a metal rod in her hand.

"I could not find anything else."

"I think this will do," Rock said. He moved the gun to his left hand and took the rod. Then he shoved it into his waist, heaved softly, and holding the rod with both hands, hit the window grill with all his strength. Bone gasped as his whole body shook. Nothing happened to the window grill.

Rock took another blow at it. Bone winced with pain as the metal reverberated and sent shock waves down his shoulder.

Rock hit one final blow and the rest of the concrete around the grill crumbled down, raining on Bone. The whole room was covered in dust, but the loosened concrete allowed him to pull the metal bars out of the splintered wall. The handcuff slipped down the grill bar. Bone was free, the cuffs dangling on his arm.

Nancy brushed the dust off his head and clothes as he flexed his biceps to get the blood flowing once again.

"God! Am I tired!" he exclaimed. One side of his body was numb. He jingled the handcuffs on his arm, perhaps wondering how he was going to remove them.

"We must get out of here," Nancy declared. "They'll come back any time now."

"Where do we go to?" Rock asked. "Ngando is a no-go zone now. I'm sure there is a war right now between Keywest and us. I suggest we find somewhere else, where they would least expect us to go. But we don't have any money."

"That should not be a problem," Nancy answered. She walked into the bedroom. When she came back, she was holding a sizeable suitcase in her hands. She opened it to show them the neatly packed bank notes inside. Rock's jaw dropped. He had never seen that much money before, yet he was the one famed for having seen the greatest amount of money.

"Where did you get all that cash?" Bone asked, totally shocked. She shut the suitcase. "My uncle in the US has been sending thousands to finance the project. I don't know why I saved it," she shrugged her shoulders.

They heard a car pull up at the gate. Everybody froze. Nancy was the first to recover. She rushed to the window, peered out, then turned to the others. The look on her face told it all. "He's come back!" she said. "What do we do?"

There was no time to plan a proper ambush. Rock moved to the broken door and pressed his body against the wall next to it, his hand gripping the pistol. Bone took the metal rod Rock had used to free him and stood on the other side of the entrance. Nancy returned to the window with her gun in her hand. Then they waited.

*   *   *

Rotich pushed open what remained of the door and stepped in, fearing the worst. His hand moved to the pistol in his breast pocket. Chebet followed immediately behind.

"Don't move!" Rock ordered him from behind. The policeman did not have to turn to know what was happening. He looked at Nancy quizzically when she aimed the gun at his huge frame.

"Don't move," she said.

He attempted to laugh, emitting something between a cough and a guffaw.

"Wha . . . what is happening here, Nancy?"

"I begged you to stop this senseless operation, but you did not listen to me. Now I have to use force," she replied.

"You can't be serious," Rotich said, dying to look behind him but afraid.

"She is!" Bone said calmly. "And if I were you, I would drop that gun, remove my mobile phone and put my hands up in the air."

Rotich turned his eyes slowly to Bone. There was no mistaking the younger man's readiness to use the metal rod in his hands. Then he turned to Rock and saw a hard face that was ready to kill and the ugly gun that he had supplied to Danger earlier that evening. Rotich was a trained man and knew when he was down. He gently placed his gun on the nearest seat, added his phone and raised his hands. Nancy picked both up and handed them to Bone.

"Move forward!" Rock commanded. He unleashed his heel into the policeman's back with a blow that propelled him to the centre of the room. One murderous look at Chebet got her scampering after the policeman.

"Kneel down and keep your hands on your heads."
Rotich obeyed, his face flushed with anger. Chebet meekly followed suit.

"Nancy! What has come over you?" Rotich asked.

"A time comes when the interests of a nation supercede personal interests," she calmly replied.

"You are a traitor! *Kipsakarindet!*" Chebet hissed.

"I should have seen it coming," Rotich said almost to himself.

"Your generation is hopeless! We should not have included you in this."

"I'm glad you did, because now we have a chance to right many wrongs," she answered.

"And what makes you think that the rest of us will not proceed with the operation?"

Nancy was calm. "You will do nothing of the sort, Uncle."

"Why not? I have not exhausted all the resources at my disposal."

As if to answer him, Nancy gracefully walked over to the music system. She pressed a few buttons and the machine purred to life. From somewhere among the pile of CDs and magazines she took an audiotape, pressed the eject button on the machine and slipped the tape in. Then she plugged in the microphone and came over to the two captives.

"Uncle, we are going to record everything you say from now on. You will answer every question you are asked."

The superintendent laughed. "Make me!"

Bone stepped forward, the metal rod firmly in his hand. "Are you sure?" he asked. Without waiting for an answer, he brought it down on the policeman's bare knuckles. Rotich howled in pain.

"Don't give us an excuse to hurt you," Bone warned him. "You'd be giving me the perfect opportunity to avenge what you have done to us. Do yourself a favour and speak up!"

Nancy pressed the remote control and the machine whirled into life. "Begin by telling us who you are," she demanded, her voice as hard as it had been earlier with Bone the captive.

The superintendent kept mum. Bone lifted the rod in the air and brought it down on the other hand.

"I'm Senior Superintendent Josiah Rotich . . ."

*   *   *

The policeman talked. He started off by saying everything about himself, then he got into the details of the plot. He gave particulars of how the whole project was conceived, financed and implemented.

Every time he showed reluctance, Bone was there to prompt him. He only paused when Nancy stopped him so that she could insert a new tape into the machine. At the end of his testimony, she said,

"Thank you very much," then turned to Chebet.

Spurred by Rotich's confession, Chebet sang like a bird. By the time she was through, Nancy had three recorded tapes.

"Good!" Bone said as he ejected the SIM card out of the policeman's phone and handed the handset to him. "You are not going to hear from us again unless you try to find us. If you do that, we will send copies of these tapes to your boss at Police Headquarters, the Kenya Human Rights Commission and all media houses in the country. We shall also forward a copy to the Office of the President."

The officer shivered.

"Nobody will believe you!" he announced defiantly.

"Maybe they won't, maybe they will. Only time will tell, not so?" Nancy asked. The superintendent looked down, unsure of what to say.

"What is more," Rock added, "we are not stopping here. We are going to approach all your hired thugs – Danger is very willing to talk – they will give the police the additional information."

"What about you?" Rotich asked Nancy. "What will you do? You think you will go back to America?"

Nancy smiled. "There are more people who need me here, Uncle, than in America." She stood up. "Let's go." She told Rock and Bone. As they walked out, she turned to her uncle.

"Saisere!" Goodbye.

epilogue

'. . . the young refuse the bonds of the past, the bonds of hate.'
David Mulwa in Redemption.

Molo South, June, 2002

The lush green landscape looked as inviting as ever. Most of the farms held long stalks of green maize as well as patches of healthy potato and bean plants. Farmers could be seen sweating it out in the mid-morning heat, meticulously weeding with strokes of their forked jembes. It was hard to believe that this area was the battlefield it had been just ten years earlier.

Bone heard some movement in the grass behind him. He took the powerful binoculars off his eyes and turned slowly.

"*Ah!* Nancy, darling."

She was dressed just like the peasants here. There was no makeup on her face, no bangles on her hands, and yet she looked so refreshingly beautiful. How much she had been transformed from the exquisite girl in the Dolce & Gabbana dress at the Los Angeles!

"What are you thinking about?" she asked softly, placing her hand around his waist and pulling him closer.

Bone savoured the environment, holding his breath back as if he did not want to let go the rich smell of the countryside.

"I can't believe I've lived without this for all these years," he said for the umpteenth time, spreading his hands to sweep the whole countryside.

Molo South looked exceptionally peaceful. He glanced up and saw the birds circling in the air above him. The scene was so different from the filth and madness in Ngando.

"Oh, I love this," he said softly. All the misgivings he had had about coming back home were dissipating with each day, and every new day he confirmed that they had made the right decision.

Presently, they watched a team of elders coming up the slope towards them. Smiling, she let go her grip on his waist and stood up to meet them. Bone followed closely behind.

"*Habari?*" they greeted warmly. The couple shook the eight pairs of hands, exchanging pleasantries. "*Karibuni.*" Welcome.

They sat down on the bench Rock had built out there for people to sit on. Nancy straightened her *kanga* and sat down on the grass next to Bone. Rock came out of his tent, shielding his eyes from the mid-morning sun. He waved at everyone.

"I'm coming shortly," he shouted. When everybody was settled, one of the elders cleared his throat and said.

"Your adventures in Nairobi have left us baffled," he began in Kiswahili. "I'm sure you have seen how the village has reacted to your return. We are glad that you have finally come back."

"We are glad too," Bone said. "We have been living a rather difficult life in the city, not knowing that home waited for us."

"Do you think it will be difficult to settle down?" the speaker was a neighbour to Bone's late father. He had held onto the family's land and when Bone came back, had offered to relinquish it. Bone had insisted on letting him have a substantial part of the land. On the remaining portion, they were putting up a house. This was where they planned to all live.

"With the great support you have shown us, I have no doubt that we will settle down easily," Nancy replied.

To recover her family land would not be as easy as it had been for Bone. Apparently, a relative had sold the land to a newcomer in the area who had put up a permanent house. However, preliminary discussions with the Luo man showed his willingness to move away after compensation. As soon as the land was recovered, Bone and Nancy planned to start intensive farming.

Rock came over with a large tea flask and cups on a tray. "How dare you start talking without tea?" he castigated them. "Words do not easily roll off a cold tongue." They all laughed.

Bone's mobile phone rang. The elders cocked their ears attentively.

Cellphones were becoming quite a sensation in Molo; they had to be respected. Bone noticed that it was a landline number.

"Hallo? Good morning?" he spoke into the phone.

"Hallo, Sir," came the voice from the other end. "My name is Doctor Owino, calling from Kenyatta National Hospital. Am I speaking to Bone?"

"Speaking," he answered, immediately alert. What would a doctor in Nairobi be calling him for? The answer to his unspoken question came after a pause.

"I'm calling you because we have a patient in our ward who has just regained consciousness after a prolonged period, and in view of the nature of the injuries he had sustained when he was brought in, it is necessary that we do a CT Scan."

"A what?" Bone asked, not understanding the jargon and puzzled at what it all had to do with him.

"A CT Scan – a test to find out if there are internal injuries in his head. Well, when we asked him about his next of kin he gave us your name and number."

"I'm sorry, but I don't have any patient in hospital," Bone said quickly, anxious to end the baffling conversation.

Dr. Owino paused, then said, "Do you know anybody called Ngeta?"

"What? Ngeta?" Bone exclaimed. Both his friends as well as the elders were alarmed. One of them inadvertently choked on his tea.

"Yes," the doctor continued.

"Doctor," Bone's hand was shaking visibly. "The Ngeta I knew died," he added.

"Sir, there is someone here called Ngeta who says you are his next of kin," the voice at the other end maintained. "He was brought in by a Good Samaritan on the night of January 18th."

Bone was stupefied. "Are you telling me that Ngeta is alive?" he shouted into the phone.

"Yes, Sir," Dr. Owino confirmed. "We need your go ahead so that we can proceed with the scans."

"Doctor, could you please do me a favour?" Bone now said. "Can you arrange for me to speak to him?"

"Give me some time as the patient is way back in the ward," answered the doctor. "I will call you back."

"Who is Ngeta?" one of the elders ventured to ask. Bone and Rock looked at each other before saying in one voice, "Lihanda-Waithaka."

"This must be a miracle!" the elder said. "You mean the Mluhya who used to speak Kikuyu as if it were his mother tongue?"

"Yes," Rock answered.

After what seemed like a whole hour, the phone rang once again. Instantly, Bone pressed the receive button. The connection took an awfully long time.

He heard a pause, then a feeble, "Niaje?" How are you?
There was no mistaking that voice.

"Ngeta?" he asked.

"Sema!"

"Is that you?"

"Yes?" came the brusque reply. Bone nodded to the others with a smile on his face. There was instant jubilation around him.

"But . . . you are. . . I mean, we thought you were . . .," he stammered.

"Dead?" Ngeta prompted him, then added, "I'm very much alive and we thank God for that!"

"How is he feeling?" Nancy whispered, unable to contain the anxiety.

"How are you?" Bone asked Ngeta.

There was a slight pause, then Ngeta said, "I'm alive. I had a broken hand and leg, and my head still feels a bit heavy. I think someone hit me with a metal bar. These people have done all sorts of tests on me. Now they want to do a head scan – I think they believe I'm mad."
A feeling of happiness shot up Bone's whole body.

"Ngeta," Bone said into the phone, "we are coming there right away." He listened briefly, then he burst out laughing. Blocking the mouthpiece, he explained to the rest.

"He says that we should not go to see him without a kilo of miraa . . . and he thinks he has been unconscious for only three days!"

Nairobi, June, 2002

Ngeta had survived death by a whisker, they learnt when they went to see him. He had become unconscious following his abduction – his attackers having used a foul-smelling chemical to immobilize him. His attackers at Keywest had beaten him up, then left him for dead.

"I think he survived because the chloroform lowered his blood pressure and the loss of blood was minimised," Doctor Owino explained. A few hours later, he came to and found himself in darkness! His whole body was shaking with pain. His left side was numb due to loss of blood.

*　　*　　*

He tried to sit up, but fell back onto the hard floor. Then a wave of dizziness hit him. His head hit the metallic floor with a mighty thud, startling his dazed senses back to consciousness. Slowly, he opened his eyes and looked round the dark place. He heard the distant sound of laughter and merriment, but it all sounded like a thousand bells ringing in his head.

His body was crammed in a small space, in an unnatural position. The moonlight streamed in from the entrance. He felt around him for something with which to pull himself up. His hands clutched a metal bench and he slowly heaved himself up. When he looked around, he realized he was in the back of a jeep. The biting cold and the quietness outside told him it was in the wee hours of the night.

He crawled towards the light and tried to kick open the door, but it was locked. He would have to jump over. He sat back and tried to gather more energy. Slowly, he collected himself and lifted one leg over the door. He tried to heave the rest of his body over, but his muscles refused to respond and he fell back into the truck in a heap.

He shut his eyes to contain the pain that shot through his body like an electric shock.

Slowly, he made another attempt to jump over. This time he managed to put his left leg out on the bumper, but then his body muscles failed him again and he could not prevent himself from falling uncontrollably out of the vehicle.

He fell for what seemed to be an eternity, and passed out immediately his body splashed into a puddle.

*   *   *

By some stroke of luck and strange coincidence, Chomelea the plastics man was passing by Revellers on his way home.

He took another sip of the *Nyota Kali* and continued his journey. Suddenly, he heard a splash near the bar and stopped, his ears pricked up for signs of a scuffle. Instead, a still bundle lying in the mud caught his attention. He peered closer.

What he saw made all the illegal brew in his veins to evaporate.

"M..m..m.. my..i..i G-o-d," he stammered. "W-w-who a-a-are y-y-you?"

The body stirred for a second. The eyes fluttered for a minute. Chomelea looked at the mask of clotted blood that was the face and cringed. The man looked awfully familiar.

"Ngeta?" he asked, worried at the possibility that the drink in his head was playing tricks on him. Mustering all his energy, he gathered up the body and labouriously put it onto his shoulders. He groaned and almost sank to the ground with the weight of the wounded man.

"Damn, the man must weigh half a ton," he mumbled.

Slowly, he made his way up to the road where he desperately flagged down all cars that passed.

*   *   *

Bone could not hide his joy as he listened to the tale.

"And we all thought you were dead," he said.

"So did I, and so did the policemen who collected me," Ngeta answered and chuckled softly. "I'm a lucky bastard. I would be lying in a mortuary this whole week now."

"Ngeta," Bone said gently, "you have been here for over six months now."

Ngeta looked at him as if he was crazed and simply asked, "*Umenoki, nini?*" Are you mad or something?

Bone smiled. Rock and Nancy were also smiling. Ngeta was obviously not fully recovered and the best would be not to excite him.

"I want you to undergo all the tests they want you to," Nancy said. "We want you to come and join us in building our house as soon as possible," she added.

"And you will have children in that house," he said. "We already have one," Nancy said. "She is called Akinyi." Ngeta smiled as he stared at his friends around him. As if to echo the mood in the room, the *Siku za Furaha* lyrics flowed out of a small radio in a corner of the ward:

"Sorry, Rock," he joked. "I am going to be around for a long time. Don't think I am about to die just when life has changed for the better."

Nancy smiled. Then she took Bone's hand in one of hers, and Rock's in the other. They reached for Ngeta's bandaged ones and formed a circle. They stayed like that for a while, making another silent vow.

For together, they would make a fresh start.

Hizi ndio siku	*These are days*
za furaha sasa ziko hapa	*of happiness now with us*
Mvua imeisha	*The storm is over*
Nayo jua sasa ishawaka	*and the sun is up*
Hakuna place ya chuki beshte	*Theres no room for hate friend*
kwa hii world ya sasa	*in this here world*